WHEN SHE WAS GONE

When She Was Gone is the second novel by Irish author S.A. Dunphy, who has previously written works of non-fiction.

ALSO BY S.A. DUNPHY
After She Vanished

WHEN SHE WAS GONE

S. A. DUNPHY

HACHETTE
BOOKS
IRELAND

First published in Ireland in 2018 by HACHETTE BOOKS IRELAND

Cataloguing in Publication Data is available from the British Library

ISBN 978 1 4736 5574 4

Typeset in Bembo Book Std by Bookends Publishing Services, Dublin

Printed and bound in Great Britain by Clays Ltd, St Ives plc

Hachette Books Ireland policy is to use papers that are natural, renewable and recyclable products and made from wood grown in sustainable forests. The logging and manufacturing processes are expected to conform to the environmental regulations of the country of origin.

Hachette Books Ireland
8 Castlecourt Centre
Castleknock
Dublin 15
Ireland

A division of Hachette UK Ltd
Carmelite House
50 Victoria Embankment
EC4Y 0DZ

www.hachettebooksireland.ie

For Deirdre – you and me and
that house on the mountain

Prologue

THE PRISONER

1

6 JULY 1999

Somewhere
Some time

HE KNEW HE HAD A NAME.

He was aware that somewhere in the mists of what had once been there was a place he called home, a family he cherished and people who trusted and valued him – he had knowledge and skills that were hard won and sought after. At one time men had listened when he spoke and jumped to his commands. But that was before reality had unravelled.

During the early days of his incarceration he turned the details of his previous existence – who and what he had been before he was taken – into a chant, a prayer to make it easier to recall, but even that simple incantation was slipping from him, and he lived in terror that one day he would awaken from a nightmare-haunted sleep to find he had no idea who or where he was.

And that would be worse than death.

Often, despite all his efforts, he drifted, unable to discern reality from fantasy, and grinning, jittering, creeping things slithered from the shadows of his dreams during waking hours too. Then, regardless of any almost-forgotten desire for dignity, he screamed, because he did not know what else to do. The cries erupted from him in waves of throat-ripping fury, and it was almost a relief, because he found he could dive down into the crests and troughs of the horror and sink to a small, silent place within himself where no one could reach him.

Or so he thought.

Finally, when his paroxysms started to disturb the other denizens of that half-world, he was taken from the room that had become the entirety of his universe and brought to a tiny, bare cell – he knew from the change in temperature and the texture of the air that it was subterranean.

The frame of a military cot stood against the back wall, and a wheelchair with a bucket fastened beneath it sat in the corner just inside the door, which was pale grey metal and had a barred grille set into it at about head height. A dim bulb glowed and buzzed overhead – there were no windows in the closet-like space, and as the light was never switched off, he lived in a kind of artificial twilight.

Food was delivered twice a day, and he made himself eat it, although it was so dull and flavourless it was more a chewing exercise than anything else. He forced the meals down, telling himself he needed the nutrition, but he came to wonder if the porridge and grey stew they brought had some form of tranquilliser mixed through them, as he habitually passed out – for how long he knew not – after eating.

Finally, he decided that he did not care, as these sleeps were mercifully dreamless, and he craved the oblivion they brought.

And the dim sense of who he had once been passed further and further from his awareness.

2

DAYS SEEPED INTO NIGHTS AND NIGHTS INTO DAYS and all were the same. He had no way of knowing how long he had been caged in the depths of the earth, so he ceased to wonder about it.

One day/night he regained consciousness to hear a sound he did not recognise in the corridor outside his cell: footsteps.

That he heard the sounds of someone's footfall was not in itself strange, as people came and went occasionally. But he knew the noises each of these individuals made and could identify them all. This tread, though, was distinct. It was faster and lighter, and he lay on his cot for a time, trying to picture who or what it might be, but the image his groggy mind conjured made no sense, so he rose and went to the door, peering out at all the metal grille allowed him to see.

Directly opposite was a wall, painted a cracked, pale green. It ended just at the second bar of the grille, and he could see the first twelve feet or so of another characterless passageway, leading away from him. If he stood on tiptoe (his people were not naturally tall) he could make out the worn red tiles that covered the floor.

Pulling himself as upright as he could and craning his neck, he looked down and saw, to his great surprise, a little girl.

3

SO OUT OF PLACE AND BIZARRE WAS THIS SIGHT THAT
for a moment he backed away from the door and considered lying
down again and turning to face the wall. He was about to do just
this, when:

'Hello? Mister? Can you help me, please?'

She spoke in a soft, almost accentless voice.

The prisoner froze, torn between his desire to hide from what
could, for all he knew, be a hallucination and his wish to learn
more about this strange visitor.

'Mister?'

Finally, in faltering steps, he went back to the grille and gazed
out.

She was perhaps five years old; her hair, which was dark brown,
almost black, had been tied into a loose ponytail. She wore what
looked to be a cheap, ill-fitting tracksuit of indeterminate grey,
and on her feet were cheap blue trainers. As generic and slovenly as
her dress was, something about this child told him that, not so very
long ago, someone had cared for her a great deal.

Which made it all the more jarring that she had obviously been
crying – her cheeks were wet and flushed and her eyes red.

'What do you want?' he asked querulously.

She sniffed and cleared her throat, peering up at him with grave
seriousness.

'Could you tell me where the Doctor is, please?'

The prisoner blinked.

'You want to see a doctor?'

'No – not *a* doctor, *the* Doctor. I need him to save me.'

'Oh.'

Somewhere deep inside the prisoner something visceral stirred – hadn't he had a child once? A little girl, not so unlike this one? He felt that he had, but the memory of it just would not come.

'Have you seen him?' the girl continued, wiping an eye with an already damp sleeve and sniffing again. 'I tried to send him a message, but I don't know if he got it. Sometimes, if you write things down – *important* things – and think really, really hard, he hears you and comes to help.'

The prisoner blinked, trying to process what she was saying. Even in his confused state, though, he knew that the child made no sense, and he was forced to consider that he might be caught in a bizarre dream – if not of his making, then possibly generated by the child's feverish mind.

He pushed the thought aside.

'You should run away,' he heard himself saying. 'This is a bad place. Find the door and get out and run far, far away.'

'But then the Doctor won't find me – when he gets here, he's going to be very cross with the bad men, and he'll make sure they are never mean to kids again. Then he'll take me home to my mammy and daddy in his blue box.'

Fresh tears leaked from the corners of her eyes at this, and he saw her fight to regain control. She was trying so hard to be brave. He admired her for it, while pitying her, too. He had been brave. For a time.

'Just go!' he hissed. 'Get out of here before they find you!'

And then he heard the sound of keys in a lock at the end of the hallway, and a look of true terror spread across the child's pretty features, and without another word she took off at a sprint the way she had come. He wanted to shrink back into his safe, featureless room, but somehow he couldn't – he was locked in place, and as he watched, a cold, bitter darkness began to work its way down the corridor, and a shape that looked like an old man but wasn't stalked past, glancing at him with reptilian eyes before making its way after the fleeing child.

'Now, Beth, dear.' He heard a deep, purring voice. 'How did you get out of your room, eh? Time for bed, my dear. Don't you want to have your story before lights out?'

He heard her screeching: '*No! I won't go! I won't go!*'

And then he was bellowing, too, and someone was opening his door and he tried to fight them, the Gods knew he did, but they were too strong.

It was months before he could get the sound of the little girl's cries out of his head.

He never forgot her, though they tried to make him.

Part One

DAY OF THE LONG KNIVES

1

3 JULY 2016

Phibsboro, Dublin
11.13 a.m.

DIANE ROBINSON WAS AWARE OF SOMEONE SHAKING her gently. Opening one eye, she saw the face of her man-friend, David Dunnigan (they had as yet been unable to settle on a proper title for what they were – boyfriend/girlfriend seemed ridiculous, as they were each either in the throes of or as close as didn't matter to middle age), grinning sheepishly.

'Breakfast is served,' he said quietly. They hadn't been together long, and had only spent the night together a handful of times, but Dunnigan had quickly learned that she was not a morning person, so a tentative approach to waking her was assuredly the best course of action.

'It's still the middle of the night.'

'It's a quarter past eleven!'

'You just made my point for me.'

He leaned down and kissed her, then went back out to the living room.

Diane stayed where she was and stretched luxuriously. Like most of Dunnigan's apartment, the room was devoid of any decoration or personalising touches: it contained a double bed (when she had first visited, there had only been a single, but she had persuaded him to scale up), a single bedside locker (which he had thoughtfully put on the side where she slept) and a wardrobe. The bedspread and pillowcases were all a neutral cream colour – the only other set he had considered buying involved characters from the *Star Wars* films, so she had steered him in the direction of something more subtle.

Getting up, she pulled on an over-sized *Bat out of Hell* T-shirt, then walked to the door. Opening it a crack, she could see the man she had come to care deeply about perched on the threadbare couch he refused to get rid of, sipping from a mug of tea and leafing through *The Sunday Times*. This room was the only one that showed any signs of individuality: on the wall above the fireplace (which she had never seen him use) hung a framed poster of Patrick Troughton as the second incarnation of the science-fiction character Doctor Who, and on the empty mantelpiece directly below was a photo of Dunnigan and his niece, Beth, who had been four years old when the shot was taken on 8 December 1998, the day she disappeared.

Beth, who was the daughter of Gina, Dunnigan's twin sister, had been about the only thing he gave a damn about other than his work – as a criminology lecturer at the National University in Maynooth and a consultant on missing persons cases and serious sexual assaults for the National Bureau of Criminal Investigation in Harcourt Street. A shared trip into Dublin city centre on the official opening of the Christmas shopping season had become a tradition for Beth and her uncle, and one they both looked forward to with great excitement. Dunnigan had prepared for it with the same degree of precision and attention to detail he applied to the criminal investigations he was so expert at – their itinerary had been carefully mapped out, he had researched restaurants they might visit for lunch and a mid-afternoon mug of hot chocolate and Beth had shown him her shopping list in advance, so he might think about where her gifts could be obtained at the most competitive prices.

All of which made it a bitter irony that a random variable had proven to be their undoing. Dunnigan and Beth had stopped on Grafton Street, just opposite the Stephen's Green Shopping Centre, to listen to a group of carol singers. The little girl had been holding his hand, but she let go for a moment, and when he looked down to check on her, perhaps thirty seconds later, she was gone.

Eighteen years later, not so much as a trace of the child had ever been found. And it had almost killed Dunnigan.

He had retreated into himself – racked with guilt, he'd pushed everyone away: family members, colleagues, the few friends he had – and started approaching the work he had always been passionately devoted to with a sort of mechanical indifference. He taught his classes and processed evidence for his police work, but with just enough effort to get by.

His career stalled. If it had not been for Chief Superintendent Frank Tormey, who had recruited him as a consultant for the gardaí in the first place and still saw something in the strange, skinny, unkempt young man, he would have been let go countless times. As it was, the university repeatedly cut his lecturing hours until he was down to the bare minimum, which meant he was dependent on the police work to simply pay his bills.

Six months ago, through a case he had been given because no one else wanted it – a series of missing persons reports involving homeless people – Dunnigan had come to the Widow's Quay Homeless Project, and there he had met the charismatic and unorthodox priest Father Bill Creedon, who had taken the lonely investigator under his wing. At the project he had also met Diane, who acted as a therapist-cum-receptionist/accountant for the charity, and after several faltering steps, the two had begun a tentative relationship that had blossomed into something special.

As they'd become closer, she'd sensed him loosening up – sharing a little more and daring to open himself to others who wanted to be there for him. He'd developed a close friendship with a young man named Miley Timoney, whom he helped to escape an abusive care home he had been placed in by a family who were embarrassed at the fact that he lived with Down syndrome.

Dunnigan had even started to approach his work with renewed vigour and had actually solved the case, which had been meant to simply keep him occupied and out of trouble. Through his efforts, he had been instrumental in shutting down a people-trafficking operation that had been snatching the homeless from the streets of Dublin and sending them into forced labour all over the world.

As she watched him through the doorway, Diane thought he looked happy. Hopeful.

'So what's on the menu?' she asked as she pushed the door open and went and sat down beside him.

Two takeout mugs of coffee, a plate with some Danish pastries, a couple of freshly baked croissants and two cream-cheese bagels and a jar of good raspberry jam he had bought at Donnybrook Fair the previous week (at her insistence) were sitting on the low, rickety coffee table that, although as much an orphan as anything else in the room, seemed somehow to have morphed into a companion piece to the ancient sofa.

'All bought with my own fair hands,' he said. 'And a cappuccino – hurry up and drink it before it goes cold.'

He passed her the Culture section of the paper, and she grabbed a bagel and slathered it with jam. They ate in companionable silence for a few moments.

'Would you consider getting a proper dining table?' Diane asked.

Dunnigan looked at her from the corner of his eye.

'I'd consider it.'

'I thought it might be nice to have Miley and Harry over for a meal.'

Harry was a ten-year-old boy whose parents were among the many forced into indentured slavery by the After Dark Campaign, the criminal group Dunnigan, Diane and Father Bill, along with

14

an army from one of the local crime gangs whom the (always unpredictable) priest maintained relations with for reasons best known to himself, had caused to cease operations. The police, to whom Dunnigan had handed over all the records recovered from the offices of an abandoned freight warehouse on the docks, were trying to trace those who had been abducted, but the trail was so convoluted the prospect of recovering them did not look very likely.

Harry was now in foster care, but Miley, who had become very close to the lad, still played a huge role in his life and saw him during regular visits. It was hoped these might turn into overnight stays in time.

'Father Bill might come over too,' Diane said, testing the waters a bit more.

'Mmm,' Dunnigan said (a sound Diane knew by now meant he was only half-listening). She poked him playfully in the ribs. 'I can't really cook, though,' he retorted.

'That's why God invented takeout menus. Would your sister come?'

Dunnigan and Gina had become very close again in recent months, and while she was still wary of Diane, there had been a gentle thawing of their relationship, too.

'She might. I could ask her.'

'Her husband still pissed at you?'

'Yes.'

Diane felt herself bristle. Obviously, she could understand why the man would still harbour some pain towards Dunnigan, but for the sake of the family, perhaps it was time to begin rebuilding bridges? She realised she was probably biased, but decided she didn't care.

'We can work on that.'

Dunnigan sat back and looked at her, his eyes clear, alive with intelligence. 'Do we need to?'

Diane shrugged. 'Only if you want.'

He smiled and took her hand in his. 'I don't.'

They continued their meal, chatting about this and that, enjoying the lazy, simple pleasure of an unhurried Sunday-morning breakfast.

Then at 12.15 p.m. (Diane had just looked at her phone, and saw it was that time precisely), the doorbell buzzed.

2

3 JULY 2016

Widow's Quay Homeless Project, Dublin
12.01 p.m.

FATHER BILL CREEDON POURED HIMSELF SOME TEA and wondered if it was a sin to add just a little Irish whiskey when the sun was barely at its zenith in the sky. He decided that, as it was a Sunday, the usual rules of etiquette didn't apply (*drinking buttermilk all the week, whiskey on a Sunday* – wasn't that how the old song went?) and discharged a modest amount into his mug.

On Sundays, the project operated a skeleton staff, a couple of elderly ladies coming in to cook lunch and Father Bill setting out cutlery and crockery on the tables and keeping endless pots of tea on the go for anyone who happened to drop by.

Because Sundays were habitually seen as a family day, a lot of the people who were regulars the rest of the week seemed to lay low. In fact, the dining room was usually filled with mums, dads and children, a lot of whom weren't technically homeless but who struggled to make ends meet and were grateful for the meal the project provided. The women who came in to cook always pushed the boat out, dishing up rustic, homemade vegetable soup and soda bread for starters, a roast of some kind with all the trimmings for the main and apple crumble (or tart, depending on who was preparing dessert that weekend) with thick custard. It was a meal most restaurants would be proud of and was wholly provided out of goodwill – various local shops donated the food, and the women gave their time and skills *gratis* and with good humour.

That quiet, gentle sense of goodwill was one of the many things that made him particularly proud to be a Dubliner.

Father Bill had grown up amid the poverty and violence of the inner city. By the age of ten he was showing promise as a boxer and knew even then that life offered him two paths: he could go into the local gangs and make a career as an enforcer, using his talents to instil fear and spread carnage, or he could enter the seminary, join a different kind of gang and serve his community in another way entirely.

He chose the church, and while over the years he had seen the organisation become more and more weighed down by corruption and the evils it claimed to stand against, his belief in a higher power, in the inherent decency that lay in the hearts of the people he worked alongside every day, had sustained him.

He could be unorthodox – he refused to toe the line when it came to sheltering sex offenders; he believed homosexuality was just another way of loving and performed gay marriages long before the state deemed them legal; he spoke out where he saw injustice and inequality and suffered the rebukes from his superiors with a stoic shrug. He understood the landscape and the psychology of the people and the environment through which he moved, and because he valued and respected those he came across, they loved and honoured him in turn. From the kids kicking ball in the narrow laneways to the rough men who ran the criminal underworld, Father Bill was seen as someone to be reckoned with.

He sipped his tea and surveyed the small office – an almost obsolete computer, some ancient filing cabinets donated to them when a nearby paper firm closed, a desk he had brought with him from Dolphin's Barn, his first parish. He had built the project from the ground up, and it meant the world to him. It wasn't much, but it was more than enough.

'Father Bill?'

One of the women on kitchen duty that day stuck her head in – a kindly, wizened face, tightly permed blue-rinsed hair, covered that day by a pink-and-orange head scarf.

'Yes, Kitty – what can I do for you?'

'Spuds, Father. We need another sack, and neither me nor Marie can heft the things. Could you go out back and grab some for us?'

'I will, of course,' the priest said, and taking another draught of his tea, he set it on the desk and followed Kitty out.

The storage room was a low shed situated behind the project. Tinned food, blankets, bags of donated clothes and fresh foodstuffs that were used quickly (potatoes rarely languished in the shed for more than a day) were kept there. Father Bill unlocked the door and went inside, grabbing a five-kilo bag. He was a tall man, over six feet in height, with a full head of dark hair that was showing some grey. He still had the slim waist and broad shoulders of a boxer, and his nose had been broken more than once. He was, however, by any standards, a handsome man, a fact not lost on his parishioners.

He turned to bring the spuds to the kitchen, when he realised there was someone standing in the doorway.

If he had looked at his watch, he would have seen that it was 12.15 p.m. exactly.

3

3 JULY 2016

Ringsend, Dublin
11.50 a.m.

MILEY TIMONEY WAS SINGING. LOUDLY. THE FACT
that music was not a talent he possessed did not prevent him from
enjoying the experience one bit. As he hoovered his small apartment,
the first home he could really call his own, Miley belted out the
chorus to 'Don't Pay the Ferryman', which he considered to be
one of the top-five best songs from his newly discovered favourite
musical artist, Chris de Burgh, whose greatest hits collection he
was playing at top volume.

Miley's life had not always been a happy one. Placed in care
when he was six, following the death of his father, he had been
moved from one care setting to another until he had ended up in a
nursing home, a residential service for the elderly. Even though he
was not yet thirty years old, Miley's family had (at least, this was
the story he told himself) believed that Harrington Nursing and
Convalescent Home was a better option than the other institutions
a young man with Down syndrome might be sent to by the state.

They were wrong. While a resident there, Miley had been
physically and emotionally abused by a thuggish caretaker. He
dreaded to think how it all might have ended if David Dunnigan,
whom he had met while being given a tour of the garda offices at
Harcourt Street, hadn't realised something was wrong. Dunnigan

had got him out and helped him to set up home on his own. He had also ensured Miley's tormentor was prosecuted for what he had done.

Now he had his own place and the freedom to be who he wanted, Miley was exploring all sorts of interests that had previously been denied him. Dunnigan, in his gruff but gentle way, had introduced him to classic horror and sci-fi, which Miley found he adored, but it was Father Bill who opened his eyes (and ears) to music. The priest had an abiding love for the songs of Canadian singer/songwriter Neil Young. Miley had bought a few of his CDs, and had enjoyed them a great deal, but he was conscious of creating his own identity, not mimicking anyone else's (in the home, the nurses on shift insisted the residents watch whatever television shows they, the staff, happened to like, and the magazines and books made available were ones they had finished reading), and while he liked the country side of Young's material, the grungy hard-rock stuff left him cold.

So deciding to find out what *he* liked, Miley had asked Father Bill if he could use the computer in the Homeless Project and spent some time on YouTube researching various musical avenues he had never gone down before.

He listened to the radio a lot, so he already had a good sense of his tastes – he tended towards gentler, lyrical music, and he was particularly drawn to songs that told stories. He also had a feeling he should support Irish musicians (Father Bill always advised him to shop locally), so he limited his search to homegrown talent.

He had been surprised at the reaction when he emerged from his online session and informed Diane, who was sitting at reception, that he thought he had found his favourite new artist.

'Chris de Burgh?' she spluttered. 'But … but he's so *cheesy*!'

Miley brushed her protestations aside.

'I like him. Have you listened to the song "Waiting for the Hurricane"? I think it really rocks.'

'Miley, sweetheart, one thing, I promise you, Chris de Burgh does *not* do is rock. But if you like him, listen away. It's your choice. You'll probably pick up his stuff pretty cheaply too – no one else much is buying it these days. He hasn't had a hit since 1988, as far as I remember.'

He'd found a shop called Spindizzy Records in the George's Street Arcade that sold secondhand vinyl and CDs. A really friendly guy called Damien worked there, who didn't sneer the way other people tended to when he mentioned the newfound object of his affections. Soon he had a decent collection of de Burgh's music, and he found that he really *did* like it – the songs had catchy choruses and told interesting tales, and he thought the singer looked to be a nice, amiable kind of chap, not really like a rock star at all. He reminded Miley of an awkwardly trendy dentist or maybe a primary school teacher.

And, Miley thought as he boogied along to the music, who cares if it's cool or not? When had he ever worried about being cool, anyway?

He switched off the hoover and looked about the room. Dunnigan called it 'compact', which Miley knew was really just a nice way of saying 'small'. It held a couch, a TV on a stand, a table and two chairs. There was a kitchen off one door, a bedroom with an en suite toilet and shower off another and the front door opened right into the living room. But it was his, and he loved it. And after that morning's efforts it was, if he did say so himself, spotless. He wanted to make a special effort because Harry was coming over for the afternoon. They were going to have lunch (he had some fresh bread, some ham and cheese and some pickles that he hated but Harry loved laid out on the table ready to go) and then they were going to the zoo.

Miley would have loved it if Harry had been allowed to live with him, and he knew Harry wanted that too, but he understood that, because of how he looked and the upbringing he'd had, the social workers had to be sure he would be a good carer. He'd met the family with whom Harry was currently living, and he had to admit, they were really good people. As long as Harry was happy and safe, he didn't feel he could really complain.

He put the hoover back in the cupboard and turned down the music. He looked at the clock on the wall. It was 12.14 p.m. – Harry was running late, but Tony, his foster dad, had called earlier that morning to say they'd be a bit delayed.

As the hands on the clock clicked around to fifteen past the hour, Miley paused – he thought he could hear footsteps on the landing outside his door.

4

3 JULY 2016

Phibsboro, Dublin
12.15 p.m.

DUNNIGAN WENT TO THE WINDOW AND PEERED out.

'Probably a mistake.'

He was almost back beside Diane when the buzzer sounded again. Shrugging, he went over and pressed the unlocking mechanism, opened his own door and waited for the caller to come upstairs. Diane cut a piece off a Danish and continued to read an article forecasting what was likely to happen in the next series of *Game of Thrones* – Season 6 had just concluded, and she was already pretty excited about Season 7, while also begrudging that she would have to wait a year for it to air. The other fly in the Westerosi ointment was that, although Diane loved the show, she was a bit dubious about watching it with Dunnigan, as he had read all the books and, whenever they discussed it, tended to point out every time the television producers made changes to the plot or (heaven save us) did their own thing completely (which is what they had chosen to do quite a lot in the recently lamented Season 6). She didn't know if she'd be able to cope with an ongoing commentary/criticism while trying to enjoy Jon Snow brooding in his leathers and furs.

'Be right back,' Dunnigan called to her when, after a minute, no one had come up the stairs.

She waved him off and munched her pastry. Moments later she heard his returning tread.

'Someone left this,' he said, and she saw he had a small cardboard box in his hand. *David Dunnigan* was printed in bold type on a piece of white paper that had been taped to the front.

'Were you expecting anything?'

'No.'

Diane took the box from him and shook it gently. There was something inside, but it wasn't very heavy and made a dull thudding sound.

'Seems safe.'

Dunnigan snorted and took the package back from her. 'And that is your professional opinion?'

'Yep.'

Diane had been in the Rangers, the Irish equivalent of the Special Forces, and had served in Chad and Northern Ireland. Dunnigan had learned during their recent activities with the After Dark Campaign that she had more than a passing appreciation for combustible materials.

'And if it explodes?'

'It won't.' Diane had already returned to her paper. The writer was suggesting that an uneasy alliance between Daenerys Targaryen and Jon Snow might be on the cards.

'We made a lot of very unpleasant people very unhappy recently, or have you forgotten?'

Dunnigan, as usual, was not going to be easily diverted. Diane looked at him sternly.

'Open it!' she said, then continued to read.

Of course, even if Season 7 proved to be complete and utter rubbish, Diane knew she'd continue to watch – she'd invested so much time and energy in it at this point, she was determined to see the whole thing to its undoubtedly bloody conclusion.

Beside her, Dunnigan made a strange strangled noise and stood bolt upright, the box falling onto the floor. She looked at him, puzzled, and saw that he was holding something in his hand. It took her a moment to register that it was a child's shoe – it looked to be a trainer. Dunnigan was now making repeated gulping sounds and had gone a frightening shade of puce – that he was naturally pale (to the point of, at times, verging on sickly) made this all the more alarming.

'Jesus, Davey – what's wrong?' She looked at him gazing at the shoe – white with pink trim. As she watched, he gently tapped the sole, and lights that were set into the sides flickered a sparkling purple.

And then she knew and felt her stomach turn over. Someone had sent Dunnigan one of Beth's – his missing niece's – shoes.

5

3 JULY 2016

**Widow's Quay Homeless Project, Dublin
12.15 p.m.**

THE MAN STANDING IN THE DOORWAY WAS AS TALL
as Father Bill and perhaps twice as wide, his body bulked up by
lifting weights and a probably not insignificant steroid habit. He
was dressed in a blue muscle shirt and some sort of light workout
pants – all designed to show off his sculpted physique. Father Bill
had only a second to take all this in, because the huge man charged
him in a sudden rush that was frightening in its ferocity.

How can a bloke that big move so fast? the priest just had time to
think as pain erupted in his ribs. He realised in an oddly detached
way that his attacker had stabbed him – further pain and an
overpowering nausea hit like a wave as the blade entered him a
second time.

Survival took over, and the priest, who was still holding the big
sack of potatoes, shoved them as hard as he could at his attacker,
knocking him backwards. Father Bill felt the blade withdraw and
slice downwards, cutting across his abdomen and momentarily
taking his breath away.

As the giant landed on his behind, two more men, smaller, but
equally vicious-looking, surged through the door. Father Bill
could feel blood soaking into his shirt and registered that it hurt
to breathe, but he pushed these thoughts aside and did what he

always did in a fight – brought the battle to his attackers. In two steps he was within range of the first of the new arrivals, a rat-like specimen in a black-and-pink-striped shell suit, and kicked him with all the force he could muster right in the testicles. Ratty gave a wheezing squeal and dropped to his knees. Without losing momentum Father Bill stepped over the fallen assailant and, using the heel of his hand, smashed the other man's nose, driving the bone back up into his skull. He keeled over immediately without uttering a sound.

Somewhere in the depths of his mind, Father Bill was aware that he was beginning to feel lightheaded and that the leg of his jeans was soaked through and blood was squelching in his shoe. He ignored all these realities and turned back to the bodybuilder. Unfortunately, the man was no longer where he had fallen. Father Bill had no time to look for him because at that moment something exploded in the back of his head– a chasm seemed to open around him, and he sank down into it gratefully.

6

3 JULY 2016

Ringsend, Dublin
12.15 p.m.

HARRY GATELY RAN AHEAD OF HIS FOSTER PARENTS and got to the door of Miley's apartment block about thirty seconds before they did. It was already open – they wouldn't have to ring up to be allowed in. This was not that unusual, as the spring mechanism designed to make the door close automatically was not as strong as it was supposed to be and always needed an extra shove to shut properly.

People who lived in the apartments or were regular visitors knew this and made sure to deliver a nudge to the lazy door, but occasional callers were not so well-informed and tended to leave it ajar.

Harry called back to Tony, his foster dad: 'I'm goin' on up!'

Tony, a short, balding man in his early fifties, called back: 'Maybe you should wait, Harry.'

Cynthia, slim to the point of skinny but with arresting blue eyes, shouted: 'Please hold on – we'll be there in a mo!'

The lad heard but, in his enthusiasm, decided to ignore their suggestions and charged in anyway.

The building had an elevator, but as Miley's apartment was only on the third floor, and the lift often took what seemed like hours to wend its way to ground level, Harry decided to hoof it and, taking the stairs two at a time, lolloped up to meet his friend.

Harry Gately was ten years old but could have passed for six. His young life had been a series of ups and downs, of traumas and challenges that would have, justifiably, caused many children to be bitter and resentful. Originally from County Clare, in the west of Ireland, Harry and his parents had come to Dublin almost a year previously. Harry didn't know why they had left their home in Ballyvaughan, but he remembered his mum and dad fighting, and he had a sense it was over money. He knew his dad used to have a job building houses, but then he didn't have one anymore, and his mum seemed to cry a lot. One day a man came to call, and Harry was told to go to his room, but he listened at the door while the grown-ups talked. He couldn't understand everything they said, but he heard something about rent, and the word bailiff was used a lot. He had asked his teacher what that word meant, and she had told him a bailiff was a little bit like a policeman who made bad people pay money they owed.

Harry thought she must be wrong about that because his parents weren't bad people. He tried to ask his mother what his teacher might have meant, but she just cried some more when he brought it up, so he never did again.

One night not long after, his dad woke him from a deep sleep and told him they were all going on an adventure. Dad dressed him in his warmest clothes (he actually put three T-shirts on him, which Harry thought was weird) and his thickest winter coat. Both his parents were similarly bundled up, and each had suitcases on wheels so you could pull them along rather than carry them. Dad put Harry's schoolbag on his back, and he knew by the feel of it that it no longer contained books, but clothes and other things instead.

They slept on benches in the railway station that night and the next morning caught the earliest bus they could to Dublin.

The first few nights they stayed in Busáras, the main terminal, wandering the city during the day, his parents taking turns sleeping and keeping watch over their belongings. Finally they were asked to move on by one of the security guards – he seemed to be more upset about it than they were and told them there was a spot only a few hundred yards up the street, adjacent to Connolly Station, where a lot of the street people camped.

This became their home for many months – Harry's dad made them a shack out of old bits of board and some strips of tarpaulin he found, and it was like they had their own little home.

Harry knew what being homeless meant, and while he was confused and embarrassed by it at first, he very quickly saw that, in a lot of ways, his family were better off this way. It was easy to get food from the skips outside supermarkets – there was always loads of stuff thrown away – and his mum didn't cry anymore. In fact, his parents seemed to love one another again, and that made him happy.

And he didn't have to go to school!

If only he hadn't got sick.

That winter nearly killed Harry. No matter how many blankets his mother packed about him at night, the cold seemed to creep like a living thing through every crack in the wall of their little home. His dad tried lighting a fire outside (it would have been far too dangerous *inside*) but it seemed to make no difference. Harry would lie on the mattress his dad had found for him, thick layers of card between it and the ground to try and insulate it as much as possible, but within an hour it felt as if his entire body was made of ice.

When the coughing began and he could not stop shivering, even during the day when it was warmer, his parents decided they would have to move. They had heard of a warehouse on the docks that was unused, and over two days they transported their gear there to a room on the second floor. After a couple of days, when it looked like Harry was beginning to perk up, his parents told him to rest and they would go out begging, in the hopes of earning enough to buy some medicine – a tonic, perhaps – to further speed his recovery.

They left on a Monday morning early, and he never saw them again.

It was two months before the man called David Dunnigan came and persuaded him to go to the Widow's Quay Project, where he had met Miley and Father Bill. Those two months had been awful – he didn't like thinking about them, although his foster parents made him visit a psychologist who tried to get him to talk about what had happened while he was alone.

Today, though, he was not going to waste a thought on those bad things. He was going to be spending the day with Miley.

Harry was aware that his friend was not like other people. He understood that Miley had a *condition*. But what did any of that matter? His friend was fun and kind and when Harry was with him he knew that Miley was listening to every word he said, and not only was he listening, he *remembered* and thought about what they'd talked about. He'd once told Miley, in passing, that he liked Honey Loops cereal. The next time he was over at Miley's, he saw a box of Honey Loops on the shelf. Miley didn't point it out, didn't make a fuss or anything, but there it was just the same, in case he fancied a bowl.

How could someone who would do a thing like that be a 'disabled'?

Father Bill was cool. Dunnigan he neither liked nor disliked – he felt safe with him and was sure he would always help him if he needed anything, but he also seemed distant and cold, sometimes. Diane was lovely, and she gave good hugs and always smelt nice. He loved his foster parents – they were really good people.

But Miley: Miley was special – and not in the way grown-ups

sometimes meant when they used that word about people like him, as if it was a bad thing. Miley was special like Christmas was special and birthdays were special.

Harry reached the landing outside Miley's apartment and ran headlong into a man who was crouched over something just at his friend's front door.

'Sorry, mister,' Harry said, staggering back a step.

The man straightened up and turned to look at him. Harry froze.

One of the things Harry didn't like to think about that happened during those two months he was alone in the warehouse was that two men had come one night. They had made him do things, bad things, and one of them, the really evil one, had looked at Harry just like this man was looking at him now.

Somewhere below, he could hear the beep that said the lift had arrived at the ground floor, which meant his foster mum and dad would be arriving in a minute or so.

The man – when Harry tried to describe him later, he couldn't; he could only remember those eyes – snorted and, shoving past him, moved quickly down the stairs, disappearing into the building below in a matter of seconds.

Harry turned to look at what the man had been doing.

There, lying against the wood of the doorframe, was what looked to be a doll of some kind. It was about the size of a teddy bear and made of rough material. A puddle of something dark was forming around it on the floor, as if it was bleeding. Harry moved it gingerly with his foot. The head lolled to one side, like it was weighted down with something, and he saw that the doll was a crudely made effigy of Miley: someone had drawn the almond-shaped eyes, the seemingly smiling mouth, and to his dawning horror, Harry saw that a tongue made of what looked to be some kind of raw meat protruded from the slashed maw.

Worst of all, though, was that a knife had been jammed into the body of the doll, which the boy now understood was little more than a sack filled with bloody raw meat.

Miley can't see this, Harry thought. *I won't let him!*

In one rapid motion he scooped up the disgusting bundle and, running to the landing window, which overlooked an alley running beside the apartment block, threw the reeking, foul thing out.

As he did, almost simultaneously, the elevator door pinged and slid open and a beaming Miley flung wide his front door.

Harry, smiling as if nothing had happened, ran to his friend and hugged him tightly.

It was later that evening when Miley saw the pool of dried blood on his doorstep. He asked Harry about it, and he knew the lad was lying when he shook his head and feigned ignorance. But he couldn't work out what the cause of such a thing might have been, and it was a day before he even knew he'd had a visitor at all, so in the philosophical way he had about such things, he set it aside and decided not to worry about it.

7

3 JULY 2016

Phibsboro, Dublin
12.25 p.m.

DIANE THOUGHT DUNNIGAN MIGHT BE HAVING A stroke.

She tried to speak to him, to calm him down, but when he responded (which was not often) all that seemed to come from him was gibberish. At one stage she tried to get him to go into the bedroom to lie down, but he couldn't seem to use his legs properly and ended up in a tangle of skinny limbs on the living-room floor.

The shoe that had started all this uproar was sitting on the coffee table among the remnants of their breakfast, looking innocent and unassuming.

'Davey, will you look at me, please?'

He mumbled something, his face pressed into the carpet, his arms and legs tucked under him at uncomfortable-looking angles.

'Davey, you're scaring me! I need you to pull it together, just for a second.'

'Shouldna ...' he said in a small, faraway voice. 'Shouldna ... let ... her go ...'

And then he was crying, loudly, desperately and uncontrollably.

Diane dialled 999 and asked for the police and an ambulance.

Then she wrapped her arms around David Dunnigan and rocked him like a baby.

8

3 JULY 2016

Widow's Quay Homeless Project, Dublin
12.25 p.m.

KITTY WENT LOOKING FOR FATHER BILL TEN minutes after she had asked him for the potatoes. She was a sensible woman who had grown up in the Liberties and was not prone to hysterics, but when she arrived at the storage shed to see what was keeping the priest, she did have a moment.

A man she had never seen before was half-lying, half-sitting against the wall by the door, his chin resting on his chest and blood dripping thickly onto the front of his sweatshirt from a wound where his nose was supposed to be.

But that wasn't the worst of it.

The floor of the shed was covered in blood, mottled with many bootprints and tracks, as if there had been an almighty scuffle. The air in the shed was dense with the coppery stench of the stuff.

Kitty paused for a second in the doorway, took in the scene and then ducked outside and threw up her breakfast.

After going to the toilet and rinsing out her mouth, she called the police.

It would be a full day before they learned the blood on the floor was Father Bill's, and two more before he was officially confirmed as missing.

9

3 JULY 2016

Ringsend, Dublin
12.32 p.m.

AFTER HARRY'S FOSTER PARENTS LEFT, HE AND Miley had a lovely lunch. There was ham and cheese rolls, and Miley remembered that he had a tube of sour cream and onion Pringles at the back of the press (he had a tendency to eat far too many, so he hid them behind the mugs and plates to put some obstacles between him and them) and they had some with their sandwiches. Harry was delighted to see that Miley had bought some bread-and-butter pickles, and he managed to persuade his pal to try some, although they weren't a huge success. Miley played Harry some of the Chris de Burgh songs he liked, and was none too surprised when the boy enjoyed 'Patricia the Stripper' the most (he was ten years old, after all), so they played it three times without stopping and laughed at one another shouting out the rude bits of the chorus. Then they strolled up the quays to the Phoenix Park and bought some ice-creams at the Spar on Ellis Quay, enjoying them as they talked about which animals they were going to go and see first when they got to the zoo.

Miley loved the African Plains, but Harry always wanted to spend ages at the penguins.

So they did both.

Miley thought it was the best afternoon he'd had in ages.

Harry did too and didn't think about the mannequin made of rotting meat once during the entire visit. In Harry's world, you didn't dwell on bad things.

By the time the two friends were discussing the dangers a hippo might present if you came across one in the Liffey (which Harry reckoned was a real possibility), a couple of stray dogs had already found the warped and cruel representation of Miley lying on the ground in the alley where the boy had tossed it. In seconds they had torn it to shreds, consuming the offal and rancid flesh with which it had been stuffed in great gulps.

Part Two

THE BEAUTIFUL SCIENCE

1

'HOW'S HE DOING?'

'Hello, Chief Superintendent.'

'What? Oh, yeah, um ... hello there. Diane, isn't it?'

'Diane Robinson, yes. Thanks for calling, Chief. I know he'll appreciate it when – well, when things calm down a bit.'

'You're welcome, Diane. How's Davey holding up?'

'Not too well.'

'He's gone into himself, I take it?'

'He's sitting staring at that poster he has on the wall over the fireplace.'

'He saying anything at all?'

'No. I brought him some tea an hour ago and he grunted something, but that's been the most conversation we've had since yesterday. Since the package came.'

'Has his sister been over?'

'No. But then, I expect she's got other things on her mind than her dysfunctional twin brother.'

'Probably does.'

Silence for a few moments. Then:

'Have you told him about Father Bill yet?'

'No. I was going to wait for him to come back to us a little before I delivered any more bad news. Anyway – we don't know what happened to him yet. He's ... well, Father Bill is not ... he's not an ordinary man.'

'The blood on the floor of that shed was almost all his, Diane. He lost buckets of the stuff. I don't want to give you false hope.'

'Do you know who the dead man was yet?'

'No. He's not on any of the databases. He's a bloody ghost. We have to assume whoever ordered the hit was sensible enough to send more than one man after the priest.'

'Good for Father Bill.'

Tormey laughed. 'He always was a tough fucker.'

'I hope he was tough enough this time.'

'You should prepare yourself for the fact that he wasn't. And Davey.'

'I know.'

'Keep him away from anything he might hurt himself with, OK?'

'Yes, I thought of that.'

'He tried it before. Nearly succeeded.'

'I know. He told me.'

'He must really trust you.'

'S'pose he must.'

'That's a pretty big deal for David Dunnigan. I didn't think he trusted anybody.'

'I'm looking after him, Chief. As much as he'll allow me to, anyway.'

'All right then. I'll keep you posted as things develop.'

'Thank you. How likely is it that you'll be able to learn anything from the shoe?'

'God, Diane … to be honest with you, I have no idea. It could tell us everything we need to know to catch the bastard, or nothing at all. We're just gonna have to wait and see what the boffins come up with.'

'OK. Thanks for the call.'

'We'll chat soon. I promise.'

Chief Superintendent Frank Tormey hung up.

2

DIANE ROBINSON SAT IN THE BEDROOM. SHE HADN'T gone home since the package had arrived – an event that seemed to have happened a lifetime ago.

The police had come and interviewed them both, but there was nothing either could offer.

Diane had been careful not to touch the evidence as they waited for the police to arrive, but she could see without close inspection that, although it had been cleaned and was spotless, it was not new, and the sole was slightly worn from usage.

If it wasn't Beth's shoe, someone had gone to a lot of trouble to play an excessively cruel prank on David.

Frank Tormey had arrived with what seemed like an army of plain-clothes men, and they canvassed every shop on the street. Footage from security cameras in the area had been taken for viewing, and Diane was in no doubt that every imaginable resource would be brought to bear on the case.

Midway through the ordeal that the afternoon had become, Tormey had received a call about an incident at the Widow's Quay Homeless Project.

If Dunnigan had heard any of that conversation, he showed no sign. He remained cold and aloof, sitting in his featureless living room on his sagging, ancient couch, gazing at the poster of the Doctor.

Diane wondered what she should do. In the end, completely at a loss, she went in to the living room, sat beside Dunnigan and stared at the poster too.

Nothing was said, but then, what was there to say?

3

MILEY TIMONEY SAT ACROSS THE DESK FROM HIS uncle, Chief Superintendent Frank Tormey, in the detective's cramped office at garda HQ in Harcourt Street. Miley was nervous and uncomfortable, but he struggled not to show it. Despite Tormey being married to Miley's mother's sister, he barely knew the man, and while he was aware the guard had played a small part in helping Dunnigan extricate him from that awful nursing home, Miley suspected the cop had done it out of a vague sense of duty and obligation rather than because he actually cared about his nephew's well-being.

Be that as it may, David Dunnigan was (after Harry) his best friend, and Miley knew he was in trouble. If that meant having some uncomfortable conversations with Davey's boss in an effort to learn what steps were being taken to find Beth, then Miley would just have to endure them.

'I don't know what I can tell you, son,' Tormey said.

The detective was a tall, spare man, his dark hair worn short in a crew cut, a thick, droopy moustache covering his mouth. Miley noticed that he had quick, sharp eyes that were not unkind, and he warmed to him slightly. 'Davey won't answer my calls.'

While Miley did speak with a mild lisp, his diction was clear and easily understood. Also, in spite of what people generally thought when they saw him, Miley was, according to the inexact methods used to measure such things, of higher than average intelligence, not just for people with Down syndrome, but for the general population. What the IQ tests failed to detect was that Miley was a sensitive and deeply moral young man.

'I don't see how I can help you with that,' Tormey said. 'And I think Davey is entitled to a little leeway, don't you? I mean, he's had one hell of a shock.'

'Is the whole thing being taken seriously?' Miley pressed. 'Beth has been missing for a long time – are the gardaí viewing this as serious evidence, or is it being treated more as a prank?'

Tormey raised a bushy eyebrow.

'We are following every possible line of inquiry,' he said tersely.

'For example?'

'I shouldn't even be talking to you.' The detective sat back and put his hands behind his head. 'You are not a member of this department and you're not a member of Dunnigan's family.'

'I'm as close as.'

Tormey sighed deeply and nodded. 'You know, you probably are, at that.'

'So?'

'So the most I can tell you is that the shoe has gone to Forensics. They'll do their thing and we'll take it from there.'

'Is that it?'

'What else is there?'

'Footage from security cameras on the street outside Davey's flat? I've read that Dublin has more cameras than any other city in Europe.'

Tormey couldn't stifle a smile. 'Is that right? Well, as it happens, there were a few cameras about. They showed a man in a hoodie stopping at Davey's door and leaving the package. Working backwards, we have him getting out of a van parked on St Peter's Road, about a hundred yards north of the flat. The plates do not exist on the system – so they were obviously fakes. Witnesses have reported a red box van parked at that location, but I think we both know it is more than likely no longer that colour. The hooded man moved up Phibsboro Road and turned right onto Monck Place, and that's where we lose him. It's one of the few spots in the vicinity without cameras, and, as he doesn't appear on any other cameras, it seems he was picked up there by another vehicle.'

'That's it?'

'I'm afraid so. You try questioning shopkeepers about a single individual on a crowded street wearing a dark-coloured hoodie and what look to be tracksuit pants. Nobody can tell us anything – I don't think anyone even noticed him. Or her. It's a dead end. So that leaves us with whatever the forensics guys come up with.'

'Are there any of *them* I can talk to?'

Tormey looked sternly at Miley. His nephew had slimmed out since leaving the nursing home – he wore his brown hair long and was dressed in a green military-style jacket and black jeans. His T-shirt bore the Batman insignia.

'Why?' Tormey said.

'Because I want everyone involved in the investigation to know there are people who care about what happens,' Miley said. 'Davey is too upset – he can't do it for himself. So I'm doing it for him. When the scientists know there's someone keeping an eye on their progress, hopefully they'll be careful in what they do. It's not just an eighteen-year-old cold case. It's something very real and very current.'

'I'll make a call,' Tormey said, smiling gently. 'I don't know that you'll understand anything they have to say – God knows, I don't – but I'll let them know you're coming.'

He scribbled something on a piece of paper and passed it across.

'Doctor Georgina Russell,' Miley read.

'Now go and annoy her,' Tormey said. 'I have work to do.'

Miley was at the door when Tormey called after him: 'You're one of Father Bill's crew – how come you haven't asked me about that case?'

Miley turned back to the detective. 'I can't think about that right now. I have to believe that Father Bill can take care of himself. Davey can't. That's all I can say about it.'

Tormey nodded. 'OK, then. Good luck with Doctor Russell. I think you two might just get on.'

Miley grinned. 'I get on with everybody.'

Doctor Phillipe Ressler

He spent his childhood wondering what he had done to make his parents treat him the way they did. Thirty-five years and six degrees later, he still did not know why.

Perhaps it was just because he was bad.

His mother would scream at him to wake up and make her breakfast, clean the house, wash the dishes, and he would do it all exactly the way she had insisted the last time he had done them, but always the rules would have changed since her last black mood, and in his effort to make her happy he would inexplicably mess up and be beaten for it.

Regardless, he tried to stay smiling and upbeat and jolly, hoping against hope that his levity might brush off on her. It never did, but he kept hoping.

In some ways, he welcomed the beatings because they heralded the end of that day's torments, and he knew he would be sent to his room for the rest of the day – there he would have his books and his peace, and he would not be bothered until the darkness stirred in her again and he would be summoned to dance to her bidding.

One of her favourite games was to set him to find some item she had lost – it could be anything from a thimble to the remote control for the television, and he would turn the house upside down looking for it, searching every place he could dream of, squeezing into every nook and crevice where such an item might have been dropped or rolled accidentally.

He came to know their house intimately during these searches, better, he told himself, than her or his stupid, indolent father, but he never found any of the things she said she'd lost. Usually they would miraculously turn up later that day – he would come into the sitting room to bring her her evening glass of vodka and she would be sprawled on the couch, the errant remote control in her hand, watching her idiotic soap opera.

'You must have forgotten to search under the cushions on the couch,' she would say dismissively.

'No, I did, Mama. I looked there first.'

'Well, that is where it was. I got tired of waiting for you to find it and looked myself, and it took me less than a minute.'

'I'm sorry, Mama.'

'Stop dawdling there and get me my chocolate. My blood sugars are very low today.'

'Yes, Mama, of course.'

'Don't just stand there – hurry up!'

He would bring her the sweets and then take whichever book he was reading and climb to the stairs at the very top of the house where there was a small landing no one ever went to except him, and he would squeeze into the corner so he felt very safe and secure, and he would read until it got too dark to see the words.

Sometimes she would call for him, and he would pretend he couldn't hear her.

Just for a few moments.

It was nice to imagine he had no mother and that he was alone in the old crumbling house.

4

DOCTOR GEORGINA RUSSELL WAS TALL AND SLENDER, with long auburn hair which she had woven into a single plait down her back. Miley thought she was very pretty, but he got the impression she either did not think so or didn't care much one way or the other. She wore glasses set into thick plastic frames that were (in his opinion) the wrong shape for her face, and a hideous woollen jumper of clashing colours glared from under her open white lab coat. The jumper had seen better days, and it looked as if she was prone to pulling her legs up under it to warm them when she was sitting down, as he had sometimes seen Diane do – the knitwear had been stretched out of all proportion and was now pretty shapeless.

Miley had announced himself first to a uniformed guard at the gate to the huge complex of garda buildings right beside the zoo in the Phoenix Park, and he was admitted through a Plexiglas door to a female officer at a reception desk, who took his details again and gave him a visitor's card on a lanyard. Then he had waited. And waited.

Finally Doctor Russell had arrived, and they made the short walk past the beautiful Georgian façade of the commissioner's building to the canteen in the forensics block to talk. The room was long and low-ceilinged and packed with staff having late lunches and mid-afternoon coffees. They had to shout to hear one another amid the scraping of furniture and loud chatter.

'So you're Mr Dunnigan's friend, then?' she said when she had a camomile tea and he a Coke.

Miley was aware of her giving him the once over – most people did when they met him first. He knew she was trying to work out how disabled he was and how much she should dumb down their conversation.

'Yes. Do you know Davey?'

'A little.'

'This has really knocked him for six. I just wanted to know if you think you'll be able to learn anything from the shoe.'

Doctor Russell adjusted her glasses and scratched her nose. 'I really don't know yet.'

'Oh. Um … why not?'

'Because I haven't started looking at it yet.'

Miley gazed at her blankly. 'Today is Wednesday. You've had it for three days already.'

'There is quite a backlog, and we are severely understaffed. I wish I could be more positive.'

Miley felt himself getting angry but tried to remain calm – he needed to get this woman onside, and losing his temper was unlikely to achieve that.

'Is there any way you could have it bumped up the pile? I mean, Davey is one of your own, so to speak.'

'He is a criminologist who is kept on retainer by the Sex Crimes Unit. That means he's not even full-time staff. I don't have time to be sentimental about these things, Mr Timoney.'

'Miley. Call me Miley.'

'All right. Miley, then. Let's speak practically, shall we?'

'I thought we already were.'

She made a sort of facial clenching that Miley assumed passed for a smile.

'I mean in terms of the science.'

'*The* science?'

'Yes. The science of what I do. Your friend's niece went missing eighteen years ago.'

'December the eighth, 1998.'

'Yes. I have only looked at the shoe briefly, but it appears to have been recently cleaned with some form of detergent – it certainly exudes a mild chemical odour. Do you know what that means?'

'I would imagine it means that finding threads and fibres and blood stains and the like will be difficult.'

Miley sensed her relaxing somewhat – he had passed some kind of test, and she seemed to have decided to speak to him like a 'normal' person. Which was nice.

'It will be *more* difficult, yes, but that is not what I mean. The average perpetrator of a crime has a cursory understanding of forensic science and the scope of what we can do, usually based on the inaccurate plots of various lurid TV serials. They *think* they know about it, but they really have no idea. You see, washing a shoe in, say, a dilution of bleach and hot water will remove certain trace elements of blood, but there will still be microscopic particles trapped in the fibres. Similarly, using a wire brush will take off larger hairs or grasses or dirt particles, but it will also push others deep into grooves and into gaps between the materials.'

'What are you saying, then?'

'Using a chemical to wash an item of clothing will not remove biological or identifying markers completely, but it can alter them. We call it cross-contamination. What it means, in terms of processing the evidence, is that it might not be usable in court.'

'What about helping to find Beth?'

'The short answer to that is I don't know. The eighteen-year time gap will, more than likely, mean that any cellular or DNA evidence she left (if she left any) will have deteriorated but could still be usable. But of course, it's not just her DNA we're after. A single item like that could hold the answer to exactly what happened to the little girl.'

'Really?'

'Oh, yes. Without a doubt. There could be blood or semen

samples on the surface of the item – even *saliva* – from the person who abducted her, which could lead us to them. I worked on a case once where a shirt worn by a murder victim had a tiny wine stain from a vintage owned by only three people in the country.'

'That's amazing!' Miley said, getting excited despite himself.

'But it could also give us nothing at all. Without examining it I couldn't begin to guess.'

Miley felt like shaking the woman, but instead he gave her one of his most winning smiles.

'Davey is my friend, Doctor Russell. I owe him a great deal. I would take it as a personal favour if you would give the shoe your closest attention as soon as you possibly can.'

'I'm due to look at it on Friday, and it's to go to the DNA people the Monday after that – if things go according to plan with the other jobs between now and then, that is.'

'I'm sure Chief Superintendent Tormey would also be very grateful if it got fast-tracked.'

'I have no doubt he would.'

'He's my uncle, you know. I have quite a bit of influence with him,' Miley lied.

Doctor Georgina Russell shook her head. 'You are a determined bloke, aren't you, Miley?'

'I am dogged.' Miley grinned. 'Everyone says so.'

The forensic scientist stood up. 'This evening.'

Miley blinked up at her. 'What?'

'I'll have a look at the shoe this evening. I had some lab time booked for a personal project I'm working on, but as you've made the effort to come over here, and because you hold such sway with a senior detective, I'll give up some of my time and look at your friend's case.'

'Thank you,' Miley said, flashing his charming smile again.

'Stop making that face,' Doctor Russell said as she walked away. 'It's freaking me out.'

5

DIANE WAS NOW ACTING MANAGER OF THE WIDOW'S Quay Homeless Shelter, where Miley volunteered most evenings. Miley sat with her in the dining room and they had dinner together.

'I don't know what to hope for,' she said when Miley told her about his day. 'I mean, if they *do* find something, he's likely to go off on a crusade chasing whatever clues it throws up … but if they find nothing, he'll be devastated.'

'I think we have to trust that Tormey won't let Davey lose the run of himself,' Miley said. 'I don't think he'll be allowed to get too involved – he can't have any perspective on this. He's too close to it.'

'I wish I was as confident as you,' Diane said, and Miley reached over and took her hand.

'How are you doing?' he asked.

'I don't know,' she said, laughing and crying at the same time. 'I just wish I could get through to him. He's still barely talking, and he won't eat. All he does is drink tea and stare at the walls. I tried calling Gina, but she doesn't answer either. There's a feckin' pair of them in it.'

'Should I call over and see him?'

'You're welcome to try, Miley, but I don't think he'll let you in.'

'You have a key, don't you?'

'I do, but he made me swear not to give it to anyone. He would never forgive me if I broke that trust, not even for you. I can't, Miley. I'm sorry, but I just can't.'

Miley nodded. He knew she was right, but he had to ask.

'Have you heard any news on Father Bill?'

'No,' Diane said. 'I don't think the police are very optimistic.'

Miley paused, a forkful of shepherd's pie halfway to his mouth. 'You know him better than anyone,' he said. 'What do you think?'

'I think he and Davey were targeted,' Diane said. 'And we both know who by.'

Miley shook his head. 'That doesn't make sense,' he said. 'How could those guys get Beth's shoe?'

'If it is Beth's shoe,' Diane said. 'It's more likely they're trying to push Davey's buttons. Maybe shove him over the edge.'

'They might have succeeded,' Miley said ruefully. 'At least we're still holding it together.'

'And we're just hanging on by our fingernails,' Diane said without humour.

'Speak for yourself,' Miley retorted.

6

THE THIRD FLOOR OF THE FORENSICS IRELAND building, where all analyses were carried out, was quiet, the bustle of the day over. The department operated twenty-four hours a day, but the night crew was much smaller and tended to keep themselves to themselves, working on whichever tasks the day technicians had left for them.

Doctor Georgina Russell loved these dark, quiet hours. She booked sessions in one of the general workrooms three times a week to do research for a book she was writing on the use of micro-organisms in forensic policing.

Microbial forensics was a relatively new field, involving the identification of microscopic life – mostly bacteria – that can be found on everything and which, if you know what to look for, can tell a huge amount about the environment from which the item originated.

The study of microbes was mostly utilised to thwart bioterror attacks, prove or disprove cases of medical negligence and track instances of foodborne disease outbreaks. Georgina contended that it had far wider applications and had begun a series of experiments to prove her point. Her efforts had, so far, been more successful than she had dared imagine – she had shown, for instance, that the microbial communities on the surface of a mobile phone matched the communities in the environment through which the phone moved (in effect, your iPhone picked up traces and cultures from each surface it came in contact with) so could be used to track the behaviours of the phone's user. Mobile phones were the ideal focus of her research, as Georgina had observed that (most) people washed their hands and changed their clothes, but few people bothered to wipe down their phones regularly, if at all.

She was excited by her studies and anxious to continue them.

But something told her the young man she had met earlier was not going to go away. Georgina's work did not often bring her into contact with the public, but she was a good judge of character. Miley Timoney was not a man to be taken lightly.

She lifted the trainer from the paper bag it had been stored in and placed it on top of the sheet of brown paper she had laid on the work table in front of her to gather any particles that might fall from the shoe while she worked. Then she did the same with the cardboard box used to transport it to Dunnigan's doorstep.

The file that accompanied the items reminded her of the facts of the case – and so the first thing to establish was whether this particular shoe *could* belong to a child abducted eighteen years ago.

A quick examination showed that the trainer had been made by a company called LA Gear, and belonged to a specific line called LA Lights. A Google search told her the brand had been highly desirable in the 1990s, until it was discovered that some of the components powering the lights set into the soles, specifically a type of metal that formed one of the switches, could be toxic to humans. Some US states even went so far as to ban the shoes, and the company went bust in 1998 – the model of child's running shoe on the desk before her was one of the last items they'd produced.

Which meant this was, beyond any doubt, a genuine relic.

That did not, however, confirm that it had ever belonged to Beth Carlton.

Another Internet search unearthed an eBay page from which she could have bought any number of previously worn or completely unworn and 'still-in-box' LA Lights shoes of all sizes and colours. So, while the trainer may well have once adorned the foot of Beth Carlton, it could also have been bought online and passed off as such by someone with a grudge against Dunnigan.

She paused and thought about that.

If she was honest with herself (and she always tried to be), David Dunnigan bothered her.

She had met him only once – at the Central Criminal Court where both of them had been giving evidence on a murder case. She had found him distant and unfocused – he delivered his testimony competently enough, it was just that he gave the impression he would rather be anywhere else, and when he had been introduced to her, his handshake had been damp and limp.

Yet it seemed Miley cared about him. And he was good enough at his job to draw the ire of some clearly unpleasant people. Perhaps she would have to reserve judgement.

Her Internet research complete, Georgina initiated phase two of her task.

She began by using the 60X lens of a special instrument called an episcope, which magnified its subject under very bright light, and examined both pieces of evidence thoroughly.

The box yielded nothing at all – she had not really believed it would. It had not been in Dunnigan's flat long enough to pick up anything sizeable (fibres from the carpet, for example), and whoever had transported it had used gloves and been very careful. The shoe, on the other hand, was another story.

Close inspection showed what looked to be tiny fragments of dried blood in the crevice between the rubber edging and the canvas of the shoe's body. Using a Frazier hook, she delicately removed them and tapped them into a petri dish.

She also spotted something wedged into one of the grooves on the sole of the shoe. It was too small to accurately identify, even under the lens, so she removed the object, along with the surrounding rubber it was attached to, with a scalpel and placed them on a microscope slide.

What she saw when she peered through the viewfinder looked not unlike a coffee bean. But of course, it wasn't.

It was a single grain of pollen.

Doctor Georgina Russell began to get excited.

David Dunnigan

The flat was in darkness – he had not bothered to turn on the lights. In fact, he had scarcely suffered himself to move since the shoe had arrived and brought all the pain and the hurt and the fear crashing back upon him.

He was surprised at how raw it still was – the guilt and the horror were as fresh and as overwhelming as they had been all those years ago. He remembered the precise moment he realised Beth was gone and that they were not going to find her – it was two days after she had been taken, and he had been sitting at his desk in the university. A wall of panic so intense it was almost a visible thing hit him, and for a full minute he could not breathe; he had truly thought he was going to die.

He knew, now, that the misery would not kill him. Though he wished it would.

He gazed at the poster of Patrick Troughton as the Second Doctor.

He'd had this picture since his parents had sent him away to boarding school in Wexford when he was twelve – his mother, in one of her rare moments of indulgence, had offered to buy something 'personal' for his new room, and this had been his choice. She'd sighed and expressed her usual displeasure at his love of something as frivolous as a science-fiction character, but she paid for it, nonetheless, and even suggested getting a nice frame, so it 'didn't look scruffy' when she came to visit, which she did twice during his six years in Good Counsel.

The poster became his constant friend. He'd brought it with him to college and to the various apartments and flats he'd leased since then. Of the many versions of his hero, Dunnigan identified most with the Second: the impish time traveller could come across as a scatter-brained buffoon, but he was always several steps ahead of everyone else, and his silliness was a way of tricking enemies into underestimating him. The Doctor could be hard and manipulative too, when he needed to be. Dunnigan believed this twinkly-eyed little man was perfectly capable of sacrificing one of his companions if the situation called for it – if there was no other way and the fate of the universe was hanging in the balance, the Second Doctor would not hesitate.

'I'm scared,' he said aloud to the poster. 'The monsters didn't go away, like I thought. They were just waiting for me to let my guard down.'

Or were they? Was this all a hoax, an attempt to break him? The photo of him and Beth had been released to the papers, as it was the most recent image of the child available at the time, so the type of trainer she was wearing was not a secret.

'But what if it's not a hoax?' he said to the darkness. 'What if she's really out there somewhere and they know where she is?'

He realised that he could not think of Beth as an adult. She would be twenty-two now, if she were still alive. He tried to picture her as a woman but found it impossible.

'If it's real,' Dunnigan said to the Doctor, 'I'm terrified of what I might find. If the shoe did belong to her, it might lead us to the fact that she's really gone. That whoever took her murdered her – or worse.'

The Doctor smiled down at him from the wall.

'I know I can't hide forever,' Dunnigan said. 'But I don't know what else to do.'

And the night wore on interminably.

7

DIANE ROBINSON LOCKED THE FRONT DOOR OF the Widow's Quay Homeless Project at 11.30, just as Georgina Russell was investigating the insole of the vintage running shoe.

It being summer, they were only about three-quarters full, but that did not diminish the quality of service the residents deserved, and before clocking off for the night she had given a thorough handover to Dominic, the night manager, and finished off the paperwork for the day. Diane knew she was keeping busy to avoid thinking about everything that was going on, and she was aware that, at some point, she was going to have to sit down and allow herself to experience it. But, perhaps luckily, just then there was too much to be done – Dunnigan needed her, even if he was too messed up to admit it or even ask for her help, and then there was Father Bill …

Frank Tormey had visited the project earlier that evening. The detective told her that, as of the next day, the priest was being treated as officially missing but (between him and her) was presumed to be dead. She did not want to believe it, but even her unwavering faith in Father Bill was starting to flag.

Diane turned right and began the walk to her car, which was parked in a yard a nearby shopkeeper allowed the staff at the project to use. She had not gone five steps when a black Lexus, which had been illegally parked across the road, slid up beside her.

The front passenger door opened and a man in a dark suit got out and unceremoniously grabbed her.

Diane had been a field nurse in the Rangers, but she'd been in the army before that and had advanced training in hand-to-hand combat. She felt something in her activate – it was like a switch in her head – and Diane Robinson, therapist and social care worker, was gone. Corporal First Class Diane Robinson stepped out of the shadows of her consciousness and drove her heel straight into the arch of her assailant's foot then, dropping slightly, put her elbow into his solar plexus with brutal force. There was a satisfying sound as all the air was pushed out of the man's lungs, and then she was running along the street as fast as she could. The car idled behind her for a second, then took off at speed, swerving across the pavement ahead of her and blocking her path. She skidded to a halt for a second, turning on her heel. She was considering jumping the barrier and going into the river when a voice said: 'Ms Robinson, please forgive my associate's rudeness. I am a friend of Father Bill's and I think I have some information you might find useful.'

She looked over her shoulder. Standing at the open door of the car was the tall, dapper figure of Tim Pat Rogers, head of one of the more aggressive and successful criminal gangs in Dublin and known locally as the Janitor.

'I can't think of any information that requires me getting into a car with you to hear it,' Diane said, trying not to sound too out of breath, though her heart was pounding and she was genuinely terrified.

She knew Father Bill liked and respected the mobster, but the truth was, as much as she loved the priest, there was a side to him that she always pretended she knew nothing about. She told herself it was in the interest of plausible deniability, that everyone was entitled to their secrets – but she knew the priest could be a violent man, and there were things he did she was better off protected from.

Tim Pat Rogers belonged to that part of Father Bill's life.

'It would be easier if you allowed me to show you,' Rogers said. 'I personally guarantee your safety. You'll be in your Honda Civic and on your way home within the hour. But I promise you, you'll be glad you came with me.'

Diane chewed her lower lip.

'Can I text my boyfriend and tell him where I'm going?'

Rogers laughed. It wasn't a nice sound.

'Tell Mr Dunnigan we are on our way to Daddy Joe's. Mind you, if he's in the state I've been led to believe, I don't know what good that'll do you.'

Diane knew he was right, but she sent the message anyway, then followed him into the back of the Lexus. If Dunnigan received the text, he never replied to it.

8

DADDY JOE'S WAS A NIGHTCLUB ON THE NORTH Wall – a long, low building that had been used for raves and acid-house parties in the nineties and mosh battles in the first decade of the new millennium. In its current incarnation it preferred to keep it country and attracted the new wave of Irish artists ploughing their furrow in this latest musical field.

It also served as base of operations for Rogers' not inconsiderable criminal empire.

Diane was ushered from the car to a door at the rear of the club by the man she had scuffled with earlier, who, she was pleased to note, was walking a little stiffly. While they were en route, Rogers had introduced him as Terry.

Within, all was dark – the trio moved through what she sensed was the wide-open space of the dancefloor and into a narrow corridor, then down stone steps to what she gathered must be the drinks cellar.

Terry turned on a light, and as her eyes grew accustomed to the glare, she saw that she had been right: beer kegs and crates were stacked all about. Rogers motioned for her to follow.

In a cleared space behind a stack of boxes was a shape that had been covered by a sheet. Diane saw that, at various points, something red had soaked through the thin material.

'What is this?' she asked, fear and anger rising in her in equal measure.

'What you might call a mutual interest,' Rogers said.

Diane glanced at the shrouded bundle.

'I don't follow.'

With a theatrical flourish, the gangster pulled the sheet away to reveal what had once been a man, bound to a metal chair with cable ties. He was naked save for a pair of bloodied and soiled boxer shorts, and his body was a mess of cuts, bruises and torn flesh. Moving closer, Diane saw that he was still alive, though his breaths were very shallow. She pressed her hand to his carotid artery, felt for a pulse. It was there, but weak.

'He needs to be brought to a hospital,' she said through gritted teeth.

As a military nurse, Diane had seen and treated many injured men. The one slumped before her was being held on the chair by his restraints alone – she could see that he was unable to support himself, meaning many of his bones were broken. The wreckage that was his soft tissue showed the marks of many different implements – he had been whipped with what was probably some kind of wire or possibly a chain, and it looked as if one of his arms had been literally skinned.

She had seen men with worse injuries, but not many.

'I think we both know that's not going to happen,' Rogers said. 'I can assure you, our friend there knows it, too.'

The Janitor was well over six feet tall and favoured expensively tailored casual suits. In his mid-fifties, his dark hair showed no grey and was swept back from his forehead. He was watching Diane with a sort of thinly veiled amusement.

'Do you want me to treat him?' she said, assuming that was why she was there. 'I don't have any equipment, but—'

'No. He's beyond help.' Rogers waved off her suggestion. 'I think you might learn something from him, though.'

Diane looked from the prone man in the chair to the mobster and then to Terry, who stood just off to the side, seemingly watching nothing but seeing everything.

'I have no idea what is going on,' she said. 'Look, it's late and I'm on shift again in a few hours.'

'This gentleman,' Rogers walked slowly over to where she stood and rested one of his large but somehow delicate hands on the bloody shoulder of his guest, 'arrived at this club, my place of business, at a quarter past twelve on Sunday last with a contingent of friends, all of them carrying weapons. If I were not the paranoid individual I am – I always keep a few carefully chosen men about the place in case I am in need of their protection – I might have come to harm. As luck would have it, events played out in my favour, and we decommissioned his four cronies. After that he seemed ... *unwilling* to cooperate with me so we brought him down here and treated him to our hospitality. Earlier today, he started to talk.'

Diane tried to absorb what she had just been told. 'They made a run at you on Sunday – around midday?'

'The shooting started at 12.15.'

'That's when the shoe was delivered.'

'Are you starting to appreciate our commonality?' Rogers said.

'You said you got him to talk?'

Rogers nodded at Terry, who strode across the cellar space and slapped the prone man hard across his mangled cheek.

'Wakey, wakey,' Rogers said.

The wounded man's head lolled back and forth, he gulped for breath, then vomited a torrent of blood and bile down his shredded chest.

'Thank you for rejoining us,' Rogers said pleasantly. 'I have someone I'd like you to meet, and I want you to tell her what you told me earlier.'

'*Fuck off,*' the man slurred.

Diane saw that most of his teeth were missing.

'Now, Ciaran – nothing would please me more than to help you spend the last few hours of your life in some degree of comfort.'

He nodded at Terry again, and suddenly the man had a syringe in his hand, the needle covered in a protective plastic sheath. The bloodied man Rogers had called Ciaran eyed it warily.

'That's heroin – not the shit stuff, not the kind that'll give you nightmares and bellyaches. What I have loaded that needle with will take you away from all your troubles and cares on a pink cloud of kindness. I *want* to give you that, Ciaran, I really do. But if you don't help me out this one last time, I'll have to give you what's in Terry's other hand.'

Rogers' associate reached behind a crate and came back up with a hacksaw.

'You probably think that we've beat you and cut you up so bad, you won't feel much else. You're wrong, Ciaran. Terry here will start on your left foot – just like in the movie – and he'll saw it off. Slowly. Then he'll get to work on your right arm – we'll probably take it just above the elbow. After that, who knows? I'll let him go freestyle.'

Ciaran's eyes had grown very wide. 'What do you want to know?' he hissed, barely audibly.

Rogers tousled the man's matted hair. 'Good choice. Ms Robinson, he's all yours.'

Diane squatted down on her haunches in front of the unfortunate man. He looked at her with hooded eyes, one of which was so full of blood as to be effectively blind.

'My friend was sent a package that contained something very upsetting at the same time Mr Rogers here was attacked, and from what I understand, Father Bill Creedon was hit at more or less that time too.'

The man continued to eye her, his head swaying slightly.

'Were you sent by the After Dark people? Was Frobisher behind this?'

Ernest Frobisher was the ancient, twisted leader of the After Dark Campaign – his family had been involved in business, politics and mayhem in Ireland and further afield for over two hundred years. By shutting down a wing of his operation, it was not unreasonable to believe Dunnigan, Father Bill, Diane and now the Janitor had drawn his wrath upon themselves.

Ciaran appeared to be struggling to process her question. The pause seemed to continue for an eternity, and finally Terry leaned over and punched him in the side of the head, an action that sprayed both him and Diane with blood and sweat.

'For God's sake, Terry, will you rein it in a bit?' Rogers said, pulling a handkerchief from his pocket and offering it to Diane. 'I apologise, Ms Robinson.'

She shook her head. 'Ciaran, they are going to cut you to pieces, and I am going to have to walk away. By the time the gardaí get here, you'll be finished, and there'll be nothing I can do about it. Please tell me what you can. My life has been turned upside down over the past three days, and I don't know what to do.'

Ciaran took in a shuddering breath. 'I don't know who paid for the job,' he said gutturally. Diane realised he had a slight Northern twang to his speech. 'All I know is my crew were called in late on Saturday night. We were told that there were four jobs needed doing: two packages to be delivered and they were to be clean – no prints, no fibres, nothing traceable – and two hits. They were all to happen at 12.15 Sunday afternoon. Someone wanted to send out a message that they were not to be fucked with.'

Diane looked at Rogers, who was standing with his hands behind his back, listening intently. He shrugged at her. She turned back to the dying man.

'Is Father Bill dead?' she asked.

'The hits were to be terminal. Lethal force.'

'He's dead,' Rogers said. 'I've told Bill a hundred times he needs to start carrying a sidearm, but he's a stubborn man.'

'They were to use a blade on the priest,' Ciaran said. 'Steve was sent – he's good with a knife. Big bastard. I don't know why they wanted it done that way. Was supposed to mean something.'

'The Yellow Man,' Diane said to Rogers. 'He pulled a knife on Father Bill when they fought down at the docks, and one of your men shot him for it.'

The Yellow Man had been Frobisher's chief enforcer. Dunnigan told her he may have been called Andrews, once, but whether that was his real name or not didn't matter anymore.

'You said two packages were delivered?'

'Yeah. One to an address in Phibsboro and one to a place in Ringsend.'

'Ringsend?'

'Yeah.'

'Did it get there?'

'How would I know?'

Diane puzzled on that – Miley had not mentioned anything.

'Who made the arrangements?' she asked. 'Who hired you?'

'I don't know. I'm a fuckin' soldier – they don't tell us stuff like that.' He looked beyond her to Rogers. 'Please … finish it now, will you?'

Rogers tutted and shook his head. 'It's up to the lady.'

Diane felt a sudden nausea. They were asking her to give the order that would end this man's life. 'Let me bring him to a hospital. He won't talk. Will you?'

'They broke my back,' Ciaran hissed. 'I can't move my legs. That bastard cut off my dick and stuck nails through my balls. Will you not let me die?'

She felt as if she was going to be sick. Instead she took his face in her hands softly.

'I'm sorry you had to die like this,' she said. 'You and your people did some bad things, but no one deserves this.'

'Thank you,' he whispered to her.

Tears welled in her eyes and she stood up. 'I'll be outside,' she said, and left the men to their horrors.

She waited in the dancehall, and after a few minutes Rogers came up the stairs.

'Terry will wait with him until he's gone. He was a tough bastard. Held out much longer than most would.'

'You could have just told me what you knew,' Diane said, tears in her voice. 'You didn't have to involve me in that … that sickness.'

'Would you have believed me?'

She paused, looking into the darkness. 'I don't know.'

'You do now, though, don't you?'

'Yes.'

'So you see why I brought you.'

They walked out to the car park.

'Do you know which organisation he works for?'

'*Worked* for. Yes. Fred Quirke's crew, over Blanchardstown way. He uses a lot of ex-IRA people.'

'Do you believe they're linked to Frobisher?'

'I think they were hired to do the job. I reckon we have Frobisher and his people on the run. He had to leave us with a little something, though, couldn't be seen to allow a slight like the one we delivered go unanswered.'

'OK.'

'What will you do with that information?'

'I don't know yet.'

Rogers opened the door for her and then got into the driver's seat. He handed her a card which was blank except for a telephone number, printed in bold italic, on one side. 'In case you need any assistance when you do know.'

Diane nodded, and they drove back to her car in silence.

Doctor Phillipe Ressler

It was the winter of his sixteenth year. He was in his hiding place at the top of the stairs one afternoon. It was proving to be a particularly bad week, and he was feeling very low. Suddenly he heard a scuffling, scratching sound, and there, peeping from a hole where the skirting boards met, he spied the face of what he at first took to be a mouse.

It had bright, twinkling black eyes and bristling whiskers, and it watched him for a few seconds before retreating into the cavity in the walls. Somehow, its being there made him feel a bit better, as if he had a friend.

He waited for it to return, but it didn't that day.

The next afternoon, when he had washed all the floors and scrubbed all the windows and been soundly thrashed for it, he took some bread and cheese and sandwich meat to his favourite spot, and he left a small piece of the cheese and some crumbs of bread just at the hole and waited.

It did not take long for the rodent to show up – he watched, rapt, as each morsel in turn was taken into the hole.

The following day he brought more food but placed it a little further away so the rat – by now he had looked it up in one of his encyclopaedias, and he knew it was not a mouse, but a Brown Rat – had to come out of the hole to get it.

Each day, he moved these offerings a little further from the hole and a little closer to himself. After nine days, the rat had to come almost to within arm's reach to get his meal, and on the tenth day, he scuttled to Phillipe's side.

As the rat ate his cheese, the boy dropped a bucket over him.

Now he had the rat, he was unsure what to do with him. He didn't want to let him go, as he had been very patient and, he flattered himself, quite clever in catching him.

He decided he was going to teach him tricks.

He found an old birdcage in the attic, and used it as a home for his new pet (he decided to call him Ben, after the mouse in Michael Jackson's song), and wasted no time in training him to follow a small table-tennis ball and bring it back to his master.

He taught him how to climb a piece of washing line and bring down a Christmas-tree decoration he had put at the top.

And he taught him how to kill things.

Sparrows would gather on a wall outside the window his little landing overlooked, and their chirping would sometimes annoy him as he tried to read. He had learned that rats were predators and would attack and eat things like smaller rodents, insects and even small birds.

He decided to apply the same techniques to the bird problem that he had to catching Ben in the first place – he put some breadcrumbs and nuts on the window sill and waited for the birds to come and partake of their feast.

He left the window open and sat, holding Ben on his lap, watching the annoying feathered pests hopping about, noisily squabbling over the morsels.

On the second day, he put some crumbs on the inside window sill too, and when one of the sparrows hopped in to get it, he let his rat go.

Ben sprang forward with remarkable speed and the sparrow, not expecting the attack, tried to fly away but misjudged its trajectory and hit the pane of glass, falling to the floor momentarily stunned.

Ben fell on it and ripped its throat out.

Within a week, the rat was patrolling the wall for him, mostly keeping the sparrows away but catching one or two and the occasional starling to boot.

Ben was a wonderful pet and a great companion.

It was too bad that Mother found out about him in the end. She beat her son until he bled from the ears, then forced Phillipe to feed his beloved pet poisoned bread and made him stay while the animal convulsed and died.

He hated his mother for it but, just to annoy her, he remained smiling and jovial throughout. Upset as he was, he found the idea of poison a very interesting one. He decided there and then to learn more about it.

9

MILEY TRIED RINGING DUNNIGAN EVERY MORNING at nine o'clock, then at lunchtime (for Miley that was half twelve) and finally again at teatime (six o'clock). By Thursday lunch he had still not received an answer and decided that it was high time he paid his friend a visit, regardless of what Diane said.

He got the bus over to Phibsboro Road and walked the short distance from the stop to Davey's building.

On arrival, he pushed the buzzer once.

No answer.

Twice.

Still no response.

Finally, he leaned his entire weight against the bell and held it there, monitoring the time on his watch. He gave up after three full minutes, which still elicited no reaction.

He stood on the footpath, squinting up at the window he knew looked out from Dunnigan's living room. One major problem flatland presented was that windows were often completely inaccessible (if you were trying to look in from the outside, at least). He pondered the problem for a moment, then had an idea. He walked to a newsagent's on the corner and bought a large bag of Galaxy Minstrels, round chocolate sweets covered in a hard sugar shell, about the size of a penny. With these in hand he walked back to his post beneath Dunnigan's window and began to toss them against the glass pane.

At first, he found the task a bit more difficult than he had expected and missed the window altogether, hitting the wall on either side, or he didn't throw high enough and the sweets fell on the ground and shattered.

After a while, though, he mastered the trick and got a good square hit each time. He also learned to catch them as they fell, which he thought was very clever indeed.

After about ten minutes he had a good rhythm going.

After fifteen minutes, the window was flung open, and Dunnigan's bedraggled head was thrust out.

'*Stop!* Will you please, please stop it?'

Miley grinned up at him. 'Hello, Davey! I've missed you.'

'I asked you a question: are you going to stop bothering me?'

'No.'

'What?'

'I said no. I've tried to call, and I've been patient, and I'm really worried about you. So no, if you don't let me in, I'm going to stay right here and continue to annoy you. I've got loads more Minstrels and three Chris de Burgh albums on my phone. I haven't listened to *Eastern Wind* much, so this will give me the chance to catch up.'

Dunnigan looked at Miley as if he was completely out of his mind. 'What are you talking about?'

'Can I come up?'

'Oh, come on, then!'

Punching the air in victory, Miley hurried to the door as it buzzed, permitting him entry.

10

MILEY WAS NOT SURPRISED TO SEE THAT DUNNIGAN was a physical wreck. The flat, as always, was neat and tidy (Dunnigan, while not a germophobe, was pathologically orderly), but the man himself was not faring so well. He was wearing a rumpled *Raiders of the Lost Ark* T-shirt and a sagging pair of jeans that showed signs of having been slept in. His hair looked like it had not been washed in days, and his face was covered in thick stubble. Miley did not have to get too close to know that a shower had not been a feature of his friend's life for some time.

'It's nice to see you, Davey,' Miley said when he was sitting on the couch beside him, and he meant it.

'Mmm,' Dunnigan grunted.

'You look awful.'

That got no answer at all.

'Have you been talking to Chief Superintendent Tormey?'

'He rings every day. They have no news yet. And there won't be any. They're humouring me by even viewing this as a real case.'

Miley nodded sagely. 'How do you know? There could be a hundred clues on that shoe just waiting to be found.'

Dunnigan, who had been staring straight ahead at nothing, gave Miley a contemptuous look. 'Why would there be no word on Beth – nothing at all – for eighteen years, and then, all of a sudden, just after I solve a case involving a very bad, very powerful man, something like this happens? It only makes sense that the shoe is a fake. There were countless newspaper and TV and radio broadcasts that detailed exactly what Beth was wearing. You wouldn't have to be a genius to pull off something like this.'

'So you aren't confident we're dealing with a real clue?'

'Don't tell me *you* are!'

Miley chose his words carefully. 'You're an expert in the field of criminal behaviour, aren't you?'

Dunnigan snorted.

Miley ignored him and continued stubbornly. 'Would it be fair to say that, while it is unusual, there have been *some* cases where children have been taken but were then found, alive and well, many years later?'

Dunnigan stiffened at that.

'I mean, I'm just an interested amateur, but I can think of a few. Like, wasn't Jaycee Dugard found after eighteen years?'

'Eighteen years, two months and three days,' Dunnigan said, almost to himself.

'So it *can* happen.'

Dunnigan nodded.

Miley ploughed on. 'It's a slim chance, but she *might* be alive somewhere.'

Dunnigan nodded again.

'What if that's what they want me to think?' he said at last, and Miley heard tears in his voice, like clouds gathering overhead.

'Let's suppose she's not,' Miley said, placing his hand on his friend's shoulder. 'Even if she isn't with us anymore, maybe this could be a chance to find out what happened to her. It's probably a slim chance, but even so ... we have to take it.'

Dunnigan put his head in his hands. 'Do you know how many wild-goose chases I've been on over the years, Miley?' he asked. 'I've lost count. I don't know if I can take another one.'

Miley put his arm around Dunnigan's shoulders. 'The difference is you've got me and Diane and Harry this time. And you know what, I think my uncle kind of likes you. If you let him, he can be your friend too.'

Dunnigan didn't move.

Miley suspected he was crying quietly, and left him to it. 'And we owe it to Beth to follow this up.'

'I know,' came the muffled reply.

'So are you going to clean yourself up and come out of your cave?'

Dunnigan nodded and got stiffly to his feet. 'You are an optimistic soul, aren't you?' he said to Miley.

'I'd have gone mental years ago if I wasn't,' Miley replied.

11

DOCTOR GEORGINA RUSSELL WAS NOT SURPRISED when she received a call from the receptionist informing her that Miley Timoney was back and that, this time, he had brought a friend.

She showed the pair to the conference room and spread her findings out across the table.

'Mr Dunnigan, I am sure you are aware that anything I tell you today has still to be confirmed – I have sent all specimens gathered from the shoe either to the relevant departments here or to our colleagues at Intertek. I expect to hear back from them before the weekend, but I am confident that my preliminary findings are correct.'

The Irish police utilised the services of a multinational testing company to carry out finer work on forensic samples, particularly pollen, seeds and other natural materials.

Dunnigan blinked at her a couple of times. Georgina thought that, between him and Miley, Miley appeared far more focussed.

'Specimens?' he asked.

'Yes. The … um … the materials I found. On the trainer.'

Dunnigan pulled over a chair and sat down. 'I was sure it would be clean.'

'It wasn't. Not at all, in fact.'

Dunnigan looked as if he was about to throw up.

'Can I get you some water, Mr Dunnigan?'

'Yes, please. And call me Davey.'

Georgina got a bottle from a vending machine outside and brought it to him. He drank a few sips and seemed to rally.

'Thank you. Please tell me, what did you find?'

Georgina sat beside him and pulled over a sheet of paper with several diagrams of the shoe, showing it from various angles.

'First off, the shoe is a genuine vintage brand, showing wear about the heel and to the rear of the inside sole, meaning the owner had good posture and was physically active. It was easy to demonstrate from this that it had been worn for a period of approximately five months by an individual weighing about 40 pounds, in or around three stones, which is the average weight for a four-year-old girl. It could also be an adult with certain kinds of dwarfism or progeria, but that is statistically unlikely.'

Miley, who had remained standing, watched Dunnigan carefully. He could only imagine how tough this must be for his friend.

'You said there were samples?' Dunnigan prompted.

Georgina indicated some photographs that she had prepared. 'The shoe had been washed in a domestic machine using a common store-bought detergent and then left to steep in a solution of chloroxylenol and caustic soda.'

'Chloro-what?' Dunnigan asked

'It's widely sold as Dettol. You may remember that the shoe had a strong aroma of it. It's quite distinctive.'

'I don't remember much about the day it arrived,' Dunnigan said.

'Well, anyway, treatment like this will remove most evidence, but I still found some interesting items. This here' – she indicated one of the photos, which showed a series of oval shapes with dark dots at their centre – 'shows a microscopic view of blood cells I was able to isolate.'

'Blood?' Dunnigan said, in a voice that was little more than a rasp.

'Please don't be alarmed,' Georgina said. 'The cells are clearly not human – human blood cells, mammal blood cells, in fact, don't have a nucleus, and these very definitely do.'

Dunnigan and Miley both leaned over the photograph – the cells were purple in colour, but Georgina explained that was due to a dye used to make them easier to see.

'So these aren't mammal cells?' Miley said, confused. 'What are they then?'

'Fish,' Georgina said. 'You are looking at the blood cells of an Arctic char.'

Dunnigan shook his head. 'Where would you come across one of those?' he asked.

'They are a species of salmon that live in subarctic coastal waters,' the forensic scientist said. 'They're extremely plentiful in that part of the world, but you won't find any in Ireland.'

'I don't know what to do with that,' Dunnigan said.

'Let's shelve it for the moment, then.' Georgina pushed on. 'Here is a magnified shot of a single particle of pollen that was embedded in the undersole.'

The shots looked to be of a giant coffee bean with a fine beading all across it.

'You're going to tell us this is from a cactus that grows in the Mojave Desert, aren't you?' Miley said.

'Not at all,' Georgina replied. 'In fact, this gives you something very definitive to work with. Here we have the pollen of *Simethis mattiazzii*, the Kerry lily.'

She pointed to a photo of a pretty white flower with bright yellow stamen.

'The Kerry lily is one of the rarer plants of its type in Ireland,' she said. 'It grows in only a few sites in Kerry and two in West Cork. It does also occur in France, Spain, Portugal and Italy, but the local option seems most plausible.'

'So Beth would have had to be at one of those places to have picked up the pollen?' Miley asked.

'Not necessarily,' Georgina explained. 'What it means is that the *shoe* was in one of those places.'

'It's something,' Dunnigan said. 'It's more than we've had before.'

'Finally,' Georgina indicated her last photograph, 'I came across these fibres inside the shoe, pressed into the insole.'

'*Inside* the shoe?'

'Yes. We would expect to find fibres in there that have been transferred from the sock or the sole of the naked foot when someone was walking about without the shoe on, picking up particles, fibres and so forth, and passing these on when the trainer is reworn.'

The photo showed what looked to be four strands of deep green cable, more or less triangular in shape with convex sides.

'What are they?' Dunnigan asked.

'They are a type of nylon,' Georgina said. 'Those types of strands – we call them *trilobal* – are very typical of what we would expect to see in certain types of carpets – specifically, carpet tiles.'

'Does that help us?' Dunnigan asked.

'I remind you, the samples have been sent for a full spectrographic analysis, but from what I can gather, the nylon we have here was used in the production of industrial flooring, mostly found in schools and hospitals, and has been in continuous production since the eighties. It's very hard-wearing and still sells.'

Dunnigan stood up suddenly, knocking his chair backwards.

'I have to ring Tormey,' he said.

'He won't act until official results confirm my analysis,' Georgina said. 'I am telling you all this out of professional courtesy.'

Dunnigan ignored her and, already brandishing his phone, virtually ran from the room.

Georgina and Miley watched him go.

'There's one more thing,' the scientist said, looking at the criminologist's friend.

'Yeah?'

'Like I said, the shoe had been washed and then soaked in an effort to clean it, and still I found the samples I've shared today.'

'And?'

'Even with the soaking, I would have expected to find more. Pollen moves in clouds. Fibre gets picked up in clumps. Blood gets splashed.'

Miley tried to follow what she was saying.

'So ...'

'What I have shown you is absolutely everything I took from the trainer. There were three particles of blood, one piece of pollen and four strands of fibre. That's it.'

'What are you trying to tell me, Doctor Russell?'

'If I were a suspicious soul, I would think they were planted by someone who knew what they were doing.'

Doctor Phillipe Ressler

They buried his mother the day before he left to go to university. His father, usually silent and vacant, cried like a baby as they lowered the coffin into the earth, and Phillipe decided there and then that he never wanted to see the man again.

The death of his mother had been another long-term project that required great patience, and he had relished every moment of it. He thought it would be poetic for her demise to be caused by the same poison with which she had made him kill Ben – arsenic.

The great thing about this substance was that it was easy to get – all he had to do was go to one of the hardware stores in downtown Utrecht and purchase some rat poison. The old townhouses on the street where his family lived were notorious for vermin, so no one questioned him.

His favourite brand was called Vertox and it was made up of porridge oats that had been infused with a chemical called brodifacoum as well as high doses of arsenic. The wonderful thing about brodifacoum was that, not only did it not show up on tox-screening in hospitals, but also it acted as a cloak for other ingested materials, so even if anyone thought of testing his mother for poison, they would find nothing.

Oats were ideal, as the only meal in the day his mother insisted needed to be 'healthy' was breakfast, for which he made her a bowl of porridge loaded with either jam or honey.

The oats that came in the Vertox box had been dyed a pretty red colour, so no one would mix them up with grains intended for human consumption, but the jam helped to disguise their presence.

And he was very careful – he didn't want to kill her outright. Only a few went in each day.

Long-term arsenic exposure does a number of interesting things to the human body – Phillipe kept careful notes on the symptoms his mother developed over the year he was poisoning her. She had constant diarrhoea and severe stomach cramps. After three months, her hair started to fall out, and at five months she became incontinent. The doctors informed his father and him that his mother had developed bladder cancer.

She survived another five painful, agonising months after that. The last three she spent in hospital, and in the final two of those she could not speak.

It was bliss.

The funny thing was that, now she was gone, he did not want the house anymore. The world stretched out before him, full of opportunity and adventure. He was going to Antwerp to study medicine, and for the first time in his life he was free.

He thought he might get another pet.

12

WHILE DUNNIGAN WAS TALKING EXCITEDLY ON the phone to a stoically silent Tormey, Diane Robinson sat in her red Honda Civic with Captain Sean Murtaugh, late of the Irish Army Ranger Wing, looking at a detached house set in its own gardens in the Dublin suburb of Blanchardstown. The Janitor had informed her that this was the location from which Fred Quirke, a gang leader slightly lower down the criminal pecking order than Rogers, plied his nefarious trade.

Murtaugh had been Diane's commander in Chad and had served in Somalia before that. He was fifty-eight years old, ran a private security company and looked as if he had been built from solid granite – he was all angles and coarse surfaces, his bald head dark and stubbled, his cheekbones sharp and prominent. He was, perhaps, the toughest man Diane had ever met.

'I don't understand why we're here,' Murtaugh said – he was from Limerick and had retained the accent despite having lived in various parts of the world since he was sixteen.

'I need to know if Father Bill is alive or dead, and I have to make sure this gang won't come after me and my friends again. I'd also like to confirm that it was Frobisher who arranged it all.'

'And we're going to walk in and ask them?'

'It seemed a good idea when it occurred to me.'

They sat in silence for a while, sipping coffee from takeout cups.

'And you don't think going in there with your friend Rogers might have been a better notion?'

'No. I don't want any more involvement with that man than is absolutely necessary.'

'Even though he's a gangster, too, and probably has more intel on what we're walking into than we do?'

'I'm told there's no love lost between Rogers and Quirke. I didn't want to walk in looking for information and end up in the middle of a bloodbath.'

'Well, it would answer one of your questions – they won't be coming after you again if they're all dead.'

They sat a bit more.

'How many are we expecting to encounter?' Murtaugh asked.

'I'm told he usually has four on site.'

'Are they trained?'

'No. Street kids with Glocks.'

'So, messy but maybe even more dangerous, for all that.'

'They're used to waving their guns around and people being scared. They won't have ever gone up against really bad individuals before. I reckon they'll freeze.'

'Maybe,' Murtaugh said. 'Or maybe they'll go apeshit and we'll have to kill one of them. Are you ready for that?'

Diane sighed deeply. 'I'm all right, Captain. Really I am.'

'You told me that when your husband died. But you weren't. You know I love you, and I'd kill everyone in the world for you if you asked me to, but one thing I will not do is put you in a situation where you're going to fuck yourself up even worse than before.'

Diane was a widow, although this was a term she never applied to herself because she thought it made her sound old and washed out – she knew this made no sense, but deep inside it was what she thought. Her husband, Geoff, had been in the Irish navy and was killed in a traffic accident five years previously. His death had brought her world to a halt. She couldn't stop crying, couldn't focus on anything but her grief and became a liability to her comrades.

It was not until she found Father Bill and the Homeless Project that she had been able to piece her life together again. She had been honourably discharged but still did some work for the army – and the Rangers in particular – as a therapist.

'I wouldn't have called you if I thought I wasn't up for it,' Diane told Murtaugh. 'Now, let's do this thing before we talk one another out of it.'

They got out of the car and went to the boot, where Murtaugh had stowed two Kevlar vests, which they put on over their shirts and then covered with their jackets.

'You brought the Steyr AUGs!' Diane grinned as the captain handed her the standard service rifle used by the Irish armed forces.

'Thought you'd be comfortable with it. I brought these along too. Stick one in your belt, just in case.' He tossed her a Heckler & Koch USP semi-automatic pistol. 'I've got a Benelli M4 shotgun as well if you reckon ...'

'I think these will more than suffice,' Diane said, and they jogged across the road to the house.

They had to climb a high wall to get into the grounds, but a tree offered a convenient aid to their efforts, and within less than a minute they were at the back door to the property.

'Security is a fucking joke,' Murtaugh said as they lined up on either side of the entrance.

'Like I said, they don't expect anyone to make a run at them,' Diane said. 'Ready?'

'Yes, ma'am.'

'I'll let you do the honours.'

Murtaugh stood back and with one powerful kick stove the door in. They surged into the kitchen to find it empty of people – although the table was still covered in plates and strewn with crumbs and gobs of butter and jam, and the sink was full of dishes.

Diane motioned towards an adjoining door and they went that way. A stairway to their right led to a second floor, and a door to their left emitted the sounds of a TV show. They could smell cigarettes.

Murtaugh didn't wait to be told this time and smashed the door just below the handle.

There were three men inside – one old guy who was very overweight and wore a tracksuit, the top open to the waist revealing a string vest, and two kids who looked to be little more than twenty, both sporting shaven heads and tattoos. A Glock 17 handgun was on the coffee table, and one of the kids made a lunge for it. Diane clipped his head with the butt of her Steyr and he ended up sprawled on the carpet.

The other two stayed where they were. *Home and Away* was playing loudly on the TV. Murtaugh took the remote from the older guy and muted it.

'Anyone upstairs?' he asked.

'Trevor is taking a shit,' the kid on the floor said.

'Let's go and get him,' Murtaugh said. 'Up.'

They went in convoy to the second floor, reaching the landing just as the toilet flushed. Slinging the Steyr about her shoulder by its strap, Diane stood to the left of the door, and as Trevor – another youngster – came out, tucking his T-shirt into his jeans, she pressed the barrel of the Heckler and Koch to his head.

'Will you check the other rooms, Cap?' she asked, and he whisked past her and did a quick recon of the three bedrooms.

'Clear!'

'Let's all go downstairs and have a cup of tea,' she said, and they trooped to the kitchen.

When all four were seated around the table, their hands placed flat on top, Murtaugh boiled the kettle. Diane hadn't really intended for them to have tea, but she figured he was just playing out the part.

'I take it you're Fred Quirke,' she said to the older man.

'I might be.'

She sighed and poked him in the chest with her gun.

'Don't be an arse. No one has been hurt yet, and with a bit of luck no one will be. Now stop playing silly buggers. I know who you are. I want you to tell me who hired your men for four jobs last Sunday.'

Quirke tried to draw himself up so his paunch was held in and he seemed somewhat taller. It didn't work.

'I can't tell you that. I have me reputation to think of.'

Diane caught him by the back of the head and smashed his face off the table, breaking his nose and cracking his front teeth.

'You fuckin' psychotic *bitch*! You can't come in here and do this! My fuckin' *teeth*!'

'I can and I have and I will come back again tomorrow if I have to. Who hired you?'

'You're a *dead* woman. You might not know it, but I'm tellin' you right now, your days are fuckin' *numbered*!'

He spat blood at her, and Murtaugh drew the Heckler and Koch from his belt and shot him clean through the shoulder. The impact knocked him back off his chair, and he landed with his legs stuck up in the air in a very undignified manner.

It did stop him shouting, though.

For a minute.

'Jesus. Jesus. He shot me. Oh my God, he shot me.'

Diane pushed him back to an upright position, then peeled his tracksuit top off, looking closely at the wound. Murtaugh was an excellent shot, and the bullet had travelled straight through the muscle – no bones were broken.

'Get me two clean tea towels, please,' she said to the kids. 'Fast, before the pain starts.'

The three boys were looking very pale and frightened, but one went to a cupboard below the sink and tossed her the towels. She folded one into a tight square and used the other to tie it in place against the wound.

'Hold it right there – put pressure on it, just like that. OK, good. Now, Mr Quirke, you can be on your way to the hospital where you will be given stitches and painkillers and an antibiotic – all you have to do is tell me what I need to know.'

'I … I don't know who they were.' Quirke was shivering now and sweating. Shock had set in, but the pain would follow shortly, and then they would get nothing from him.

'How were you paid?'

'All in cash up front.'

'Who? Who gave it to you?'

'A man in a suit. He came to the betting shop I own and said he wanted a job done, some gang or other had become a problem to his business and he wanted them to stop.'

Diane nodded. It was as she had suspected – he hadn't named the After Darkers, but it could be no one else.

'Is Father Bill dead?'

'Stevo said he threw his body in the river.'

'Where?'

'Near the Memorial Gardens. There's a spot there where you can't be seen from the road.'

'His body hasn't been found.'

'Weighted him down. Tied bricks to his ankles. Stevo says he cut him bad. He was bleedin' like anythin'.'

'You delivered two packages.'

'A scary doll to Ringsend and a box to Phibsboro.'

'A scary doll?'

'Don't fuckin' ask – I was just told to have it delivered.'

'And it was?'

'My man was disturbed by some kid, but he said he left it where he was told.'

Diane shrugged. Miley claimed to know nothing about any delivery on Sunday. Didn't seem to matter much now.

She leaned in very close to Quirke, speaking right in his ear.

'If you, or your associates, bother me or my friends again in any way, the captain here and I will come back with even more of our friends, and we will fuck you up *really* badly. Are you absolutely certain you understand me, Mr Quirke?'

'Yes.'

'And you boys?' Murtaugh punched one of the kids on the shoulder. It looked like it was not a gentle punch.

'Yeah!'

'Deffo!'

'Absolutely!'

'All right then,' Diane said. 'Is the car out front yours?'

'Yes.'

'Are any of these three old enough to drive?'

'I am!' Trevor piped up.

'Connolly Hospital is on Mill Road. They have a fast A&E there. He'll be all right. It's a clean wound.'

The boy nodded and hurried over to help the trembling, sweat-drenched gangster to his feet.

As they were leaving, the young man she had knocked down motioned to her.

'What is it?'

'Who do youse run for?'

'What?'

'Which gang, like?'

'We're not a gang.'

'Only, I'd like to come over to work with yiz. I mean, you're fairly fuckin' bad, y'know what I'm sayin', like?'

Diane sighed and looked him dead in the eye. 'Go back to school. Get a job. Get some therapy, if you think you need it. The next people who bust in here won't be as nice as we were.'

The kid looked highly confused when she left him. She hoped some of what she'd said made an impression, but she doubted that it had.

This time, she and Murtaugh left by the front gate.

13

'BUT WHAT DOES IT ALL MEAN?' TORMEY ASKED.

He, Dunnigan, Diane and Miley were sitting in Captain America's diner on Friday evening. The results had come in from the Phoenix Park and Intertek, whose laboratories were based in Bremen, in Germany, confirming everything Doctor Georgina Russell had said.

'It means we have somewhere to look,' Dunnigan said, picking at a chicken fajita.

'Where? I mean, are we looking for a primary school in Kerry that happens to have a pond with its own school of Arctic char?'

'That would work, but no. I have another suggestion.'

'What?'

'The Kerry lily is known to grow on cliffs around the coastal region of West Cork. There is, according to HSE records, a private psychiatric hospital situated near the coast, right in the area where the flowers proliferate.'

'For it to be of any use to you at all, it would have to have been in operation in 1998.'

'It's been there since the late nineteenth century.'

'And they have char there?'

'Probably not, but it's by the sea – that's as close as I could get. The fish blood doesn't bring me anywhere useful, so I'm working around it.'

Tormey pursed his lips and looked at Diane. 'You tell me that all this was down to Frobisher and the After Dark people.'

'Yes. According to my sources.'

'And they are?'

She shook her head.

'I could arrest you, Diane. See how that sits with you.'

She grinned. 'You could, Chief. I wouldn't take it personally.'

Tormey took a bite of his burger and raised an eyebrow at Miley, who was ignoring them all and tucking into a plate of baby back ribs. He was wearing as much of them as he was eating, but he seemed to be enjoying himself. 'Do you have anything to add?'

Miley paused and put down the rib he had been gnawing. 'Doctor Russell seems to think this may be some kind of trap – that the forensic evidence was put there on purpose.'

'She told me that too. Thinks it might be a good idea to simply set the case aside and see if anything else emerges.'

Dunnigan shook his head. 'We're not going to do that.'

'Aren't we?'

'No. I'm going to West Cork to see what I can find.'

'On whose authority?'

'I can go with the unit's blessing, or you can give me some leave and I can go under my own steam. I don't care which.'

Tormey dabbed at his voluminous moustache with a napkin and sat back. 'I can't stop you going, and if you head down there without police backing you're at even greater risk, so I am going to authorise it.'

Dunnigan nodded. If Tormey had been expecting a 'thank you', none came.

'Now let me be clear – you two,' Tormey looked at Miley and Diane, '*cannot* go with him. You are not employed by the unit, and I am not going to deputise you, as Miley here suggested to me on the walk over.'

'We're going to focus on keeping the Homeless Project up and running,' Diane said. 'Aren't we, Miley?'

'So says you,' Miley said glumly, and returned to his ribs.

'Good. That's settled then.' Tormey reached for the menu. 'I fancy something sweet.'

'Any word on Father Bill?' Diane asked as he perused the dessert options.

'We sent divers down in the spot your famous fucking sources indicated,' the detective said. 'Nothing. The currents are pretty strong there. If he did go in at that point, he could well have been washed out to sea.'

Diane smiled weakly and said nothing.

She still hadn't stopped hoping.

Doctor Phillipe Ressler

Antwerp was everything he had hoped it would be, and university was wonderful.

He had been a solitary boy at school in Utrecht, but now, without the feeling that his mother was looking over his shoulder all the time, he was free to be himself.

It took some time to discover what that was, and when he did, he found that the happy-go-lucky, upbeat, jolly character he'd adopted for her seemed to fit him well and that people responded to it.

He made friends. He became, in fact, something of a social animal, helping to run several societies for the students' union, taking up amateur drama in a small theatre near his flat and trying to hit as many parties as he could each weekend. He developed a love of Scotch and rough sex and indulged in both pathologically – he had never touched alcohol and was a virgin before leaving home, so these were new and exciting experiences for him.

They proved a potent combination, though, and after a one-night stand became so violent it left a classmate permanently disabled, he made the decision to moderate his drinking and maintain a celibate lifestyle. He did not want to risk losing everything he'd worked for, and while it was easy enough to cover his tracks and make sure poor Sven would not be able to tell anyone what had happened, it had been tedious and had completely ruined his evening.

And he had so much to live for now. So much he wanted to do!

He adored his studies and consistently finished top of his class. He completed his MD with first-class honours. He had taken undergraduate psychiatry and knew within a matter of weeks that this was going to be his postgraduate specialisation.

The mind, he came to understand, was humanity's real engine – it was *what drove us. He wanted to know more, not just about others, but about himself, too.*

He met the boy during his first residency, an attachment to an orphanage in Delft.

'What's wrong with him?'

'Nothing biological – he's as strong as an ox. He was abused as badly as any kid we've ever seen. Sexually, physically, emotionally … parents never even bothered to name him.'

'What do you call him?'

'He's Johann on the books, but he doesn't answer to it.'

Phillipe looked at the boy pacing his room like a caged animal, thirteen years old and barely verbal, his body a patchwork of scars and welts, the most recent ones self-inflicted.

'I'd like to work with him.'

'Be my guest. No one else wants to.'

Later, when everyone had gone to bed, he went to the lad's room. Without a sound the boy came at him, broken nails bared like claws.

Phillipe shot him with a Taser and shocked him until he wet himself and passed out.

'I'm going to call you Benjamin,' he said, looking down at his new project. 'I think we're going to be wonderful friends.'

Part Three

FAR BEYOND THESE CASTLE WALLS

1

DUNNIGAN'S TWIN SISTER, GINA, HAD NOT BEEN
in contact with him since the shoe that may or may not have been
Beth's had been delivered, and he had not made any attempt to call
her, wrapped up as he was in his own grief and uncertainty.

He and Gina had been as close as a pair of identical twins
might be expected to be growing up. Their parents – their father
was a psychoanalyst, their mother an educational psychologist
– had realised their mistake in having children after the pair had
been born, which was, by any standards, too late. Dunnigan
had adopted the role of carer for his sister as soon as he was old
enough to realise someone needed to, and they had grown up in
a house where they could only rely on one another for emotional
support.

When Beth disappeared, Gina never blamed her brother,
although her husband, Clive, from whom she was now estranged,
was not so understanding. Dunnigan had been unable to share
Gina's belief that they might help one another through the trauma
of the child's loss and had broken off all contact for more than
a decade, either ignoring the attempts she made to rebuild their
relationship or sabotaging them by making things so difficult Gina
sporadically gave up and retreated from his coldness and feigned
apathy.

To her credit she had persevered, and over the past year things
had improved, partly due to Gina making a Trojan effort to break
down the walls her brother had constructed around himself, but
also because Dunnigan had been slowly thawing as people like

Miley, Father Bill and Diane gave him a reason to get up in the morning.

So not speaking to Gina for seven consecutive days was, by then, an unusual event for Dunnigan, and one he was surprised to find he wished to remedy. He struggled to understand the emotional worlds most people inhabited, but his sister's absence over the turbulence of the past week suggested to him that she was hurting. He realised there was still a chance he would arrive to find she had become ensconced in a good book or a box set of the original *Star Trek* series, but he felt this was unlikely in light of the delivery of the shoe and the emotions it would probably have triggered. Also, Gina did not like *Star Trek*.

When she was a child, chocolate cake had always helped when she was sad. Something told him baked goods might not be as effective now, but he went to Tesco and bought the most spectacular confection he could find anyway, then drove to Gina's house in Greystones.

When he got there, she was in the garden pulling weeds from a flowerbed with more aggression than the task required, an AC/DC baseball cap keeping the sun from her eyes.

She looked up as he got out of his beloved 1983 3 Series BMW and walked across the lawn towards her, the cake box held out before him like a talisman.

'Are you sad?' he asked her by way of a greeting.

She sighed and continued her weeding.

'Because if you are, I have cake.'

She put her trowel down and sat back, resting her bum on her heels. Striking rather than pretty, Gina had the same slim build, dark hair and blue eyes as her brother.

'What kind of cake?'

He opened the lid of the box and angled it down so she could see he had chosen her favourite: chocolate fudge.

She laughed in a dry kind of way and shook her head. 'Put the kettle on. I'll be in in a second.'

'OK.'

So it still works, he mused as he walked to the house. *Who'd have thought?*

He made coffee for his sister and tea for himself, then cut two generous slices and put them on plates. She came in after about five minutes and sat opposite him at the kitchen table.

'Thanks for coming,' she said as she sampled his offering, and he could tell from her voice that she meant it. 'I've been all over the shop. I don't know what to feel or how to express it, so I thought I was best away from other human beings. Sorry.'

'I didn't come for an apology,' Dunnigan said. 'I wanted to see how you are before I go.'

She raised an eyebrow. 'Where are you going?'

He told her about the pollen and the fibres and the blood, and the different theories about what they might mean.

'Shit,' she said when he had finished.

He waited for her to say more. She put down her fork and sat back, folding her arms across her chest as she always did when she was being forthright. 'What are you walking into?'

'I am following up on the first – the *only* – leads we have had in eighteen years.'

'We have no reason to believe that shoe has anything to do with Beth,' Gina said. 'It might be – let's be honest here, it *probably is* – a horrible joke. Those bits of fluff and what-have-you your scientists found are either random crap or were put there by someone you pissed off who wants to torment you. And they're tormenting me, too, Davey!'

Dunnigan tried to hold her gaze and couldn't, so he looked

down at his plate and scraped up some ganache with his finger instead.

'I can't let this go,' he said. 'I know very well it might be nothing, and it could be an attempt to isolate me and put me at risk, but it may be something real that will help us get a clearer picture of what happened. You must understand that I can't let that pass me by.'

'What if you go down there and end up hurt or killed – or, worse still, *you* disappear? What do you think that will do to me?'

'I promise I will not allow any of those things to happen.'

'How can you make that promise?'

Dunnigan took a deep breath and voiced what he had been unable to admit to Miley or Diane: 'Because I am expecting the worst. I agree with you – I think someone *wants* me to go to this asylum in the middle of nowhere. But I also believe that really is Beth's shoe. I don't know why, but I do.'

'It's wishful thinking, Davey,' Gina said. 'Tormey brought me in and had me look at it. Maybe it's hers, but who knows? You know how much I want her found, and in other circumstances I'd be begging you to go down there and poke around, but in this context, with everything you've been through recently, I think it's madness.'

She leaned forward across the table and took her brother's hands in hers. 'Don't go! It feels all wrong – I don't believe this will end well, Davey. Can't the local police down in Ballydehob or wherever the bloody hell this place is look into it and report back to you?'

'The asylum is called St Jude's and is outside the town of Donbro,' Dunnigan said.

'Whoop de doo! Don't they have guards down there?'

'They do, and I'll call on them if I have to, but I don't trust them to do a thorough job. This may be a huge deal to you and me, but to everyone else it's an eighteen-year-old cold case.'

'If you really have to go, take some backup with you.'

'Once again, I remind you that this is old news. Tormey is going above and beyond, and will probably catch hell, for even agreeing to let me go.'

Gina looked very unhappy.

'Promise me you will at least keep in touch with the local gardaí when you get there, that you won't go all weird and try to do it by yourself.'

Dunnigan scowled. 'I work best alone.'

'Swear to me, Davey! I'll bloody well follow you down there myself if you don't give me your word.'

'OK. I promise.'

Gina squeezed his hand and grinned.

'Good. Now give me some more of that cake.'

2

ST JUDE'S ASYLUM, A RAMBLING, RED-BRICKED building with gothic arched windows and an ornate clock tower, was situated on five acres of its own land amid the undulating countryside of West Cork, about two-thirds of the way between the town of Donbro and the village of Goleen. It had been built in 1805 by the Devaney family, direct descendants of William Penn, a famous Quaker who came to the county from Pennsylvania in the seventeenth century to settle his father's estate.

St Jude's had been established to cater for members of the Quaker community who were of a 'nervous or sensitive disposition' – essentially, its mission was to deal with psychiatric illness in as humane a manner as possible in an age when the mentally ill were commonly shackled and flogged as a 'cure' or were subject to the most brutal surgical procedures as a response to symptoms the medical profession simply did not understand.

While many asylums had, over the years, been purchased by the state, St Jude's remained privately run and was still under the management of the Devaneys – Roderick, the great-great-great-grandson of the original director, was the current proprietor.

Tormey had rung ahead to inform the staff that Dunnigan would be arriving that morning, but he found the black iron gates closed and padlocked when he pulled in to the driveway.

'No one informed me of any visits from the police,' a humourless voice at the end of the phone informed him when he dialled the contact number on the asylum's website.

'My chief superintendent called yesterday,' Dunnigan said. 'Would someone please open the gate?'

'This is a private medical facility. We don't allow just anyone in. I'll have to consult with Doctor Ressler.'

'To whom am I speaking, please?' Dunnigan snapped, losing patience.

'I am Chief Nursing Officer Olive Jules.'

'Very well. I am parked across your gates – would you please make whatever inquiries you need to and send someone to let me in?'

The line went dead. Dunnigan rolled all the windows down. It was a brilliantly sunny day, and he realised that all he could hear was breeze, birdsong and the occasional baa of some sheep. He couldn't remember the last time he had experienced such quiet, and he wasn't sure he liked it.

On the drive from Dublin he had been listening to the BBC's radio adaptation of *Lord of the Rings*, which he had on MP3, so he switched it back on and continued to wait. Half an hour passed, during which deep matters were discussed in theatrical English accents at the Council of Elrond. Finally, he spied a figure coming down the winding driveway – an elderly man, dressed in shirtsleeves and baggy jeans kept up with a pair of red-and-blue braces.

'Are you the guard?' the man asked, peering through the bars of the tall gate. He had a Cork accent so dense it was barely penetrable.

Dunnigan held his identification out through the car window. 'I am, as I have already explained, a civilian consultant with the Sex Crimes Unit of An Garda Síochána.'

'All right, all right. They'll see you now.'

With great ceremony, the padlock was undone and the long, well-oiled chain unwound. It fell to the ground with a clatter, and Dunnigan was in.

3

NURSE JULES MET HIM AT THE DOOR. A TALL, sturdily built woman, she appeared to be in her late forties and was dressed in an old-fashioned white nurse's uniform.

'Thank you for waiting, Mr Dunnigan. Our director, Mr Devaney, is available to speak with you.'

A tiled entrance hall held a reception counter, behind which was a line of grey filing cabinets. Four simple wooden chairs sat opposite it against the wall.

'You may wait there.'

Dunnigan ignored her. The walls were adorned with portraits he presumed depicted patrons of the asylum through the years. He was looking at a painting of a friendly looking, bewigged fellow in a frilly collar and frock coat when he heard steps echoing behind him.

'Mr Dunnigan, please forgive me. I failed to inform Nurse Jules that we had an appointment.'

Dunnigan turned and found himself looking at a smiling, round-faced man with a receding hairline and ample girth. He was dressed in a dark suit that had been tailored to hide his corpulence, but somehow only made it more obvious.

'Do you have an office where we can talk?' the criminologist asked.

'Of course. Would you like tea or coffee?'

'Some tea would be good, thank you.'

'Nurse Jules, would you have Pru bring us some tea?'

'I'm busy. You'll have to call her yourself.'

The director did not seem bothered by such open insubordination and called for refreshments when he and Dunnigan arrived at his office, all shiny, lacquered wood and dusty ledgers, a very expensive and top-of-the-range computer seeming out of place amid all the period features.

'So how can I help you?' Devaney asked when an ancient-looking woman had brought a tray with their drinks.

'I'm here following up on a missing person case dating back to 1998,' Dunnigan began, and he told his host about Beth, the circumstances of her disappearance and the shoe and what had been found on it. There was no reason he could think of to be circumspect.

'Well, I'm terribly sorry about your niece,' Devaney said when he was finished, 'but I really don't know how I can be of any assistance to you.'

'Were you working here during the Christmas of 1998?'

'Yes. My father was still director back then, but I served as the accountant for the place, so I was here regularly.'

'And did you then, or at any time you're aware of, have children here?'

'We are solely an adult facility. Our policy is that you must be over eighteen to be admitted.'

'What about as visitors?'

'Well, I suppose it's not beyond the realm of possibility that a child might be brought in to visit one of the patients – a family member, you understand – but even that is quite rare. I can think of one case – old Robert Holmes, his grandson used to visit very occasionally, but he was eleven or twelve, if I remember correctly. I honestly can't recall any little girls.'

'Do you have set visiting hours?'

'The relatives of our patients pay quite handsomely to send their loved ones here, Mr Dunnigan. I don't think it would be very decent of us to place limits on their access.'

Dunnigan blinked. 'I was presented with a padlocked gate when I arrived. It was not at all easy to get in.'

'I beg to differ, Mr Dunnigan.'

'Please call me Davey.'

'All right – Davey, you made a phone call, your identity was confirmed and we allowed you in. I don't think that could be described as particularly difficult. We work with sick, vulnerable people, and their families trust us to provide for their safety. If we had a free-and-easy open-door policy, well, I think we'd be negligent in our duty of care, don't you?'

'So, people can visit twenty-four hours a day, seven days a week?'

'In theory, but in practice, visitors are generally all gone by ten at night. If a resident is very ill, or is expected to pass away, family members are permitted to be here around the clock. We try to facilitate that difficult period where we can.'

'Of course. So what I'm hearing is that there could be children here that you don't know about.'

Devaney blanched. 'I'm sorry?'

'Well, you don't actually live here, do you?'

'No.'

'Which means there are periods when you aren't in St Jude's. You admit that in 1998 you were in and out of the building a good deal, as you only came to do the books. A little girl could have been here and you wouldn't have known about it.'

The director laughed nervously. 'We have a visitors' book that everyone coming in and out has to sign.'

'And that is a reliable record?'

'I would say so.'

'I didn't sign it.'

'You are not here to visit a resident patient. Your presence has been logged in the daybook.'

'I see. And would your visitors' book make a note of, say, a visitor being a child as opposed to an adult?'

'To be honest, I don't know.'

'Can I see these books?'

Devaney shifted uncomfortably. 'I am not sure that you can.'

'I am a civilian consultant—'

'I know who you are, Davey, and who you represent. But I, too, serve the law, and I am bound to protect the confidentiality of my patients and their families. The Data Protection Act 2003 safeguards the privacy of manually held files relating to medical confidentiality.'

Dunnigan shifted in his seat. 'In Ireland, confidentiality is not considered an absolute requirement. And even if it were, I don't believe visitors' records would fall under that remit.'

'Are you a lawyer, Davey?'

'I am a criminologist.'

Devaney spread his hands wide. 'If you wish to see any records, I will need to be legally compelled to release them. I'm sorry, but that is our position.'

'Do you think I won't be able to make that happen?'

The director laughed. 'St Jude's has been operating as a private institution for a very long time, Davey. This is not the first occasion the state has sent a representative prying into our affairs.'

'You seem to have misconstrued the reasons I'm here,' Dunnigan said. 'I'm not inspecting your facility – I'm looking for links to a missing child.'

'And I will facilitate you in any way I can, but to view our records you will need a warrant. Now, is there anyone else you'd like to talk to?'

'Whoever was here in 1998.'

'I'll have Nurse Jules set you up in our common room, and we'll send any staff from that period down to talk to you. How's that?'

Dunnigan shrugged. 'It will suffice for now.'

'Good stuff.' Devaney grinned.

Dunnigan did not return the smile.

4

THE COMMON ROOM WAS LARGE AND HIGH-ceilinged, carpeted in the green tiles Dunnigan supposed had – either here or elsewhere – yielded the fibre found in his niece's trainer. Huge windows should have looked out on the fields and woods behind St Jude's, but someone had placed plastic sheets across the lower half of each pane, opaque enough to permit light but dense enough to obscure any view of the outside.

The room was full of chairs and tables, each of which had either a board game or a selection of magazines artfully arranged on them, most of the publications years (some even decades) out of date. The space was clearly meant to be a gathering point for the patients but was empty save for Dunnigan and Nurse Jules.

'Sit here and I will send for Brendan.'

Dunnigan sat in the chair she had indicated and waited. For the second time that day, he was surprised at the depth of the silence. Even though he knew there must be many other people in the old hospital, he could not hear any signs of human life – there was the occasional creak as the building shifted in its foundations, a pipe clanging somewhere and beyond that a drip, drip, drip, perhaps from a tap, perhaps condensation. Other than these noises, there was nothing. He was a man quite comfortable in his own company and not prone to flights of fancy. But sitting alone in the old asylum, even with the sunshine sending a beam of dust-flecked light onto the tabletop before him, he thought the place eerie.

Brendan turned out to be the old man who had opened the gate. He informed Dunnigan that he had worked for the Devaney family all his life, as had his father.

'Yes, I was here in 1998. I can tell you now, without even having to search my memory, there was no little girl. It is a rarity to see a child in this place, and thank God for it. I bring my grandson with me to help out in the gardens sometimes, when he's on holidays from school, but he doesn't go into the wards – I keep him on the grounds where it's bright and there are growing things. He's the only child you'll encounter hereabouts. This is no place for children.'

'You're certain? Mr Devaney said there might be an occasional one as a visitor.'

'As I said, it's a rarity. Rare enough that I would remember, and I remember no four-year-old girl. And don't think I'm a feeble old man who is losing his memory – 83-D-4004. Do you know what that is?'

'It's the registration number of my car,' Dunnigan said.

'And I only saw that for a few seconds.' The old man laughed, showing that, along with his mental faculties, he also had all his teeth. 'You never know when a piece of information might come in useful,' he said. 'Now, you might find a lot that is useful at St Jude's. You'll have to keep your eyes open, but if you do, you could learn a lot.'

Dunnigan blinked, not sure what he had just heard, but the gardener was already walking to the door, so he filed it away to ponder later.

The morning turned into early afternoon. Nurse Jules brought him some tea and a ham and cheese sandwich. He spoke to seven more people – four nurses, two porters and a cook. None knew anything about a little girl being in or about the hospital in 1998 or ever. At four o'clock, Dunnigan realised he had reached a dead end and went to find Devaney.

'Sorry we couldn't be of more help,' the director said as he walked Dunnigan to the BMW. 'I hope you have more success elsewhere.'

'Could you recommend somewhere I might get a room?'

'Well, there's the Seaside Hotel in Donbro. It's pretty decent, I believe. Not driving back this evening, then?'

'No. I'll see you tomorrow.'

'Whatever for?'

'I'm going to interview everyone again.'

Devaney couldn't seem to find anything to say to that, and he was still standing there, his mouth hanging open, as Dunnigan drove away.

Doctor Phillipe Ressler

Benjamin came on in leaps and bounds under his tutelage.

It seemed the boy's parents had considered him on the same level as the family dog, and he had, in fact, received most of his care and affection from the animal. The only creatures among God's creation he had any love for were dogs, and Ressler thought that getting him a puppy might be a good way of bringing the lad out of himself.

This had not been as successful as he might have hoped, as his young charge did not seem to know his own strength and had crushed the little thing within hours of being handed it. To the psychiatrist's surprise, he was heartbroken.

'Where's my dog?' he asked, one of the first proper sentences he had ever uttered. (Ressler had been using reward and punishment to encourage verbalisation – sugar if the boy attempted words, a dose of pepper spray in the eyes if he growled or snarled.)

'They've taken him away,' Ressler said. 'You did not learn your vocabulary, so they took him. Be a good boy, and they might bring him back.'

To the psychiatrist's pleasure, this inducement seemed to work better than anything else he'd tried. Benjamin would do almost anything to get a dog again.

The potential this offered did not become fully evident to Ressler until a company named Kaiser Care advertised locally for a research position he was interested in – alas, so was another member of staff at the asylum, Doctor Wilhelm, who was much more experienced.

When it became obvious that Wilhelm was likely to be awarded the post he coveted, Ressler let it slip while he was with Benjamin that his rival may be hiding a dog that had been purchased for the boy. In fact, he told the bereft lad, Wilhelm had indicated that he had no intention of ever giving it to him.

All it took after that was to leave Benjamin's door unlocked that night and remind him that Wilhelm would be working in his office late.

Leaving a Stanley knife lying on the carpet near the door to that office was a final stroke of genius on Ressler's behalf.

Benjamin made a terrible mess, though he never did find his dog.

When Ressler, with the only real competition out of the picture, was granted his new post, he petitioned the management at the home to transfer Benjamin to the new state-of-the-art hospital where he would be working in Berlin. They agreed immediately.

'You are going to be staying with me from now on,' Ressler told the boy when he came around from the sedatives they had given him for the journey. 'You will be like my son.'

'I will be with you always,' Benjamin said.

And he was – when Kaiser Care sent Ressler to London to run their operations in the UK and Ireland, Benjamin travelled with him.

5

DONBRO, THE NAME OF THE NEAREST TOWN, IS derived from the Irish words *donn* meaning 'brown' and *brú* meaning 'riverbank', referring to what was now just a stream that flowed through the town centre down into the sea – apparently it had been much more impressive during the medieval period. The town was very quaint and there were plenty of tour guides more than happy to take an interested visitor on a stroll through the narrow laneways, showing them sites of interest and telling them stories about famous names who had made the place their home.

David Dunnigan had no desire to take a tour and didn't care about rivers, small or large.

He took a single room in the Seaside Hotel, which, as the name suggested, overlooked the bay. A mile off shore the shape of Tully Island, a five-kilometre strip of land that still had a few residents eking out a living, sat, a spearhead of rock against the sky. Dunnigan paused to look at it through the window of his room, drawn to the dark shape for reasons he could not explain.

He thought about calling Diane, but for some reason felt very far away from her and cut off from the part of himself that came out when she was around. He considered this for a few moments and reached the conclusion that he was putting all of himself into finding Beth and working out what had happened to her. In short, he just didn't have space for Diane just then.

This settled, he took the folded pieces of paper on which he had recorded his thoughts during the interview process, turned on his laptop and compiled a Word document on what he had learned from his day's activities. It made for depressing reading, and he was finished by seven.

The sun was still shining, and it was a lovely, warm summer's evening in the south-west of Ireland. He might have gone for a walk up the town's picturesque main street. He could have taken a swim in the ocean. He might even have had a sauna in the hotel's spa.

Dunnigan did none of these things. He had a chicken sandwich and a pot of tea brought to his room and watched *The Wrath of Khan* on his laptop. He was asleep by ten o'clock.

6

DUNNIGAN WAS AT ST JUDE'S BY NINE THE following morning and began re-interviewing the staff immediately.

Devaney complained bitterly about what he saw as the repetition of a fruitless exercise, but Dunnigan assured him he was operating standard police methodology: even people who are telling the truth can forget details of an event, particularly one that happened a long time ago. Asking an interview subject the same questions in different ways and from various perspectives can often yield unexpected results.

So, on day two of the interviews, he decided not to focus on the presence of a strange child at all – he asked instead about what had been going on in St Jude's in 1998. Had anything unusual or out of the ordinary occurred? Had any new staff started working that year or any changes in policy been introduced?

Dunnigan's interview style could be described as functional, bordering on disinterested – he asked questions in a monotone and kept only sporadic eye contact, making the odd note here and there on a tightly folded piece of paper, resting his chin in his hand and often appearing to be bored. He found that this put people off their guard – what did it matter what you said if this guy was only barely listening anyway? People who were used to commanding attention went onto auto-pilot, forgetting to be careful about their answers, and individuals who craved approval worked even harder, bringing up little nuggets of information they thought might pique his interest.

Of course, the criminologist was listening to every single word and filing everything away.

'So when did Nurse Jules come here?' he asked Pat, one of the porters.

'Oh, I reckon it was in 2000,' he said.

'She definitely wasn't here in 1998?'

'No. The CNO back then was a lady called Delia – what was her surname? – oh, yes, Delia Tarbuck. But she retired in late '99, and I'm pretty sure Olive, Nurse Jules that is, started in the January of the new millennium.'

'What was Nurse Tarbuck like to work for?'

'She was old school. A tough lady. Ran a tight ship, so she did.'

'Liked by the staff?'

'Respected.'

'You weren't pals, then?'

'She didn't want or need us to be her friends.'

'Who was she close to?'

'What do you mean by "*close* to"?'

Dunnigan shrugged. 'Take it any way you wish.'

'She was pally with the local sergeant. It was rumoured they were more than just friends, though he was a married man. There were stories that he used to … ahem … visit her here when she was on nights.'

Dunnigan made an idle note on his piece of paper and sighed as if he was so bored he could barely stay awake.

'I caught them in a clinch once,' Pat said abruptly.

'You just said it was all a rumour.'

'It was more than that. They were shaggin' each other.'

'Wasn't she at retirement age?'

'Old people shag.'

'I suppose they do,' Dunnigan said.

Nurse Tarbuck's steamy night-time encounters with the local sergeant – a man named Ormonde – received three more mentions that day. He didn't know whether such a mundane scandal was relevant, but he thought he might look into it before returning to Dublin.

His third interview of the day brought the first mention of the deaths.

'There was a storm on Christmas Eve of that year,' he said to Martina, an attractive ash-blonde nurse in her late forties.

'Yes. And I think it was the day before that — the twenty-third — when poor Sid died.'

Dunnigan did not even look up. 'Sid was an old man?'

'No. He was twenty-four. He took his own life, the poor dear.'

Dunnigan wrote the words *Sid — 24 — suicide — 23/12/98*, then refolded the page so he had a fresh blank square.

'Sid was ... um ... very disturbed, I take it?'

'He was depressed — I mean, that was why he was here. But he suddenly had a complete breakdown. Had to be restrained.'

'Not enough, clearly,' Dunnigan said, looking at his nails.

'Sorry?'

'Was there anything else unusual about that Christmas?'

'Well ... Kettu came to us in December. It wasn't Christmas week, but it was around then.'

'*Kettu?* Am I pronouncing that correctly?'

'Yes.'

'Is that a nickname?'

'No. That's his name. He's Indian or something like that.'

'I see. Is he still here?'

'Yes.'

'Could I speak with him?'

'Well, I don't think Doctor Ressler or Nurse Jules would allow it — and he wouldn't talk to you, anyway.'

'No?'

'He doesn't say much, and when he does, it's in his own language.'

'Hindi?'

'I don't know. Not English, that's for sure.'

Subsequent interviewees spoke of two more deaths – both suicides and both of young people – in early 1999.

'Robert was a nice lad. Never gave us any trouble. It was like something just snapped and he couldn't face another day.'

'Hilda was such a sad thing. But we thought she was on the mend. Then one night … she decided she'd had enough.'

At three o'clock Brendan, the caretaker, was sat in front of Dunnigan – he'd reversed the order of the previous day's meetings, so this was his last interview.

'I've got nothing to say to you that I didn't say yesterday,' Brendan drawled. 'You're chasing a ghost, so you are, and there's no good can come of it.'

'Why do you say that?'

'They tell me you're here because a piece of a lily was found in some shoe s'posed to belong to the missing child.'

'Yes.'

'Have you looked at the ditches and *sceach*s hereabouts?'

Dunnigan realised, with a sinking feeling he managed to avoid showing, that he had not – he had been so anxious to hear someone say that a child matching Beth's description had been seen at St Jude's that he had failed to confirm that rather significant detail.

'No. But then, I'm not a botanist. If the plant wasn't in flower I would miss it. I am reliably informed it grows on the coast in West Cork.'

'There's a lot of coast.'

'What are you trying to tell me, Brendan?'

'I know a thing or two about flowers, Davey. I wouldn't go so far as to declare myself a botanist, but I am the next best thing.'

'I don't know what the next best thing to a botanist is,' Dunnigan said.

'I'm a gardener. I know my plants and my flowers, both wild

and domestic. Now, I'll ask you again: you've been here for two days, and in that time have you seen any Kerry lilies in the vicinity of St Jude's?'

'You're going to tell me there aren't any.'

'That I am. Do you know where you will find them?'

'Obviously not.'

'You'll find them in sparse patches on the cliffs around Donbro harbour, but where they grow in abundance is out on the island.'

'You mean Tully Island?'

'I do.'

Dunnigan made a mark on his page.

'You've been most helpful, Brendan. While we're chatting, I don't suppose you know where I might find an Arctic char around West Cork, do you?'

'You'd have to ask Kettu about that.'

'The Indian gentleman?'

Brendan laughed. 'He's no Indian.'

'I was told he was.'

'Don't know who said that. Kettu is an Eskimo.'

This time Dunnigan could not hide his surprise. 'Excuse me?'

'Kettu is a pure-blood Eskimo. From the North Pole, like.'

Captain Sean Murtaugh

All his experience told him the threat against Diane was not eradicated, and he decided the only course of action was to keep a watchful eye on her.

He would have liked to think she was safe at the project during the day, but then he remembered that was where her friend the priest had been hit, so he gave one of his men – a youngster who had just joined the firm and was anxious to show willing – the job of watching her from seven in the morning until seven at night.

Murtaugh did the nights himself.

He and Diane had become close during their time in Chad. He had been her commanding officer, but he believed the way to encourage your troops to function at their best was to make them want to do your bidding: not out of fear, but because they liked and trusted you and wanted to make you happy. He insisted on regular social gatherings wherever they were billeted and was not beyond striking up sing-songs on long marches – he favoured the music of the Dubliners and the Wolfe Tones, but he was democratic in his choices and allowed everyone to add their tastes to the battalion's musical repertoire.

Diane enjoyed Bryan Adams, Bruce Springsteen and Bob Seger. And she could sing, which helped.

She was a great addition to his crew. She was a talented medic and a great counsellor – no one minded going to her with any issues they had, as she had such an easy, matter-of-fact way about her – but she was also a really good soldier. She was tough, resilient and dedicated, and, like so many young people he had worked with in the armed forces over the years, she believed she was totally invincible.

The death of her husband in a stupid road accident had brought home to her with crushing force that this was not the case. He had watched her fall apart before his eyes – this amazing, powerful woman became a quivering wreck almost overnight.

He did what he could, petitioning the powers that be to give her an honourable discharge and to permit her to continue as a referred counsellor for their unit. When she found the project and Father Bill, he was relieved and grateful to see her regain some of her spark.

Now it looked like she had walked into something very unpleasant, and he wasn't sure she was equipped to deal with it. Since he had gone into private practice, he had tangled with a number of underworld figures, and in his experience you did not walk into their headquarters and push them around without there being some sort of retribution, usually of the swift and brutal variety, soon afterwards.

It came a week and a half after they had been to Blanchardstown. He was parked across the road from her house in Kilmacanogue when he saw the lights of another vehicle pull in about a quarter of a mile up the road on the other side. Using night-vision binoculars, he watched as two figures got out, jumped the fence and disappeared into the field that adjoined Diane's garden.

It was no great difficulty to jog across the road and be waiting in the shrubbery for them to come over her wall. But they never came.

Fifteen minutes later, he climbed the wall himself and found the men, their necks broken, lying in various positions in the long grass. They had never even got a shot off.

'You're her friend, aren't you?' a voice said behind him.

He made to spin around, and something pressed into his back.

'Don't!'

He stayed where he was, squinting into the darkness. 'We're old army comrades. She asked me to go with her to Quirke's place. I knew it wasn't over, so I kept an eye out.'

'You're going to keep watching?'

'Yes.'

'Good. I'm needed elsewhere.'

He waited for more, but nothing came. After five minutes of silence he turned and saw he was alone but for the bodies.

7

'NO, I AM VERY SORRY, DAVEY, BUT YOU CANNOT see Kettu.'

Devaney had dropped any semblance of his previous geniality and was glowering at Dunnigan across his office desk.

'According to what your staff tell me, he arrived here almost a fortnight to the day after Beth disappeared.'

'I don't see the relevance.'

'Forensics found particles of blood from an Arctic fish on the trainer.'

'Do you honestly think we have a fur-clad Inuk gutting fish here? Please be reasonable! This is all some ridiculous coincidence.'

'I don't believe in coincidences, Mr Devaney. How can a fisherman afford to be here in the first place?'

'That is none of your concern. Kettu is under my protection. He has no family that we know of and has not spoken English in close to twenty years. Allowing you to interview him would be pointless.'

'Why not let me, then? What harm could it do?'

'By law I must observe my patients' right to confidentiality and privacy unless they direct me to do otherwise.'

'Yet you tell me that Kettu does not have the capacity to make such a direction.'

'Which means I have to act in his best interests.'

'And speaking to me would act against those interests?'

'I believe it would. I suspect Kettu's psychiatrist, Doctor Ressler, would agree with me.'

'I don't think I've met him yet.'

'You specifically asked to speak to staff who worked here in 1998. Doctor Ressler did not come here until the end of 1999.'

'He is the only psychiatrist here?'

'We are a small facility. He is a gifted practitioner – very respected within his profession.'

'Ressler isn't an Irish name.'

'I believe he's Dutch.'

'Could you ask him about my request to speak to Kettu? He may feel it would be beneficial.'

Devaney smiled simperingly. 'No, I could not.'

Dunnigan reached into the pocket of his long grey overcoat and took out his phone.

'Hello. Boss, it's Davey. Yes. Can you get me a warrant please? I need the management at St Jude's to let me into their records. And while you're at it, I would like to interview one of their patients. A gentleman by the name of Kettu. As soon as you can, please. No, they're not being terribly cooperative. Thanks, boss.'

He ended the call and looked at Devaney. 'I should have a legal writ granting me access by tomorrow afternoon.'

Devaney smiled, regaining his composure. 'Well, we'll just have to wait and see, won't we?'

'It looks like we will.'

Dunnigan left without saying goodbye. The fact that Devaney looked so smug made him feel very uneasy.

Dunnigan's mind was still on the altercation with the asylum's director as he walked briskly down the stone steps that led to the car park and his old BMW. So distracted was he that he was at the vehicle before he noticed the man sitting on its bonnet, swaying from side to side as if to music only he could hear. The interloper was deathly pale, dressed in what looked to be a pair of blue overalls that seemed to button down the back. He was probably in his mid-thirties. His hair was short and had been cut in a jagged, uneven manner, and Dunnigan could see patches where clumps had been pulled out, exposing raw, bloody scalp. A steady river of green mucus, much of which had caked onto his upper lip, flowed from the man's long, crooked nose, and there was a thick layer of drool down his stubbled chin. As he rocked and bobbed on the bonnet of the criminologist's classic car, his gaze seemed to be fixed on a point in mid-air: whatever it was he saw there, it appeared to fascinate him.

Dunnigan was unsure what to do about this strange figure. 'Um ... excuse me, please,' he said, gently opening the door. 'I need to go now.'

The man did not move, just remained sitting cross-legged, moving to his own private rhythm.

'I'm sorry – sir, could I ask you to sit somewhere else?'

Still no response. Hesitantly, Dunnigan reached out and gently touched the nearest bit of the strange person he could reach – which happened to be his arm. It was as if the contact had generated an electric current: the man jerked spasmodically, wailing loudly, and slid awkwardly off the bonnet of the car into a heap on the ground. Thinking he might have hurt him, Dunnigan walked around to help the fallen individual up, apologising as he went, but suddenly, in a burst of motion and with unnatural speed, the man sprang to his feet, glowering at his would-be helper.

'Don't touch me,' he said, his voice sounding strange, liquid almost – and was that an accent behind the words? German, perhaps? 'You do not touch me!'

'I'm sorry,' Dunnigan said, moving backwards with slow, steady steps. 'I just want to be on my way.'

His back hit the open car door, and he tried to negotiate his way around it without making a sudden movement.

'Where's my dog?' the leering, drooling man said. 'Have you seen my dog?'

'No.' Dunnigan tried to sound sympathetic. 'I haven't seen a dog anywhere around here.'

'I want you to give me back my dog now!' the strange man shouted, and before Dunnigan could fend him off, he shoved him, hard. Suddenly the criminologist was nose-to-nose with the dog-lover, breathing in his scent of sour milk and aniseed.

'Let's go for a drive,' the man said, so close Dunnigan could feel him pressing into his thigh.

He has an erection, Dunnigan thought. *That cannot bode well for me.*

'Where did you see your dog last?' he asked, trying to keep his attacker talking.

'I lost her so long ago,' the man said, and licked Dunnigan's cheek in a long, slow lap.

'Now, Benjamin, what are you doing out of your room?'

Nurse Jules's voice had never sounded so sweet.

'I am going for a drive.'

'Has he been bothering you, Mr Dunnigan?'

Dunnigan was clearly in an uncomfortable situation, but the nurse remained standing a bit away, leaving her errant patient pressed against him.

'Yes, I am extremely bothered, Nurse.'

'Perhaps I should tell Doctor Ressler about your behaviour, Benjamin. What do you think?'

It was as if she had slapped him – the man shrank away from Dunnigan, cowering on the ground in a paroxysm of terror. 'You no tell! Please!'

'Don't let me see you out of doors again today, and I'll reconsider.'

Moving in a sidelong rush, like a human crab, Benjamin scuttled back up the steps and into the asylum.

'You need to be more careful,' Nurse Jules said. 'Never forget, this is a home for the mentally ill.'

'I'll watch my step,' Dunnigan said, taking a tissue from his pocket and wiping his face where Benjamin had touched him.

'You should,' Nurse Jules said, and followed her patient back inside. 'He's had a taste of you now. And who knows when someone may leave his door unlocked again?'

8

DUNNIGAN DID NOT WANT THE NURSE TO THINK he was spooked (though he actually was) so he did what he knew he should have done the previous day and spent an hour combing the grounds of the hospital for Kerry lilies. As Brendan had forecast, he found none.

He walked for a kilometre up and down the road outside the gates, checking both sides, and found no flowers there either. Even if the area had been blanketed with them in 1998, in 2016 there were none in evidence.

Dunnigan's gift – if it could be called that – was a laser-like ability to focus on the apparently insignificant aspects of a case and find patterns others had missed. Details were his speciality, his occasional flashes of brilliance proving instrumental in solving many hopeless cases over the years.

The criminologist had travelled south and dedicated two days to interviews because he was certain the location met specific forensic criteria: the pollen and the fibre. With the pollen no longer certain and his link to the fish blood tenuous at best, it seemed he had repeated a behaviour that had caused him nothing but pain in the past: he had gone off half-cocked, chasing the spectre of his lost niece.

In disgust, he drove back to Donbro and an hour later was pacing his hotel room. Nothing else made sense but that he had got it wrong.

But what about the presence of the Inuk? Two Arctic references were just too much to write off.

He called police HQ in the Phoenix Park.

'Doctor Russell, it's Davey Dunnigan.'

'Yes. They told me before putting you through.'

'I'm confused.'

'Do you mean generally?'

'I've been investigating an asylum in West Cork. I've located the carpet – I've even found a link to the Arctic. There are, however, no Kerry lilies in the immediate vicinity.'

There was silence at the end of the line for a long moment.

'Are you still there, Doctor Russell?'

'I don't understand why you're calling me.'

'I don't know how to articulate the problem any more clearly, Doctor Russell.'

'Try.'

'If the flower is not on site, surely I have identified the wrong location!'

'I don't understand why you think that.'

'Doesn't it make sense—'

'No! No, no, no! For all those items to be present on the shoe, they don't need to have been picked up in the same place at all! The owner of the trainer could have been out for a walk, miles away from where the carpet was laid, picked up the pollen, come back to the hospital, come in contact with the fibres, and the next day or the next week or even the next month stumbled across the fish blood. I'm surprised at you, Davey, thinking it all had to happen at the same time and in the same place.'

Dunnigan's mind was racing. 'But I have a site *near* the hospital where there are lots of those flowers.'

'If you have a reasonable link to the fish, if you've got the right carpet and are in proximity to the pollen, I expect you are, in all probability, in the correct location. Now can I please get back to work?'

'Yes.'

And he hung up, feeling relieved and a bit stupid all at once.

9

DUNNIGAN STILL HAD TO BE SURE.

The hotel receptionist directed him to the bar, where a young man wearing a Big Tom and the Mainliners T-shirt, a woollen cap at a rakish angle atop his head, was drinking a pint of Guinness.

'You're Donal,' Dunnigan said. 'I want to go to Tully Island. Will you take me?'

The youngster looked at him from the corner of his eye. 'When?'

'Now.'

'I'm having me pints.'

'I want to go now.'

'Well, it's a pity then that I'm not goin'.'

'I'll give you fifty euro.'

The glass of porter, which was three-quarters full, was downed in two gulps.

'Follow me, sir. Do you want me to wait for ye out there or will I come back when your business is done?'

'I expect I'll be a couple of hours.'

'No problem, lad. I'll drop ye and come back.'

The dock was a five-minute walk from the hotel. Dunnigan, who was downwind, noticed that his pilot was reeking of alcohol.

'Are you safe to navigate?'

'To do what, like?'

'Can you get me to the island in one piece? You appear to be drunk.'

Donal guffawed. 'If I have a problem it's that I'm not drunk enough. This is my vessel, right here.'

Tied to the pier and sitting low in the water was a wooden rowing boat with an outboard motor.

'Are you serious?'

'It doesn't leak, if that's what you mean. And if the motor gives out, we have two fine oars.'

Drunk or not, Donal descended from the dock and was in the boat, standing at the stern, with two sure steps. It took Dunnigan a good deal of wobbling and swaying, and eventually the assistance of his pilot, to do the same.

'I'll take that fifty now, if you don't mind.'

Dunnigan handed it over, already feeling seasick.

'And we're off!'

The trip took about ten minutes and, once Dunnigan became accustomed to the movement of the boat, was surprisingly pleasant. The sun made the water sparkle as if there were jewels just below the surface, and at one point a school of harbour porpoise surfaced only a few yards ahead of them. Dunnigan was surprised at how ungainly they looked – not long and sleek like dolphins, but short and stubby.

'The islanders call them harbour hogs because they're a bit pig-like,' Donal told him. 'I like them. They're friendly animals.'

Dunnigan disembarked at the stone pier on the island – quite a few boats of various sizes were tied up there, and several groups of people were sunbathing and having picnics nearby.

'It's half six now,' his new friend said. 'I'll be back for you around eight thirty.'

'I'll be here at that time precisely.'

'I probably won't be, so don't rush,' Donal said, and waved as he steered back towards the mainland.

A pathway led from one end of the island to the other, and many smaller lanes tapered off it through heather, bracken and scrub to cliffs, inlets and quiet beaches. Dotted about were houses in various states of repair and dereliction. It took him fifty minutes to make the walk from point to point, and in that time he found four clumps of lilies. A further excursion into the interior yielded six more. He took photographs of each specimen on his phone and logged their locations on Google Maps.

Sitting on a rock, he looked at one of the flowers closely. Its petals were radiantly white, almost glimmering in the sun. The stamen were white also and looked furry, with yellow anthers on the tops heavy with pollen. He brushed one gently with his finger, and a fine, powdery residue came off. He knew that if he were to examine this residue under a microscope, each individual grain would look like a coffee bean.

Dunnigan was rarely impressed by nature – in fact, he usually didn't notice it at all. He was puzzled to find that he did not just find this flower beautiful – he was actually awestruck by it. He realised, after a few moments of gazing stupidly, that he was deeply moved to be touching something Beth might have come in contact with after she vanished, and he thought that, even if she were afraid and upset, she might, even for a moment, have been impressed by this flower's delicate beauty too.

It was while he was sitting on his rock, marvelling at the lilies, that he noticed a figure standing atop a rocky outcrop about a hundred yards to his left. It was difficult to discern from this distance, as all Dunnigan could see was a silhouette, but it looked to be a man. And the man seemed to be watching him closely. Dunnigan stared right back, and they remained motionless for a minute before the person on the higher ground turned and was gone. The criminologist couldn't decide whether to be alarmed by the man's presence or not, but concluded that he was feeling too relaxed and content to be upset, so he tried not to think about it – for the rest of the evening, at least.

Satisfied, almost at peace, he walked back to the pier and waited for his lift to return. It was a quarter past nine before it did, Donal florid-faced and jolly with stout, but Dunnigan didn't mind. The sun began to drop as they rode the waves back to shore, turning the sea a rich crimson.

The criminologist thought that was a very beautiful sight too.

He had a bowl of seafood chowder and some brown bread at the bar, then brought some tea back to his room. It was almost fully dark, and he unlocked the door and put the tray with his tea things down on the small table before turning on the light. He took his coat off and was about to toss it on the bed when he froze.

There, lying on his pillow, was a Kerry lily.

10

'HI, DAVEY.'

'Hello, boss.'

'I have some good news and some bad news.'

'Are you telling me a joke?'

'No. I really do have some good news and some bad news.'

'Oh.'

'Which would you like to hear first?'

'I don't care.'

'You're not very good at this, are you?'

'At what, boss?'

'I have a warrant directing St Jude's to give you access to Mr Kettu.'

'Good.'

'But you can't see any written or digital records relating to patients.'

'Why not?'

'They're protected under an obscure piece of law dating back to 1875, the Lunatic Asylums Act. It cements privacy and confidentiality rights for privately owned psychiatric facilities in ways state-owned institutions couldn't dream of – basically, back in the day, a family who could afford to have their son or daughter or alcoholic mother locked up somewhere like St Jude's wanted to be completely certain no one found out they were there. This law makes sure of that by prohibiting anyone – even the gardaí – from accessing their files. It's a fucking relic of the Victorian class system, but it's there, and it has us rightly screwed.'

'Can we mount a legal challenge?'

'I have our lawyers looking for a loophole, but it seems this is a new one on them, too. I think your Mr Devaney might have us by the short and curlies.'

'What am I to do, then?'

'Shit, I don't know, Davey. Have you tried investigating? Looking for clues? Talking to people? Rumour has it that some members of the force have found that to be an effective course of action.'

'I'll keep digging.'

'There's a good lad.'

'Someone left a Kerry lily in my room last night.'

'That's the flower that sent you running down there?'

'Yes.'

'Do you think it was left by a friend or a foe?'

'I haven't a clue, boss. But I think it means I'm close to something.'

'Be careful, will you, for the love of God?'

'I'm trying to be.'

'Try harder.'

Tormey hung up.

11

NURSE JULES LOOKED AT THE WARRANT DUNNIGAN presented to her with disdain. 'What do you want me to do with this?'

'I'd put it on file, if I were you.'

The nurse sniffed and set the sheet of paper aside. 'Is there something you require?'

'I would like to see Kettu, please.'

'Mr Dunnigan, we do not—'

'Nurse Jules, the warrant I just showed you, signed by an officer of the court, obliges you to give me access to a person we believe might have information pertinent to an ongoing garda investigation. Now, if you do not observe the letter of the writ, I will be forced to bring members of the local police force here and compel you to do so – by force if necessary. Am I being clear, Nurse Jules?'

Giving him a look that was tantamount to a physical assault, the woman picked up the phone.

'The gentleman from the police is back,' she said (he assumed she was addressing Devaney and wondered that she seemed more deferential this time). 'You have already received a copy of the legal document, sir? I see. Yes. All right. I shall bring him upstairs. If you're certain.'

She stood. 'Very well. I will show you to Mr Kettu's room.'

'Is Kettu his surname or his Christian name?'

'Inuit do not have surnames, Mr Dunnigan. Kettu is what he answers to – when he answers at all.'

They climbed a flight of stairs with dark wooden bannisters and traversed a corridor, stopping at a room at the end. Nurse Jules didn't bother to knock.

Inside, sprawled on an armchair and gazing out the window, was a dark-haired man with a lined chestnut-brown face, dressed in a tracksuit in the Cork colours of red and white.

'*Kettu*,' the nurse said in a voice that was several decibels louder than it needed to be, as if shouting would induce the room's occupant to respond, 'this is *Mr Dunnigan*. He is from the *police*. He wants to *ask* you some *questions*.' Turning to Dunnigan, she said, 'He rarely speaks and when he does it is in his own dialect. I can't make head nor tail of it.'

Then she was gone.

Dunnigan looked about the room and, finding no other chair, sat on the bed. Kettu had neither looked at him nor acknowledged his presence in any way. The criminologist noted that the room contained no books, no photographs, and did not have a radio or a television. It was as if no one lived there – he wondered if the man had been recently moved and his belongings had not made the transition yet.

'Is it OK if I call you Kettu?' he asked. 'You don't have a title or anything?'

The man shifted in his chair, which Dunnigan took to be a response, of a kind.

'I'm Davey,' he said. 'I know you don't speak much anymore, and that's OK – I went for a long time without saying a lot, too, a few years back. But I'd be very grateful if you'd listen to what I have to say and think about it. If you know anything, I'd appreciate any help you can offer.'

A pause, then a sigh. He soldiered on.

'I have a niece. Her name is Beth, and around the time you came here, someone took her away. A couple of weeks ago, her shoe was left at my front door. The scientists were able to tell that the shoe had been here at some stage, but no one I talk to claims to know anything about it. So what I want to know is, when you came to St Jude's first, in 1998, if you can remember seeing a little girl?'

This speech elicited neither noise nor movement. He tried repeating it slowly, using simpler language, reasoning that the man's grasp of English might not be very good. Still nothing.

After an hour, he realised he was wasting his time: the wizened man appeared to be virtually catatonic. Dunnigan stood so he was in front of him. 'I'm sorry I took up your time,' he said, and then stopped dead.

Kettu was crying – though he had not made a sound, tears were streaming down his face. '*Sinnektomanerk*,' he said, his voice harsh and rasping from lack of use. '*Sinnektomanerk*.'

In a flurry of movement, Dunnigan dragged some paper from the pocket of his coat and scribbled down the word.

He gently urged the man to say more, but that was all he would utter.

As soon as Dunnigan was outside the door, he put the word into Google Translate – he had to alter his spelling a few times before he found the correct letters, but finally he did.

Kettu had spoken the Inuit word for *dream*.

Doctor Phillipe Ressler

He saw his job as a simple one – to oversee the application of certain procedures and methodologies on a specified target group; to monitor trials carried out in the name of medical research; and, perhaps most importantly, to protect the interests of his employers at all costs.

This he had done successfully for fifteen years – he and Benjamin.

And then this strange man had come, asking questions.

Ressler had looked into him, of course.

The criminologist's history and psychological profile suggested some possible courses of action, yet the two gentle hints that had been made had not deterred him, and it was beginning to look as if harsher measures needed to be implemented.

He would have to begin priming Benjamin – withholding his food, beating him occasionally, suggesting that this Dunnigan might be hiding his dog somewhere. It wouldn't take much.

Benjamin could be a blunt weapon, but he could be subtle, too. He could be used to frighten the unwitting and the weak-minded, or he could be a deadly force.

Ressler hadn't decided which would be needed to address the threat posed by David Dunnigan.

But he knew the time would soon arrive when he would have to make up his mind.

12

'WHO IS HE, MR DEVANEY?' DUNNIGAN ASKED THE director.

They were seated opposite one another in the virtually empty canteen – which was like none the criminologist had ever been in before, bearing a closer resemblance to the dining room of a fine hotel. Devaney was eating a roast beef dinner, complete with perfectly risen Yorkshire puddings. Dunnigan had not been offered a morsel.

'He is one of my patients,' Devaney said, pouring a little more gravy on his roast potatoes.

'I'm forty-four years old,' Dunnigan said. 'I have lived in Ireland that entire time, and I have never met a member of the Inuit before now. They don't, as a rule, migrate this far south. How did you end up with one resident here?'

'Why don't you ask him?' Devaney retorted. 'Now, please leave me alone. I'm trying to have my lunch.'

Brendan was sitting astride a ride-on lawnmower, cutting a patch of grass by an old stone folly when Dunnigan found him, a little boy of about six seated in front of him, his small hands resting on the wheel, helping the old man to steer.

'Did you find any o' them lilies yet?' he asked as the criminologist approached across the freshly cut grass.

'I did, thank you.'

'Well, isn't that grand,' the oldster cackled. 'Amazing what you can see when you know where to look, isn't it, Cormac?' This to the boy, who nodded, looking at Dunnigan with liquid eyes. 'This is my grandson. Say hello to Mr Dunnigan, Cormac.'

'Hello,' the lad said obediently.

'Hello,' Dunnigan said, extending his hand for the child to shake, which he did enthusiastically.

'I met your resident Inuk this morning,' Dunnigan said.

'Ah – Kettu the Eskimo,' Brendan said. 'Interesting chap.'

'I don't think you're supposed to call them "Eskimo" anymore,' Dunnigan said. 'It's considered racially insensitive.'

'Is that right?' Brendan said. 'Well, we wouldn't want that, would we?'

'How did he come to be here – Kettu, I mean?'

'Did you put that question to Doctor Ressler, by any chance?'

'I haven't had the pleasure of meeting him yet.'

'Oh, I'm sure he'll introduce himself to you soon enough. What about Mr Devaney?'

'He's very busy.'

'Our director is most likely shovelling food down his throat in the lunch hall about now, wouldn't you think, Cormac?' Brendan said, ruffling his grandson's hair. 'They serve beef on a Wednesday, you know.'

'You don't partake?'

'These days we're referred to as "ancillary staff",' Brendan said. 'They used to call us servants, but I suppose that would also be considered insensitive. Amounts to the same thing, though. We get soup and sangwidges in a different canteen below stairs. Cormac and I've had ours, thanks.'

'Do you know how Kettu got here, Brendan?'

'Oh, that I do.'

Dunnigan tried a smile – it was not a facial expression he was accustomed to, so it probably looked a bit odd. If Brendan thought so, he didn't pass comment. 'Do you think you might tell me?'

'You know, there's some brack in the servants' quarters. I could take a sup of tea, and I know Rosie keeps some fizzy pop for our younger gardeners, if you'd care to take some with us.'

'The tea would be very nice,' Dunnigan said.

'Well, let's do that, so, and I'll tell you all about our northern friend.'

13

THE BELOW-STAIRS CANTEEN WAS A SNUG ROOM dominated by a large wooden table, a couple of armchairs and an ancient Aga. The ceiling had been stained a yellowish brown from tobacco smoke. Brendan hung the keys for the lawnmower on one of a series of hooks, each of which had a similar key dangling from them, all labelled to indicate which door they opened or vehicle they set in motion. As he brewed a pot of strong tea, the gardener spread thick slices of spicy currant bread with butter and Cormac curled up in one of the chairs with a *Power Rangers* comic.

'When Kettu came to St Jude's he was a broken man,' the caretaker said in his slow, musical way. 'I would like to think that, for a while, at least, he considered me his friend. A lot of the patients are locked in their own private torments, and there isn't much a fella like me can do for them, but in those days Kettu was happy to speak English and he enjoyed being out of doors and walking in the grounds.'

'Besides Kettu, I've only seen one patient since I arrived here,' Dunnigan said. 'That was Benjamin, and Nurse Jules said he'd escaped and wasn't meant to be out. Is it common for them to use the gardens?'

'Benjy isn't exactly a patient, as I understand it.'

'What is he, then?'

'He's more of a special project of Doctor Ressler's.'

'Wouldn't that still make him a patient? Anyway, it doesn't matter – Kettu changed?'

'By the time he was here six months, he had stopped talking.

Then he was whisked off to one of their private wards, and I hardly saw him after that.'

'Why did he come here in the first place? What's wrong with him?'

'Do you know anything about the Eskimo peoples?'

'We shouldn't call them that—'

'*Arah whisht*, young fella! 'Tis only us talking now, and I don't think you're the kind to easily take offence.'

'Well – no. I suppose not.'

'Good. Now, what was I saying?'

'You asked me what I know about the Inuit. Other than they live in Arctic regions, I don't know very much.'

'They're an amazing bunch, the Eskimo! Kettu told me that he was reared *on the ice*! And that is not a euphemism, Davey. He literally grew up on a sheet of feckin' ice. Think about that, for a moment. The whole of Ireland shuts down if we get a powdering of snow, but Kettu and his sort work and eat and play in conditions we could not even dream of.'

'Remarkable,' Dunnigan agreed.

'Our friend was – *is* – a master fisherman. He went to college and he has degrees in biology and marine husbandry or something like that. He worked for a fishing company out of Greenland – he was over their fleet of boats. A company from this part of the world bought that company, and they wanted to expand into the North Atlantic, so Kettu was brought from his home to run things here – they wanted to use his skills to develop a new fleet.'

'I still don't know what's wrong with him.'

'Have patience, lad. Part of what he did for this company was to go out with the fishermen and observe what they caught and how they caught it. Now, Kettu had no fear of the sea. He'd spent his life on boats in all conditions, and this day the wind was a bit high and the water a bit choppy, but he thought nothing of heading out in it. That night their boat was hit by hurricane winds. It broke in half, and all hands were lost, all except Kettu, who managed to inflate a rain jacket somehow and kept himself afloat. Search and Rescue found him by sheer luck, almost dead from the cold.'

'He was lucky to have survived,' Dunnigan observed.

'He was,' Brendan said. ''Twas a freak storm. There was a lot of them that December. It wasn't on any of the forecasts, and it blew out as fast as it stirred up. No one saw it coming.'

'Meteorology is not an exact science.'

'No. It took him a week in hospital to recover physically, but the whole experience had done something else to him. He couldn't sleep. He couldn't eat. He kept having what he called visions – he'd be talking to you just as I am, and then, suddenly, he'd be back in the ocean fighting for his life.'

'Flashbacks,' Dunnigan said. 'He was suffering from post-traumatic stress.'

'That wasn't his take on it. He told me that he was meant to die with the others,' Brendan said. 'His time had come, but he was too afraid to accept his fate. He had cheated death.'

'Wouldn't most people be glad about that?'

'Not Kettu's people. You see, when that ship went down, our Eskimo friend was standing on the threshold of the other world – all he had to do was step over. But he didn't. Instead, he drew back. And Kettu believes that when he did that, he brought something back with him.'

Dunnigan looked bemused. 'What? A ghost?'

'A demon. Kettu believes he's cursed, and he thinks that the deaths of those fishermen, and all the bad stuff that happened here, too, are all down to him.'

'But that's nonsense,' Dunnigan said. 'Didn't you say he was an educated man?'

'He is. Doesn't mean he's wrong.'

'We'll have to agree to disagree on that point,' Dunnigan said. 'What "bad stuff" happened here?'

'There was a cluster of suicides around the time Kettu came.'

'I heard something about that. In a psychiatric hospital, are such things really so strange?'

'Twelve people took their lives. They were all young, and none would have been considered a risk to themselves.'

'*Twelve* deaths?'

'Seems a bit less commonplace now, doesn't it?'

'Can I ask you one more thing?'

'Why stop now?' Brendan said, pouring them both some more tea.

'Why are you telling me this when you know your boss would sack you if he found out?'

'I'm seventy years of age, Davey, and I'm the last of my family to work in St Jude's. When I started working here, the custom was to keep your head down, do your job, and let the doctors and the men with degrees do theirs – you didn't ask questions or pass comment on what you saw. Working-class people knew their place and kept their silence. But things are different now, and so am I.' The old man sat back and rubbed his chin. 'I come here to tend the gardens and fix the odd leaking tap because I like to, not because I need the money. Kettu was a good man. Whatever they did to him, they sure as hell didn't make him better. I don't know if it has anything to do with this missing niece of yours, but if you can do something about the evil that's here while you're looking for her, I won't complain. Because there is something bad going on in St Jude's. I don't know what it is, but it's been here a long while. It's time it was stopped.'

'I'll do my best,' Dunnigan said.

'I wouldn't ask you for anything less.' Brendan grinned.

14

THE GARDA SERGEANT FOR DONBRO IN 1998 – WHO had allegedly enjoyed a torrid affair with Chief Nursing Officer Tarbuck – was a man named Finbar Ormonde. He had retired in 2004, but he and his wife still lived in a fisherman's cottage a short walk from the Seaside Hotel.

'What do you want me to tell you?' Ormonde growled when Dunnigan asked him about the deaths at the asylum. 'It's a hospital that deals with people who are mentally ill. That type of person sometimes does irrational things, like taking their own lives.'

The front room of the cottage looked as if it had been decorated by Angela Lansbury – it was all bone china ornaments, lace trim and pressed flowers. The retired sergeant, who was a bear of a man with a large gut and a square head, looked ungainly and out of place.

'Twelve people who had no history of suicidal ideology?'

'Jesus, you know the way these things go,' the former guard said. 'One of them tops themselves, and the others get the idea too. It's a copy-cat thing.'

'Was there an investigation?'

'We looked into it.'

'Can I see the paperwork?'

'They'll have it at the station. I don't imagine it'll tell you much, though – there would have been a few questions asked at St Jude's, maybe a chat with the families, but probably not much else. There was the whole confidentiality thing too – you know how it is.'

'You're telling me that there *wasn't* an investigation.'

'I am saying we looked into it, and the deaths were found not to be of a suspicious nature,' Ormonde said, his voice betraying the beginnings of anger. 'The individuals concerned died in tragic circumstances.'

'I see.'

'Why are you asking about this? I thought you were following up on a missing person case. What the hell has this to do with it?'

'It's out of the ordinary. So I ask questions until something pops up, and then I'll probably ask questions about that. Hopefully in the end I'll know something I didn't at the start of the process.'

'There's nothing *to* know. You should go back to wherever you came from and leave us in peace.'

'Maybe I should speak to Ms Tarbuck.'

Ormonde's eyes narrowed, and Dunnigan thought he saw something low and mean in them. 'Why?'

'She was head of the nursing staff in St Jude's at the time of the deaths, wasn't she?'

'She's not well.'

'Still, she might be able to help me.'

'Leave her alone.'

Dunnigan could feel something unpleasant radiating from the big man. He was probably in his seventies, but the criminologist was in no doubt that he could still hurt him badly if the mood took him. 'Thank you for your help, Mr Ormonde.'

'You know the way out.'

Dunnigan did, and took it.

15

THE FILES WERE, AS ORMONDE HAD SUGGESTED, OF little help. He made a note of the names of the twelve deceased, scribbling ages and times of death beside each one: the youngest was nineteen, the oldest twenty-seven. While he was at it, he recorded the numbers of the corresponding death certificates, so they could be pulled up on the system when he got back to Harcourt Street.

The sergeant had dealt with the cases himself, which Dunnigan ruefully admitted was probably normal enough for a rural police station. With nothing left to learn, he asked the uniformed officer on duty where Delia Tarbuck lived.

'You can walk there from here easy enough,' the young officer said, carefully writing the address for him. 'She's not a well woman, though. Alzheimer's – awful bloody disease. Her husband cares for her as best he can, and they have a nurse who calls in most days.'

The Tarbucks occupied a beautiful three-storey townhouse on the waterfront. The retired nurse was having physiotherapy when Dunnigan arrived. James, her husband, had renovated the lower floor into a self-contained flat so his wife, who had become quite frail, did not have to tackle the stairs to go to bed or use the bathroom. He was a tall, thin man with a prominent Adam's apple and a curly frizz of white-blond hair about his ears, the top of his head freckled and shiny.

'She was the brightest, most able woman you could hope to meet,' he said, sitting with Dunnigan on a wooden bench outside their front door, a glass of lemonade in his hand. 'She retired in 1999 – we thought we'd welcome the new millennium together with a fresh start. We had plans to travel, see all the places we

150

hadn't visited yet. But she was already showing signs of dementia by that first Easter.'

'I'm sorry,' Dunnigan said.

'I am too. I love her. I've never loved anyone else, if I'm honest. I know she found me a bit staid, a little boring. If you've been talking to Ormonde, I expect you're aware he and she had a thing going for a time.'

Dunnigan cast him a glance.

'Oh, yes, I knew. It nearly ate me up, but I knew I could wait them out. Ormonde's a horrible man, and he used her and cast her aside. He was jumping in bed with half the women in town in those days. It devastated her, but I was here to offer comfort when it ended, and we muddled through.'

'You weren't angry?' Dunnigan asked.

'I was furious.'

'But you loved her more than you hated her.'

'I never hated her. I wanted to, but I couldn't.'

They drank their lemonade and watched herring gulls squabble over discarded chips across the street.

'Does she remember much of her time at St Jude's?'

'She remembers everything that happened twenty years ago,' James said. 'Twenty *minutes* ago, well, that's another matter.'

'So I might be in luck?'

'Only if you can catch her when she's able to articulate what she wants to say.'

'How is she today?'

'Changeable.'

'Is that good?'

'None of this is good, Davey,' James said without humour.

Delia Tarbuck had probably once been beautiful, but now resembled a skeleton that someone had put a wig on. She sat in a wheelchair on a patio at the rear of the house, a shawl across her bony legs. James sat a little away from them, half-reading a copy of *Little Dorrit*, half-listening to make sure his wife didn't become too upset by Dunnigan's questions.

'Nurse Tarbuck, I would like to talk to you about the last year you were in St Jude's,' Dunnigan said. 'Can you tell me anything about that?'

'Are you from the agency?' she asked – her voice was still strong and commanding. 'Did they send you to cover for Gerry?'

Unsure how to answer, Dunnigan decided to play along. 'Yes, they did. I'll be working with you for a while.'

'How long? I need to know how long.'

'I'll be here until Gerry comes back.'

She wrung her hands and chewed on her lower lip with yellowed teeth. 'OK. You can work his hours.'

'I'd be happy to. Nurse, one of the other staff told me that there have been some deaths: suicides among the patients.'

'Yes. They got sick. Shouldn't have happened.'

'Why did they get sick?'

'Treatment. The treatment didn't work. We need to change it.'

'Were you trying something new?'

'Yes. Not working, though.'

Dunnigan didn't know what to do with that. It wasn't so strange that a hospital might try a pioneering method – medicine as a field was always bragging about new initiatives that revolutionised the way this illness or that condition was viewed. 'OK. Will we change the treatment then?'

'Doctor Ressler. Have to talk to Doctor Ressler.'

'We can do that.'

Dunnigan had been labouring under the belief that the psychiatrist had arrived at St Jude's after Nurse Tarbuck's retirement. He would have to double-check that.

'Nurse, before I start work, could you tell me if you've seen a little girl around the hospital? She'd be about four.'

The woman's breathing quickened. James looked up from his book, sensing her agitation.

'Lights,' she said, 'in the dark.'

'What do you mean?' Dunnigan said.

'Lights in the dark. You can see them across the bay. The lights.'

'No, I was asking you about the hospital. St Jude's. Did you see a little girl in the hospital?'

'Yes,' she hissed, looking about her anxiously, as if she expected to see someone hiding in the shrubs, eavesdropping on their conversation.

'You did?' Dunnigan was suddenly terrified she would lose her train of thought.

'They came by bus, the little ones,' Nurse Tarbuck said.

'To St Jude's?' Dunnigan tried desperately to keep her on track. 'Little ones – children – came by bus to St Jude's?'

'Lights. You could see the lights.'

'Yes, you said that. Please think – it's very important: you said the little ones came to the hospital in a bus.'

'They did. The children came to us by bus. The men took them downstairs.'

And then, with no warning, Delia Tarbuck, former chief nursing officer at St Jude's Asylum, started screaming.

16

IT TOOK JAMES THREE-QUARTERS OF AN HOUR TO
get her settled.

'Does she do that a lot?' Dunnigan asked once the woman was
safely in bed.

'No. I've never known her to do it before.'

'I'm sorry if I upset her.'

'Not your fault.'

Dunnigan thought that maybe it was, but he shook the man's
hand and walked back along the quayside to the Seaside Hotel.

When he got there, the girl on the desk told him he had a visitor.

'There's a man waitin' for you in the bar.'

'Who is it?'

'Foreign bloke in a suit.'

'Did he leave a name?'

'He says he knows you,' she said.

'I am Doctor Philippe Ressler,' the man in question said,
standing up from his seat at a table by the window as Dunnigan
approached him. 'I wish to apologise for not introducing myself
before, but I have many pressing duties.'

'Yet you decided to come and see me now,' Dunnigan observed.

'I did.'

'Why?'

The psychiatrist was of average height but radiated coiled,
suppressed energy. He had a high domed forehead and hair so
black Dunnigan wondered if it was natural. His skin was very
pink, as if he had just stepped out of a hot shower, and his eyes

flashed a deep amber, giving him an almost feline quality. His suit was of straw-coloured linen, and the criminologist found it impossible to put an age on him – he could have been fifty, but there was something about him that seemed much older than that.

'Shall we have a drink, Mr Dunnigan?'

'Call me Davey. I've been drinking tea and lemonade all afternoon.'

'Would you be offended if I had a little something?'

'Why would that offend me? We're sitting in a bar.'

'You're sure I cannot tempt you?'

'I'm fine.'

'I will be back in a moment, then.'

He returned with a large glass of Scotch over two cubes of ice. 'This is my vice. I keep it under control, but I acknowledge that it would be such an easy thing for me to let it loose and then: *pow*! I would be in a mess.'

Dunnigan didn't know what to say to this admission, so he said nothing.

'I wish to speak with you because you have become a feature in the life of one of my patients.'

'Really?'

'Come, Davey – this is not a surprise announcement. I know Roderick mentioned me in your conversation of this morning.'

'He did.'

'You met with Kettu.'

'Yes.'

'And I hear from the grapevine that you made quite the breakthrough with him!'

'Did I?'

'He spoke to you! He said a word in answer to questions about your niece who has been missing.'

Ressler's speech bounced along, punctuated by smiles and

energetic hand movements. It was all a bit discomfiting. Dunnigan didn't know why.

'He said one word.'

'Yes! He said to you *sinnektomanerk*, the word for dream! What do you think that means, Davey?'

'You're the psychiatrist. How would you interpret it?'

'That is a very, very good question! But I think we might be jumping ahead of ourselves in this game, Davey. We need to go back a few steps.'

'We do?'

'Oh, yes. A far more important question to consider is not what Kettu said, but *why he chose to speak to you at all.*' Ressler leaned in close to Dunnigan as he said this, bringing his voice to a hushed whisper.

'Isn't it just because I talked to him?'

'*Yes!*' This was almost shouted, and punctuated by a loud hand-clap. 'Yes, this is a possibility! But you must consider that Kettu has been a resident in St Jude's for almost twenty years. For most of that time he has hardly talked at all, and the people he does communicate with are a select few: me, Nurse Olive Jules, sometimes Rosie Malone, the lady who brings his food to him. These are all people he sees every day of his life. Then, you come along. And *wham*! He speaks to *you*!'

'Doctor, my interest in Kettu is rooted in the case I'm investigating. I'm sure you find this an interesting psychological puzzle, but it isn't one I have the time or the inclination to pursue.'

Ressler sat back, feigning shock. He took a swallow of his drink. 'Davey, I do not know what to say to this untruth. You injure me!'

'Untruth?'

'Yes! I know what you say does not reflect what you think or feel.'

'I promise you it does.'

'No.'

'Yes.'

'No. I am sorry, but it does not. You are a detective.'

'I am a civilian consultant with the Sex Crimes Unit—'

'Come, David Dunnigan, this is a *label*. It has no value in the world of reality. You are a detective and your interest in this life is to solve puzzles. Kettu is a puzzle. You must agree with me! Come now, say you do!'

'What are you getting at?'

'I think my friend and yours, Kettu of northern Greenland, spoke to you because he feels you are kindred spirits. He sensed a *bond*.'

Dunnigan would have laughed at this had he not been so wrong-footed by the psychiatrist's odd manner. As it was, he sighed irritably and said, 'I grew up in Dublin in a big house surrounded by a forest of fir trees my father planted because he had notions about being a smallholder. Those trees are as close to the wilderness as I have ever been. I have never gone fishing in my life, and I don't like snow. How are Kettu and I in any way the same?'

Ressler held up his hand to silence him. 'Shall I tell you, David Dunnigan?'

'I just asked you to.'

'You wish to know how you and this strange, alien man are really very much alike?'

'I'd like to know why you think we are, yes.'

'What binds you together like brothers of the blood, is *loss*.'

'Pardon me?'

'You are both defined by loss.'

Dunnigan struggled to read people, but somehow he knew this odd man was trying to goad him. He decided to let the shrink play his hand and see where it led. 'Go on.'

'The world has taken away something precious from each of you, and this has been done in a most tragic yet also splendidly *apt* way. It would almost be funny if it was not so sad! David Dunnigan the criminologist, you work for the police. You specialise in finding people who are lost, you chase the bad criminals and you stop them from perpetrating violent acts. If you cannot stop them, you make sure they are caught and punished for doing their nasty things. But what happens in your life? A wicked person comes and takes your niece, this little girl you love so much. The predatory man takes her right from your side, and there's nothing you can do to stop it. Even though you try to capture this horrible person for many years, you cannot find them. It is as if all the evil things in your job came together and smote you down! Ha! Just like so.' Ressler chopped the air like a karate expert.

'You could look at it like that,' Dunnigan said through clenched teeth.

'Kettu is a master of the sea. His job was to find the best places to catch the fish, to seek out spots where the boats could fill themselves up and get back to port in safety. And one day, out he goes onto the ocean, and the sea rises up and takes his boat and the fish inside it and even the fishermen whom he was supposed to protect! Like you, all the dangerous things he was to prevent, they happened to him. He could not stop them.'

Ressler motioned to the waitress for a refill.

'And you think Kettu saw that parallel?'

'Perhaps. The Inuit are an instinctive people. A *soulful* people. You know he believes that he is cursed?'

'I heard that.'

The waitress placed the second glass in front of the psychiatrist, who gave him a jaunty thumbs-up.

'Did you ever think *you* might be cursed, Davey?' Still the jolly tone remained, though Dunnigan sensed an edge to it now. 'Were there times you believed the universe was trying to crush you? Did you despair? Perhaps, in a moment of great dread, you tried to end your life?'

Dunnigan experienced a moment of extreme rage. It was as if a wave of heat crashed across him.

Ressler smiled. He had seen it too. 'Poor old Kettu, he has been without a tribe for many long years now.'

'And?'

The psychiatrist drained his glass and put it down on the table with a bang. 'Maybe you can be his tribe. What do you think, Davey? You and he, united in your grief.'

Dunnigan stood up and, without looking back, walked out of the bar. He suddenly needed to get away from this awful man. He was afraid that if he stayed, he would either start crying or hit the psychiatrist with a chair.

'I cannot wait to work with you some more,' Ressler called after him.

Dunnigan didn't wait for the elevator. He took the stairs at a run.

Part Four

INTERLUDE

1

DUNNIGAN LAY ON THE BED IN HIS ROOM, STARING at the ceiling.

The psychiatrist had got under his skin. He would have to be more careful, keep his guard up – next time, he would be prepared.

He might have dozed off, because the next thing he knew the texture of light was different and his phone was ringing. He picked it up, his fingers clumsy with sleep. 'Yes.'

'Hi, Davey.'

'Diane. Hello.'

'Have you been missing me?'

'I've been busy.'

'Are you safe?'

'Only one person has tried to physically molest me.'

'Only the one? Have you learned anything? Anything important?'

'I've learned a lot of things. I don't know if any of it is relevant. Maybe.'

'When are you coming home?'

'I don't know.'

'The residents at the project want to have a thing for Father Bill. Sort of a ceremony.'

'It seems a little soon for a memorial – it's only been a couple of weeks. He hasn't officially been declared dead.'

'It's not a memorial. It's more a "we hope you come back safely" sort of thing. I suspect Miley might be behind it. He's been like a little lost puppy with you away, and you know what he gets like when he's at a loose end. He starts worrying at things.'

'When is this event taking place?'

'Tomorrow night. I – *we* – would love it if you'd come.'

Dunnigan held the phone to his ear. He didn't want to leave Donbro; he felt he had the tail end of something, and he needed to dig just a little deeper to have a firm grasp of it.

But he didn't want to let Diane down. Or Miley. Or Father Bill, for that matter.

'I'll come.'

'Thanks, Davey.'

'Goodbye. I'll call to the project tomorrow.'

'I ... I'm looking forward to seeing you.'

'Yes. Tomorrow, then.'

He threw what few belongings he had brought with him into a bag and left his room without informing the hotel. For some reason, he did not want anyone to know he had gone.

He played his *Lord of the Rings* on the drive back, but heard little of it. Ressler's words were still playing in his head, and he could not stop them. The effort of keeping the fear and the anger and the wild panic at bay since coming to Cork suddenly became too much, and as he drove, he wept.

By the time he reached the outskirts of Dublin, he was exhausted and sweating, even though all the windows were rolled down and the night air was cool.

He went straight to the flat and spent half an hour going through every room and touching each item he owned, a ritual he had not had the need to enact for more than a year. When he felt that he was somewhat grounded again, he stripped, threw everything, including his grey woollen overcoat, into the washing machine and put it on a rinse cycle. Then he got into the shower, turning the heat up as high as he could tolerate, and scrubbed himself until it hurt. When he was afraid he would draw blood, he towelled off, put on a Flash Gordon T-shirt and a pair of pyjama bottoms, and watched Jon Pertwee and Katy Manning in *Doctor Who and the Curse of Peladon* on his laptop. By the time he reached the third episode, he was beginning to feel better. But he still slept on the couch that night, under the watchful eye of his poster, the photo of Beth clutched to his chest.

2

'YOU'RE A SIGHT FOR SORE EYES!' TORMEY SAID when Dunnigan arrived to the office the next day.

'Thanks, boss.'

'I was being sarcastic – you look like shit. Have you slept?'

'A bit.'

'So what's been going on?'

Dunnigan told him.

'Jesus,' Tormey said when he was finished.

'Exactly.'

'Well, it's all very nasty, but you don't have anything we can act on.'

'The suicides weren't properly investigated.'

'Death by suicide is a delicate matter – in the late nineties it was still fucking taboo, especially in rural areas. Add to that the fact these kids were all in a loony bin, even a swanky private one, and you've got yourself a right can of worms. We can probably have the cases reopened, but I'm not at all sure what we could prove.' While he talked, Tormey cross-referenced the death certificates to pull down the relevant coroner's reports. 'Look at the causes of death: eight of them were asphyxiation – they hanged themselves, Davey. Where can we go with that?'

'I don't know, boss. Something's off. I know I'll find it.'

'You're probably right, but *what* will you find? You're looking for Beth, Davey. Come on, son – we've been down roads like this before. All they ever do is mess you up.'

'What about Nurse Tarbuck's comment about the children?'

'It's certainly interesting, but it's the interesting ramblings of a woman in the throes of Alzheimer's.'

'Combined with the evidence on the shoe, though, and the presence of Kettu, surely we could get some more men down there?'

'I don't see it, Davey. Sorry. To be honest, I can only give you a couple more days and then I'm gonna have to bring you back to base.'

'Give me another week.'

'Can't.'

'Then grant me leave. I can't walk away from this. Not yet.'

Tormey sighed. 'If you keep working off your own bat, it will be without the unit's backing or authority.'

'I know.'

'I won't make a fuss about it, but if the management of the asylum call us, or the local gardaí down in Donbro, I'll have to tell them you're not there on our behalf.'

'I appreciate that, boss. Will you do something for me before I'm off the clock?'

'What?'

'Will you have the money boys check into St Jude's?'

'Why?'

'It's like a bijou hotel from the fifties – the staff are served up a three-course lunch every day and everywhere I look there's antiques and original artwork. But I don't think they've got more than a handful of patients. Even if they're paying through the nose, it doesn't add up. I want to know where the money's coming from.'

'I'll call in some favours. When are you going back down there?'

'Tomorrow. Are you coming to the thing for Father Bill tonight?'

'I'll pop along. Is that why you came home?'

'Yes.' He paused for a moment. 'And I was scared.'

Tormey smiled. 'As good a reason as any.'

3

DIANE AND MILEY CRUSHED HIM IN A GROUP HUG.

'How have things been here?' he asked when they put him down.

'Pretty good, considering,' Diane said. 'Everything is running as it should. In fact, I would go so far as to say the project is doing better than it was before because Father Bill was terrible at keeping his receipts in order.'

'I gave the TV room a coat of paint – it was long overdue – and we cleaned out the gutters in the yard, so the improvements have not just been financial,' Miley said.

'Very impressive,' Dunnigan agreed.

'There's been no news on Father Bill, though,' Miley continued glumly. 'Which is not so impressive.'

'The plan is to have a candlelight ceremony tonight out by the river,' Diane said. 'Some of the residents want to say a few words, there'll probably be some singing and we'll have tea and sandwiches afterwards. Everyone wants to make a gesture, acknowledge the fact that he's such a huge figure in the local community.'

'That sounds perfect,' Dunnigan said. 'I think he would like that very much.'

'Thanks for not using the past tense,' Diane said.

That evening a crowd of people gathered at the railings right across the road from the Widow's Quay Homeless Project. They were staff, friends and service users, many of whom had worked with

Father Bill for years – some had known him when he was a child growing up in these same streets. Diane spotted Tim Pat Rogers standing a little aloof from the group and nodded at him. He raised his hand in recognition. Tormey, who was standing a little apart on the other side of the crowd, looked at the gangster coldly.

Neil Young songs were sung. Candles were lit and Chinese lanterns were released to the sky.

Dunnigan had never been to a ceremony like it.

'Father Bill is more than just the guy who ran the shelter,' Gizzy, a man who had been living rough for as long as anyone could remember, said. Diane had kitted him out with a shirt and tie and a new jacket for the occasion. 'Everyone who uses the Widow's Quay Project thinks of him as a friend. He always has a kind word, and no matter what else is going on he'll sit down and share a cup of tea or a cigarette, or just take a second to give you a hug – he seems to know when you need one, sometimes before you even know it yourself.'

'He found me when I was at my lowest point,' Vincent, a young man who had only been coming to the project for six months or so, said. 'I know I'd be dead today if he hadn't stopped that day and talked to me. Do yiz know, I don't think I'd talked to anyone for maybe three weeks? When you're on the street, people look right through you. Father Bill had eyes that saw everyone, and each person he saw, he loved.'

'Father Bill has never told me what to do or how to be,' Miley said, when it was his turn to speak. Harry was standing beside him, holding his hand. 'I didn't come to Widow's Quay to help people, even though that's what I said. I came here because I was afraid to be alone – see, I was homeless. I had a roof over me, but I didn't have a family and I didn't have friends and I didn't know what to do. Father Bill understood that, and he, and all of you, became my friends and my family and you gave me a purpose. I can never repay you for that. Father Bill, please come home.'

The last person to speak was a young woman who looked to be in her late thirties. Dunnigan didn't think he had ever seen her around the project before – she was nicely dressed and artfully made up, her brown hair fashionably cut. Yet there was something about her that said she had suffered, that life had not always been kind.

'A couple of years ago, I didn't know Father Bill,' she began, looking about her uncertainly. 'I'd heard of him – everyone who lives in this part of Dublin has – but I'd never met him. I don't go to Mass and I was livin' in one of the houses on East Wall Road, so I wasn't homeless or nothin'. But I had me problems.'

She cleared her throat, and shuffled uneasily.

'My man – you don't need to know his name – he useta like to box me around the place when he'd had a few drinks on 'im. Which was most of the time. He'd been doin' it since we met. Fifteen fuckin' years – sure I thought it was normal. Me da, he was quick with his fists too, and I s'pose I just thought it was how fellas behaved. But see, last year, I got pregnant by 'im. I was on the pill, but one mornin' he hit me in the stomach so hard, I puked, and I must have thrown up the pill along with me breakfast, so when he wanted some of his conjugals later that week, he knocked me up.'

She was sobbing in between sentences now, and Miley moved gently through the crowd and put his arm around her.

'I din't tell him for a coupla weeks. I wanted to wait till he was in a good mood. That oughta tell ya somethin'! Two fuckin' weeks I had to wait for him to crack a smile at me. So I cooked 'im this steak dinner, I even spent me savin's on a nice bottle o' wine – one I heard them talk about on *Saturday Kitchen* on the telly – and when he's tuckin' in, I says that I've some good news.'

She laughed, or at least, it seemed to be somewhere between a laugh and a cry – Dunnigan wasn't sure.

'He threw the table at me. Broke me jaw. Kept punchin' me

in the guts until I was vomitin' blood. Needless to say, I had a miscarriage. I think he actually scared 'imself, though, because he brought me to the hospital. The story we cooked up was that I'd been jumped by a bunch o' lads on the way home from visitin' me ma, and none o' the nurses questioned it. They'd just given me a bed and he'd gone home for the night, when I looked up and who should be pullin' a chair up beside me only the best-lookin' priest I ever seen.'

That got a laugh and more than a few nods from the group.

'"What happened to you?" he says, and I gives 'im the story about the gang. "I know most of the crews working along the waterfront," he says. "What did they look like? I'll make sure they don't even think about mugging a woman again." I made up some shite about this tattoo and that haircut and one o' them havin' a skull ring, and I'm certain he knows I'm bullshittin' 'im. He sits there listenin', though, and he says he'll look into it.'

She looked around the group, all of whom knew exactly where the story was going.

'Father Bill arrived the followin' day, just as they're dischargin' me, and says he'll give me a lift home. I din't have the money for a taxi, and I was still pretty sore and couldn't face the bus, so I was kinda pleased. He chats away, pleasant as you like on the drive over, and he carries me bag for me and walks me right up to the door. Well, doesn't your man open it before I put me key in, and before he gets a chance to say "hello", Father Bill nuts him right between the eyes. He goes down flat on his back, and Father Bill steps in and drags 'im by the scruff of his neck into the livin' room and puts 'im sittin' on the couch. Then he pulls up a chair and lights a fag. It takes a minute or two for me fella to come back to his senses. "How much would you say Janet here weighs?" Father Bill asks him. Your man starts to give out: "You can't come into my house and assault me!" and Father Bill slaps 'im hard, right across the face. That shuts 'im up. "How much does Janet weigh, give or take?" he asks 'im again, all friendly like. "I dunno, seven stone. Maybe eight." "I'd say you're about right there," Father Bill says. "And you?" Yer man says he's thirteen stone. "That's a whole different weight class," Father Bill says. "I mean, you're almost twice what she is. Now, I'm fourteen stone, so I've got some weight on you, but we're a hell of a lot closer than you and Janet. And see, *I hit back*." And he reaches over then and puts a hand on me man's shoulder. "You're only a short walk away from where I work," he says. "So I'm going to be checking every day to see how this young lady is doing. If it looks to me like she's walking a bit stiffly or seems out of sorts in any way, you and me will be having a chat again. And I won't be as gentle next time."'

All eyes were on her. The whole group knew Father Bill and how he did business. Many had similar stories.

'I woke up the next day and my fella was gone. I was relieved and terrified all at the same time. I couldn't leave the house that first day – I was scared shitless he'd be waitin' for me somewhere. On the second day, Father Bill came to visit about lunchtime. He had a cardboard box full of groceries, and he cooked me a meal. He didn't say a whole lot, just sat with me, made sure I was OK. He came every day after that, and he always brought somethin' – food or a cylinder of gas; the odd time he gave me money. And one day, about a month later, he told me about a job – a solicitor he knew needed a receptionist. I'd never done anythin' like it before, but Father Bill said this guy owed 'im a favour. He gave me some money and told me to go out an' buy meself a suit, and that they were expectin' me the followin' day.'

She smiled through her tears.

'I have two girls who work under me now, and in September, the company are payin' for me to study law at night in Trinity fuckin' College.'

Miley started to clap, and everyone joined in.

'Father Bill took me when I was so broke I didn't believe I could ever be fixed, and he gave me a new life,' Janet said. 'If I had all the money in the world, I could never repay 'im.'

They filed back across the road and had tea in the dining room of the project. People began to drift away in dribs and drabs, and only those who were either working or sleeping in the building were left by nine.

'I'm not on tonight,' Diane said. 'Want to wait and we can go over to yours when I've finished here?'

Dunnigan looked at his shoes. 'I think I'd rather be by myself,' he said. 'If you don't mind.'

Diane couldn't hide her surprise. 'Oh. OK. If that's what you want.'

'Thanks.'

'Um ... is everything OK? Have I done something to upset you?'

'No. I just need a little space.'

'And what if I don't?'

'I don't have an answer for that,' Dunnigan said, and left her holding a tray of mugs.

4

'DAVEY?'

'Hello, boss.'

'Have you left yet?'

'I'm going now.'

'I wanted to let you know that you've been granted extended leave.'

'Thank you.'

'We can't pay you – you know that? You're a part-time employee, so you only get a salary for whatever hours you work.'

'I know that, boss. I'm paid by the university over the summer, so I'll have money coming in.'

'While we're talking about such things, the accountants are checking into how St Jude's manages its funds. We should hear back from them in a day or two.'

'You know how to reach me.'

'I do. Please be careful down there, Davey. I'm not going to pretend to be happy about all this.'

'I'm not either. Which is why I need to shake things up a bit more.'

'What's your plan?'

'I'm going to spend as much time as I can with Kettu and see if I can get him to talk to me.'

'This Inuk who hasn't said anything much in two decades?'

'Yes.'

'You might want to ask Diane for some help. She's a counsellor, isn't she?'

'Yes.'

'Might have some advice. You're … um … you're not exactly a people person, if you get my drift.'

'I'll drop in on her before I go.'

'I think that's a good idea. OK – happy hunting. I'll be in touch.'

'Thanks, boss.'

Tormey hung up.

5

DIANE LOOKED UP WHEN HE WALKED IN, BUT DID not acknowledge him. She was sitting behind the reception desk at the project, a PLO scarf tied about her head like a bandana.

'I'm heading back now,' he said.

'Good luck.'

'Thank you.'

She continued to write in the day book. When he didn't move, she put the pen down and looked up, exasperated. 'What do you want, Davey? I'm busy, and last night you didn't seem all that interested in talking to me … or doing anything else with me, for that matter.'

'I need your help with something.'

'Jesus Christ, you've a fucking nerve.'

'Can I tell you about it?'

She seemed to think about this for a few moments, then called into the office that adjoined the welcome area: 'Joanne, I'm heading out for half an hour. Can you hold the fort here?'

'Go ahead!' a voice responded, and Diane stood and took her leather jacket from the back of her chair.

'It'll probably take more than half an hour,' Dunnigan said.

'Don't push your luck,' Diane snapped.

He knew her well enough to realise he was walking on thin ice and said no more. He followed her from the project, keeping his opinions to himself.

6

'DAVEY, I KNOW NOTHING ABOUT INUIT psychology,' Diane said when they were sitting opposite one another in the nearest Starbucks.

'No, but you're good with people. They like you.'

'Maybe it's because I pay attention to their feelings and don't act like a prick.'

'That's a part of it, I expect.'

'Not like some who just clam up and won't talk about what's going on in their heads.'

'That's just it. I need to get Kettu to talk. I think he was trying to tell me something when he said that word, the one that means dream. If I can just get him to speak some more—'

'I was talking about you, Davey!'

'What? Oh … But I'm not clamming up! I'm talking to you now.'

'Not about anything important.'

'There is nothing more important than this.'

Diane looked out the window of the café and tried to force back tears that had risen unbidden. 'I see.'

'Good. Now, tell me – what should I do to get through to Kettu? Are there methodologies I could study? Techniques to draw individuals like him out?'

Diane sighed and realised she was on a hiding to nothing. He was so wrapped up in the case and the challenges it presented, all he saw when he looked at her was a source of information, not a woman he was in a relationship with. She thought that he had changed, had grown since they had been together. Maybe she was fooling herself.

'The obvious approach would be to use things he's familiar with,' she said, resignation sounding in her voice. 'You say he's a fisherman – maybe bring in pictures of boats, books about fish, watch some episodes of *Deadliest Catch*, tie some sailor's knots, if they use them anymore – that sort of thing.'

'Could I bring him fishing?'

'Do you know how to fish?'

'No, but how hard could it be?'

'Probably harder than you think.'

'You get a stick, tie some string to it, put a hook on the string, a worm on the hook—'

'I think you may be over-simplifying it. And would the staff even allow you? This is a patient who has been highly dependent for many years. They may be reluctant to let you just wander off with him.'

'If it's to aid in the investigation—'

'There are lots of things going on in people's lives other than this investigation, Davey,' she said, her anger close to the surface.

Dunnigan remained oblivious. 'Would it help to show him movies about the Arctic?'

'If you can find any, I expect that could help, yes.'

'I've been looking for some online primers for Inuktun – that's the Greenlandic Inuit language – but I can't find any.'

'Are there any anthropologists in the university that could point you in the right direction?'

'Everyone is on holiday – I already thought of that.'

'I'm fresh out of ideas, then.'

'You've been of some help.'

'Don't heap the praise on too thick, Davey, you'll give me a big head.'

He drained what was left in his teacup. 'I should go.'

'I think that might be a good idea.'

He stood. 'Say goodbye to Miley for me.'

'Of course.'

'Thank you.'

And placing the exact change for his drink on the table, he walked out and didn't look back.

Part Five

IN MY TIME OF DARKNESS

1

HE HAD PAID FOR HIS ROOM IN THE HOTEL A week in advance, which left him two more days until the money ran out. However, as he was no longer on the police payroll, Dunnigan was aware this was an extravagance he could ill afford. He had no idea how long he'd be staying, and was beginning to think the move could be an indefinite one.

He arrived in Donbro late in the afternoon and called at an auctioneer's to enquire about rental properties. A florid-faced man in a suit that might have fit him fifteen years and twice as many pounds ago told him that he had just the thing and showed him a small two-up, two-down property off a side street from the main thoroughfare. It was furnished in the loosest sense of the term (a bed in one of the upstairs rooms, a couch in the living area, a table and two chairs in the kitchen and no television), but Dunnigan assured him it was ideal for his purposes. He paid the deposit and a first week's rent on the spot. With a set of *Spiderman*-themed bedding he purchased at the town draper's shop under his arm, he moved in that night – there seemed no reason to spend any more time at the hotel, and to his delight he discovered the Wi-fi for a café at the top of the street was unprotected.

He passed the evening researching fishing in the North Atlantic and the lives of the Inuit of Greenland. When the clock in the corner of his laptop screen showed eleven, he had a folder full of files – images, films and pages upon pages of text – saved to a flash drive he had purchased for the purpose.

Satisfied with his solid night's work and stiff from sitting over the computer for so long without a break, Dunnigan decided to go for a walk before bed, following the path along the seafront to where it met the cliffs. Deep in thought, he was a mile outside the town before he realised he had gone so far. It was a clear night and he could see Tully Island distinctly across the water. Lights in a couple of the houses there – some people lived on the island only in the summer months, a few all year around – glistened in the dark like tiny flames.

As he watched, he thought he saw movement near the eastern end of the strip of land – a part of the island he knew had no houses. Something twinkled for a moment, bobbing and weaving before vanishing and then appearing again for a second, only to extinguish after a few moments. This continued for about ten minutes, then the lights vanished completely.

Dunnigan stayed where he was, watching, for an hour before giving up and making for his temporary home.

Lights in the dark, Nurse Tarbuck had said. *Lights across the bay.*

2

HE STOPPED AT THE LOCAL POLICE STATION THE next morning and used their printer. Then, with a bundle of papers in his bag, he drove the short distance to St Jude's.

He paused to inform Nurse Jules that he would be spending the morning with Kettu and, ignoring her protestations, mounted the old staircase. The man was in the same position he had been the last time Dunnigan had met him – dressed in a baggy tracksuit, gazing out the window. Dunnigan had paid him the courtesy of knocking first, but when he received no answer, he tentatively pushed open the door and went in. Kettu's dark eyes fell on the criminologist and then flicked back to the view of the garden.

Dunnigan set up his laptop on the bed and plugged in the flash drive, opening one of the files he had downloaded the night before.

'Kettu,' he said, when it was ready, 'I have something you might like.'

The man paid him no heed, remaining with his back to Dunnigan.

'Um … don't you want to look?'

Still nothing – it seemed he was just not prepared to move.

A heavy wooden chair stood on the landing at the end of the corridor outside, and Dunnigan hefted it back to Kettu's room, setting it down right in front of him. He put the laptop on that.

'Now. You can look out the window and watch the slideshow too.'

Dunnigan had combed Google Images for as many photographs of life in Greenland as he could find – he tried to focus on the tribal people, but he threw in a few pictures of the local wildlife and some scenery too – and using Windows Movie Maker had made these into a short film, accompanied by some sounds of Inuit speech he had downloaded as well as what he thought was tribal music and singing. The whole thing went on for about fifteen minutes.

He was quite proud of it.

While the video was rolling, he took the freshly printed pages from his bag and stuck them up at various points around the room. They were all images (sadly in black and white, as the police station didn't have a colour printer) – some of which featured in the slideshow, but the rest of fishing trawlers, nets full of fish, a ship's radar screen, ocean waves.

This done, the featureless room seemed a lot more vibrant. And Kettu's eyes were now definitely fixed on the screen. The film finished playing.

'Well?'

Kettu muttered something, almost to himself.

'I didn't catch that.' Dunnigan sat up attentively.

The man spoke again, in little more than a whisper. This time, though, Dunnigan heard.

'*Inerkonartok*,' Kettu had said.

'I'm sorry.' The criminologist reached for his phone. 'I don't know your language. I've found a phonetic dictionary online, but I'm not sure how reliable it is.'

'*Inerkonartok*,' Kettu said again, more firmly this time.

Dunnigan sounded out the word and scrolled through the letter 'I'.

'It says that *inerkonartok* means "pretty" or "fair",' he said. 'Is that right? You enjoyed the slides?'

'*Inerkonartok*,' the man said, almost affirmatively (or was Dunnigan being wishful?).

'Will we watch them again?'

And now – and there could be no doubt – Kettu nodded.

Dunnigan grinned and pressed play.

3

FOR THE NEXT FEW DAYS HE ARRIVED AT ST JUDE'S at nine in the morning, and he and Kettu began the day with a viewing of the slideshow. After that Dunnigan would have something different to show his new friend – one day he brought a miniature ship in a bottle; another, a framed picture of various sailing knots; once, he brought a whole salmon he had got from the local fishmonger's (he gave it to the hospital kitchen when he and Kettu were finished with it).

He sensed the man slowly thawing towards him – he liked the image of that, the idea that the ice that had formed in the man over the years was gradually melting, allowing the true, educated, articulate person who was trapped beneath to escape.

Slowly, painstakingly, he was experiencing more interaction. On day two, the man was facing the door when he arrived. On day three, he smiled when Dunnigan produced the ship-in-the-bottle. On day four, he laughed when the criminologist tried to say the word *turska*, the Inuit word for 'cod'.

Dunnigan sensed they were building a relationship, although this was a concept he struggled with in the easiest of circumstances, so he did not really trust himself to interpret the signs correctly.

On the eighth day he arrived to find Ressler waiting at reception, whispering conspiratorially to Nurse Jules.

'Hello, David Dunnigan,' the psychiatrist said, bounding over to him, hand outstretched.

Dunnigan ignored it and continued towards the stairs.

'You are here to see my patient Kettu again today?'

'Yes.'

'What activities have you planned this fine morning to try and massage his memories?'

'None of your business.'

Ressler stepped about the criminologist, blocking his progress up the stairs.

'I am his doctor. What he does is my concern in every way.'

'I will simply be talking to him.'

'Talking about what things, David Dunnigan?'

'I am going to ask him to teach me Inuktun.'

Ressler guffawed with laughter and slapped Dunnigan on the back so hard he almost winded him.

'You tell me the funny joke, I think, Davey! Well, good luck in your lessons. I will see you later today.'

'I have an appointment this afternoon. I won't have time.'

'Who said I meant this afternoon? I am like the penny that is bad – I am always popping up when you least expect to see me. Pop! Just like so.'

'I'll keep that in mind,' Dunnigan said, and continued up the stairs.

'How are you settling in to your new house down that lonely side street?' Ressler called, just as he reached the first landing.

Dunnigan stopped.

'Do you know that you have no neighbours next door to you on either side?'

Dunnigan turned to look at him. 'What are you telling me, Doctor Ressler?'

'I am only passing the pleasantries with you.' Ressler grinned.

Dunnigan spun on his heel and left Ressler standing on the first step, a rictus grin across his pink face.

4

ALL THE PICTURES DUNNIGAN HAD PUT UP around Kettu's room were gone. He was annoyed, but tried not to show it. He made a note to replace them and to make enough copies that he could put up fresh ones every day if he needed to.

'Good morning, Kettu,' he said.

The man waved at him, which was a first.

Dunnigan pulled out his laptop and, pushing a chair over so he was sitting beside Kettu, put it on his knees. He opened a file and got an image of a polar bear on the screen.

'*Nanuk*,' Dunnigan said.

Kettu looked at the picture and then at Dunnigan.

'*Nan-UK*,' he said, placing the stress on the second syllable.

Dunnigan repeated it, trying to mimic him, until Kettu seemed satisfied he had achieved the correct pronunciation.

He changed the photo to one of a child.

'*Frittongak*,' he said.

'*Fritt-ON-gak*.' Kettu laughed this time, stressing the middle syllable and making a guttural, popping noise in the back of his throat for the final part of the word. Dunnigan struggled with this one, but he persevered, and finally could make a reasonable attempt at saying it correctly.

And so it went on: fish; boat; snow; ice; ocean; whale; net; fur … They spent two hours exploring Kettu's world and the sounds he used to describe it. Somewhere in the middle of it all, the fisherman patted Dunnigan's chest and looked at him quizzically – Dunnigan realised he was asking for his name.

'I'm Davey,' he said. '*Davey.*'

'*Angasartok?*'

Dunnigan turned to his phone again and found that Kettu was asking him what his name meant.

'Our names don't really mean things in the same way yours do,' Dunnigan said.

Kettu shook his head, not prepared to accept this answer.

'All right,' Dunnigan said. 'Well, Davey is short for David, and in the Bible – you know what that is?'

Kettu nodded.

'In the Bible, David was a shepherd boy who killed a giant – uh,' referring to the phone again, '*Jättiläinen?*'

Kettu nodded.

'All the people were very happy when he did this, because without this giant, an army that wanted to take over their lands was powerless and had to leave their country. David was made into a king and he did many great things, and some things that were bad and hurt people, but, by and large, he is remembered as a good leader and the first of a line of famous rulers.'

Kettu patted Dunnigan on the back, congratulating him for having such an auspicious name.

'So what does *Kettu* mean?'

Kettu nodded at the phone.

'You want me to look it up?'

A nod in response.

'You could tell me.'

A shake of the head.

Dunnigan acceded.

'All right. Let's see. Well, it says here that Kettu means "fox". That's pretty cool.'

The other man beamed.

'Yes. I am Kettu the Fox,' he said, his speech stilted but very clear.

Dunnigan had to bite his tongue not to whoop with delight.

5

DUNNIGAN WOKE IN THE MIDDLE OF THE NIGHT.

This was unusual – generally when he closed his eyes, sleep took hold immediately and he knew nothing until morning. His inner clock was very accurate, and though he set an alarm, he tended to snap into consciousness fifteen minutes before it went off.

He lay in the darkness for a moment, gazing at the ceiling, listening to the sounds of the house and the sleeping town outside: a car going past on Donbro's main street; voices somewhere in the far distance; the wind; and, beyond that, waves from the waterfront.

What had disturbed him?

He picked up his phone from the floor beside his bed and checked the time: it was 3.37. He was rolling over to return to his slumbers when he heard a bang somewhere below him.

Dunnigan was not of a nervous disposition, nor was he prone to flights of fancy. He had lived alone his entire adult life and was used to the noises houses make at night. He was not frightened or upset by this nocturnal occurrence, but, in an academic kind of way, waited to see if it was repeated. A minute passed, then another. He was closing his eyes when he heard what he took to be footfalls followed by a door banging.

He was out of bed in an instant and down the stairs.

A fan of horror movies, Dunnigan was familiar with the well-worn trope of the hero (or more usually the heroine) getting up in the middle of the night when there is a suspected intruder about, leaving all the lights off and the place in complete darkness, all the better to be attacked with a knife/axe/machete when their back is turned.

He turned on the landing light as he passed it, then the one in the hall, flooding the place with electric illumination. He paused for a second, listening: silence.

He pushed open the living-room door and, reaching in, hit the light switch. Peering inside, he saw the place was just as he had left it: the floor was covered in notes and papers and his laptop was sitting closed on the arm of the couch. There were no curtains for a serial killer to hide behind – this room, at least, was clear.

He moved on to the kitchen.

It was also undisturbed and free from any foreign bodies: his bowl, plate and mug were upside down on the draining board, and a box of Cheerios (half-empty) sat unassumingly in the middle of the kitchen table. He checked the back door and found it locked and bolted.

Trudging back upstairs, he popped in to the bathroom to empty his bladder – no one was hiding behind the shower curtains or crouching in the bath. He was about to go back to bed when he realised that he had not checked the other upstairs room – it had no bed or any other furniture, so he'd had no cause to go in there since the estate agent had shown him the house on that first day. He peeped in.

There was no need to turn on the light, as the moon was shining in through the window and a streetlight just outside was adding its orange glow to the scene.

The room was empty.

Thinking he must have dreamed the whole thing, Dunnigan closed the door.

'Have you seen my dog?' a voice Dunnigan recognised immediately said behind him and, before he could respond, impossibly strong arms were wrapped around his throat and he was being dragged to the stairs. 'I just want her back,' Benjamin said, in tones that were almost reasonable. 'Tell me where she is, and there won't be any trouble.'

Terror inserted itself like a needle into his consciousness, but he pushed it away, walling it off – it was of no use to him now. He needed to remain rational – he could hear by his captor's breathing that he was in a state of high agitation, and knew he didn't have long before things spun out of control.

As they reached the top step, Dunnigan felt something cutting into his cheek and did the only thing he could think of: he twisted his body and wrapped his arms around his captor's mid-section, then flung them both backwards, head over heels down the stairs, Benjamin wailing at each thud on the way down.

Dunnigan landed on top of him and pulled his fist back to try and stun his opponent, but the intruder was already moving and squirmed out from under him.

'You stole my dog,' Benjamin said in deep resignation. 'Now I'm going to have to take something from you.'

A blade sliced across Dunnigan's shoulder – the pain was so great it seemed to swallow up everything else, and there were white lights behind his eyes. When he could see again, the man was dancing before him, a butcher's knife held loosely in his hand. He boogied forward and put his foot on the criminologist's chest – Dunnigan realised he was lying flat on his back now and wondered how he'd ended up in that position.

'I'm going to take your insides out,' Benjamin said, giggling. A gob of something that had oozed from his nose was hanging loosely from his chin and swung back and forth as he moved. 'Maybe my dog's in there somewhere. Let's see if we can find her!'

Dunnigan tried to kick out but couldn't seem to put any strength into his legs. The deranged man leaned down and licked his left eye.

'Gonna suck it out,' Benjamin hissed.

Then Dunnigan heard the sound of glass breaking, and someone shouting, and then everything went dark.

6

HE CAME AROUND TO FIND HE WAS STILL
stretched out on the floor in the hallway. Doctor Phillipe Ressler,
a leather case full of medical equipment open beside him, was
applying a dressing to his shoulder.

'You have been wounded in the flesh, but it is not so serious. I
am going to drive you to the hospital and there I will give you a
shot for tetanus.'

Dunnigan didn't know whether to be relieved to see the
psychiatrist or if he should be even more afraid. He decided to go
with relief – for the moment, anyway.

'Where's Benjamin?'

'He has been taken away.'

'By whom?'

'One of my staff. The poor man somehow believed you were
hiding his dog, and he made good his escape and came here to get
it back.'

'How did he know where I live?'

'He is more resourceful than one might think, is he not?'

'And how did you know he was here?'

'He has been talking about you a lot since you met him last
week – it would seem he has become fixated. It was not a difficult
guess.'

'Did he ever even have a dog?'

'Oh, yes.'

'Where is it?'

'Long dead.'

Dunnigan winced, and not just from the physical pain.

'Don't you think perhaps you should be going home, David Dunnigan, back to Dublin's fair city? Cork is turning out to be a dangerous place for you.'

Dunnigan struggled into a sitting position and pushed himself up. He realised his face hurt and touched it delicately.

'He butted you with his head – *pow!* – just as we broke in,' Ressler said. 'You will have a blackened eye in the morning, I suspect.'

Dunnigan glanced at the front door and saw that it was closed and locked.

'You got in through the living-room window?' he said.

'Yes, I'm afraid my man had to break it to gain access. We have removed all the glass – it would not have been very good to cut poor Benjamin as we took him out of your home.'

'How did he get in, then? I checked the place, and everything was as it should be – it doesn't make sense.'

Ressler shrugged.

'And where did he get the knife?'

Ressler shook his head, his face a perfect picture of confused innocence. 'These are mysteries,' he said. 'I told you this was a lonely and dangerous place. You are lucky the night nurse noticed poor Benjamin was gone and had the sense to call me, or I fear you would not be in the land of the living now.'

Dunnigan looked at the man, feeling a fury building in him – the fear was still there, too, but the anger was becoming greater.

'I would be very concerned that, the next time, I might not be able to get here on time,' Ressler continued.

'And you think there'll be a next time?' Dunnigan said coldly.

'Oh, Benjamin's condition is very entrenched – when he gets something in his head, it is beyond my skills to root it out. I *assure* you, David Dunnigan, that poor, sick Benjamin will do his very best to visit you again.'

'Get out of my house, Doctor Ressler.'

'But you need the injection, or you will be at risk from blood poisoning.'

'I said get out.'

Ressler smiled and closed his medical case. 'You have had a mighty shock,' he said genially. 'You should rest. Of course –' he chortled '– you have a bloody great hole in your living-room window, so anyone might get in while you're asleep! I'd try and fix that before you nod off. Pleasant dreams, Davey.'

And he left him standing in the hallway, feeling utterly powerless and very alone.

Benjamin

He remembered fear.

When he was just a pup, he was frightened all the time. The big people beat and burned and sometimes did worse things to him. It did not matter what he did, if he was good or if he was bad, he got hurt anyway.

He remembered that he was always hungry. There never seemed to be enough food, and he sometimes thought he had a hole inside him that it was impossible to fill.

He sensed that the fat woman was his mother, but he could not think of her as that. He had only a vague understanding of what 'mother' was, but it was not a word that should be used to describe someone who tortured you.

The dog was his mother.

She let him curl up beside her at night when it was cold, and when they beat him and he bled, she licked the wounds and made comforting sounds, and he knew somehow that she loved him. It was a simple love, but that was all he needed.

When they took her away, he stopped being afraid.

Without her, he was only angry.

The big people brought him to a place where they locked him up and tried to tame him, but he fought and bit and scratched and spat.

Then Doctor Ressler came. He said he would help him find the dog that was his mother, or he might get him a brother or a sister. All he had to do was help Doctor Ressler. And he did that just by being who he was.

7

DUNNIGAN FOUND SOME CARDBOARD AND PUT
it up across the hole where his living-room window had once been
– luckily a couple of cereal boxes did the job. Holding his shoulder
where the knife had done its work, he swept up the broken shards
of glass and dumped them into the bin, then stretched out on the
couch and closed his eyes.

He must have slept because it seemed that only moments had
passed when someone was knocking on his front door. He paused
in the hallway, wishing there was a peep-hole so he could see who
had come to call so early. Gathering his courage, he flung the door
wide, stepping back as he did so to create some space between him
and whatever awaited him.

'Surprise!'

Miley Timoney, wearing a Chris de Burgh Irish Tour 1989
T-shirt and looking not at all certain of the welcome he would
receive, was standing on Dunnigan's doorstep. His face dropped
when he saw the state of his friend (the criminologist didn't know
it yet, but his cheek and forehead were coming up in a deep blue
bruise, and he had bled through both the dressing and his pyjama
top), and then lifted into a grin when, quite uncharacteristically,
Dunnigan flung his arms around him, hugging him tightly.

'I have never been so happy to see anyone in my life,' Dunnigan
said, tears coming to his eyes quite unexpectedly.

'I told Diane you'd be pleased!' Miley said. 'She said you'd send
me straight back home.'

'Let me get dressed and then we'll have some breakfast.' Dunnigan gave him one last squeeze.

'Do I want to know what happened to you?'

'I'll tell you all about it while we eat,' Dunnigan said. 'I've got a plan, and I think you can help.'

''S'why I came!' Miley said, and followed his friend inside.

8

THEY WENT TO THE CAFÉ WITH THE UNPROTECTED Wi-fi, which was called Boylan's, and Miley tucked into a full Irish, while Dunnigan picked at a scone and told him everything that had happened since he had arrived in West Cork.

'Well, it's pretty clear this Ressler guy wants rid of you,' Miley said when he was finished.

'I think we can safely say that,' Dunnigan agreed.

'So that probably means they're afraid you're going to find out something,' Miley continued, mopping up some egg yolk with a piece of toast.

'Or that I've already found it out and just don't know it yet.'

'What, though?'

Dunnigan rubbed his one good eye (the other was swollen and bloodshot) and shrugged. 'I don't know. Here's what I think: we have two different events that seem to be linked – Beth being here at some point in 1998/1999, and the deaths of twelve young people. Mixed up in all of that is Kettu. I have Nurse Tarbuck telling me that children were brought to St Jude's by bus, and it would seem from what she was saying that Doctor Ressler was involved in things at the hospital long before the date I was led to believe he started.'

'But what does any of it mean?'

'I haven't got a notion.'

'You said you had a plan.'

'Yes.'

'Feel like sharing?'

'So far, I've been running around, asking questions, knocking on doors and being fairly polite about it.'

'Really?'

'Yes, really. And by doing so, I've somehow pushed Ressler into making a run at me.'

'Using this Benjamin guy as his weapon.'

'Yes. So I've been thinking: what if I change my tactics?'

'In what way?'

'What if I stop being polite?'

'Davey – and I say this with love – from what I know of you, you're the least polite person there is.'

Dunnigan seemed to consider this. 'Well, I never said it was a good plan.'

His phone buzzed, the word TORMEY flashing on the screen under a picture of the cartoon character Deputy Dawg.

'Does he know you have that as his photo?' Miley giggled.

Dunnigan shook his head and shushed his friend, picking up the handset.

'Davey, how are you?'

'I'm all right, boss. Miley has come to visit for a few days.'

Dunnigan considered telling him about his night visitation but decided against it – Tormey would just tell him to come home, and that wasn't going to happen.

'I had a suspicion he might end up down there eventually. You two behave yourselves. C'mere, the money boys have got back to me *finally* – apparently the asylum's accounts are a right tangled mess and there's still a few leads they want to follow, but I have something I think you'll be interested in.'

'I'm listening.'

'OK. St Jude's has a long and glorious history going all the way back to the 1800s – sure you know that already. There was never any problem making ends meet until the previous manager took over – we're talking mid-1990s.'

'So *not* Roderick Devaney?'

'No, this would be his father, Templeton. Seems he had a few, shall we say, issues.'

'Issues?'

'He liked to drink vodka at eleven o'clock in the day. He was also partial to a bit of gambling, and while he was losing his shirt at the roulette table, he enjoyed snorting cocaine off the arses of prostitutes. To top it all off, he felt it was quite acceptable to pay for his hobbies with cash taken directly from the accounts of St Jude's.'

'Well, he would have done – his son was the accountant.'

'And a bloody good job he did of burying his father's indiscretions,' Tormey said. 'Our lads had a hell of a time rooting through all the records. He has a gift, does old Roderick.'

'I take it they ran into debt?'

'They dug themselves into a massive feckin' hole – owed money left, right and centre to just about every institution they could borrow from. In the end, though, it caught up on them, and the piper wanted to be paid. Unfortunately, there just wasn't anything to give him.'

'But they're still running.'

'Indeed they are, but what you've been seeing is basically a front.'

'How so?'

'Roderick Devaney is director of St Jude's in name only. The asylum is owned by a company called Kaiser Care, who bought their debts in 1995. In fact, Kaiser Care own 80 per cent of the asylum's interests.'

'I've never heard of them.'

'Their head office is in Switzerland, and that's also where they do all their banking, so it's difficult, but not impossible, to access their records – our boys are on it. What we do know is that they specialise in running private medical facilities, most of them in the field of psychiatric care, and they also run drug trials for all the major pharmaceutical companies. Their MO is to come in when a place is in trouble – they hoover up any debt and take over the running of the hospital, and they seem to be able to turn these facilities around in a remarkably short space of time. They've got about forty St Jude's all over the world.'

'If Devaney isn't managing the place, who is?'

'Go on – have a guess.'

'I don't play guessing games, boss. You know that.'

'Humour me.'

'No. Who's the real manager?'

'You're no fun. St Jude's is run by Doctor Phillipe Ressler.'

9

DUNNIGAN USED MILEY'S VISIT AS AN EXCUSE TO have Kettu show him around the garden.

Somewhere not far off, Brendan was clipping some shrub or other and the staccato clacking of his shears drifted to them on the wind every now and again. The three men sat on an old bench beside a flowerbed, an ash tree offering some shade. They had not been able to walk far, as inactivity had stiffened and atrophied the fisherman's muscles, but he seemed eager to be in the sunshine and made a noble effort to get around.

'This must be very different from your home,' Miley said as the older man tried to get his breath back.

'Yes,' Kettu said, after a brief pause.

Dunnigan did not want to lose momentum and followed up with another question rapidly. 'Do you miss Greenland?'

'I miss it very much.'

'What part are you from?'

'I grew up on an Inuk reservation, about a day's journey from the town of Faringen, in the north of the country. Up near the pole.'

Faringen, Miley thought. *Why do I know that name?* He pushed the thought aside but determined to come back to it later. 'Davey tells me you grew up "on the ice".'

'Yes.'

'You liked it?'

'I did not like it or not like it, then. I did not know any different. Now, I know that I was very happy. I should not have left.'

'You can always go back,' Miley said. 'It's something to work towards, isn't it?'

'No.'

'Why not?'

Kettu looked at Miley. 'Do you know what *tonrar* means?'

'No.'

'You would say *devil* or *demon*.'

'I don't believe in things like that,' Miley said. 'I've known some bad people in my time – some who were *really* mean – but they were just people.'

'It does not matter whether you believe it or not. I have a *tonrar* on me, and if I leave this place, it will follow and its evil will spread.'

Dunnigan shook his head. 'You haven't caused any evil.'

'Everything bad that has happened since the storm is because of me.'

'Your boat sank and your friends drowned – you cannot be held accountable for a storm and the damage it did. I don't yet know why those young people killed themselves here, but I cannot see how you believe your presence caused it – did you even have anything to do with them?'

'I knew some of them, yes.'

'But not all. Don't you see, Kettu? Your thinking this way is all a part of your illness.'

'I saw him, Davey. I *saw* the devil.'

'Where?'

'In the dungeons.'

'It probably felt like you were in a dungeon, Kettu,' Miley said. 'I was locked away too, for a long time, and there were days it really seemed like I was in jail.'

'It felt like it because that is what it was. The people who died, they took them to small, dark rooms under the ground, and they never came back from there.'

Dunnigan looked at the hospital building – they could see a

side-on view of it from where they sat. 'The hospital doesn't have a basement.'

'This was not a basement or a cellar. It was a prison.'

'So they took them to another place – another building?'

'When I could not tell who I was anymore, when the visions got really bad, they brought me down there, and I thought I would die.'

'But you didn't,' Dunnigan said.

'No. The devil would not let me die.'

'Why would he let you live and not the others?'

'To torment me more.'

'The only reason you are alive, Kettu, is that you choose to be. Somewhere deep inside is a part of you that wants to be here.'

'You are wrong.'

'I know more about it than you might think,' Dunnigan said.

Kettu looked at him again. 'Maybe you do,' he said.

Dunnigan stood up. 'It's a beautiful day.'

'Yes.'

'You up for a bit more of a walk?'

'I will try.'

'I know you will.'

10

WHEN THEY HAD DONE ANOTHER CIRCUIT OF THE grounds, Dunnigan brought Kettu back to his room, where he promptly lay down on his bed and fell asleep.

Back outside, he and Miley followed the sound of the shears and found Brendan. 'Hey,' he said, approaching the oldster as he trimmed a laurel bush.

'Hello, Davey.'

'This is my friend, Miley Timoney.'

'Howya doin', Miley?'

'Well, thanks.'

'I need to ask you something,' Dunnigan said.

'I'm a bit on the busy side today.'

'It won't take more than—'

'I can't be talkin' to you!' Brendan hissed at him, his eyes still on the shrub but his tone tense and urgent.

'But I only—'

'I have a grandson!' the old man said, fear entering his voice now. 'Please go away and forget I ever spoke to you at all!'

Dunnigan and Miley exchanged glances. 'They threatened Cormac?'

'Not in so many words ... I had the lad here with me yesterday evenin' – we were cleanin' the pond over by the south field – and suddenly Ressler was there. He had Benjamin with him. They just stood and watched us, but as they were leavin', Ressler came over. He had yer man by the arm, and he put his hand on Cormac's head, and he says to me: "I wouldn't bring your lovely grandson in here anymore, Brendan. Asylums can be dangerous places, for the young." He turned to go, and as he did he says: "Loose lips sink ships. Remember that." And then he was gone. All the time, Benjamin was watchin' wee Cormac. Never took his eyes off him for a second.'

'I'm sorry, Brendan.'

'I ought never to have talked to you. Go on home, now, and leave us in peace. Please!'

They drove back to Donbro.

'What will we do now?' Miley asked.

'Let's go on one of the historical walking tours,' Dunnigan said.

'Seriously?'

'I'm always serious.'

'That's true.'

They parked and walked up the town. It wasn't long before they spotted a group of loudly clad tourists gathered around a plaque that hung on the wall of the post office, proclaiming that Saint Finbarr had once preached there. To Dunnigan's surprise, the person discoursing on the historical relevance of the location was none other than Donal, his pilot from the previous week.

They fell in behind the group and followed them at a discreet distance for an hour until they reached the final point on the tour, the Seaside Hotel, where Donal passed his ragged woollen cap around for any contributions his followers felt moved to make and then sent them on their way.

'How much of that was true?' Dunnigan asked, sitting down on one side of the sailor/historian, Miley on the other, as he ordered his first pint at the bar, the coins and a solitary five euro note he had collected spread out in front of him.

'All of it,' Donal said. 'I did local history in college.'

'Which one?'

'The only one that matters, University College Cork.'

'Who taught you?'

'Fuck off.'

'Why would I do that?'

'Because you are being a snobby cunt. You don't think I look clever enough to have been to university, so you're trying to catch me out in a lie.'

'If I may,' Miley said, giving Dunnigan a hard look, 'Davey wants to know something relating to the history of the area, and he just wants to establish how well trained you are, and therefore how reliable the information will be. Isn't that right, Davey?'

'Um … yes, of course.'

Donal sniffed and downed half his pint in a single gulp. 'Why didn't he just say that, then?'

'He probably thinks he did,' Miley said, shrugging. 'Pretend he has Tourette's if it helps. I sometimes do.'

Donal had a long drink of his porter, and then turned to look at Miley. 'What's your name, pal?'

'I'm Miley.'

'It's nice to meet you, Miley. How'd you fall in with this guy?'

'That's a long story.'

'I'll bet it is.' Donal shook Miley's hand and turned back to Dunnigan, whom he had been roundly ignoring during the last exchange. 'Did you get hit by a car?' he asked, referring to the criminologist's battered visage.

'Something like that.'

'You're lucky your pal here is a nice guy, because I'd guess a lot of people want to aim their vehicles at you.'

'Will you help me?'

'What do you want?'

'Is there a series of subterranean rooms on the grounds somewhere in St Jude's?'

'Why do you want to know that?'

'Because someone I'm trying to help claims they were locked up in them.'

The man finished his drink and nodded at the barmaid for another. 'The direct answer to your question is that I don't know. But there's someone who might.'

'Can I speak to them?'

'Any fuckin' time you like. I'm talking about Cedric, runs the local library. There isn't an old building within a forty-mile radius he hasn't studied.'

'It's the weekend – will the library be open tomorrow?'

'No, but that doesn't matter – he's sitting over there.'

The librarian, greying hair gelled straight back on his head, wire-rimmed glasses balanced on the end of his aquiline nose, was at a table by the window, bent over the local newspaper, a pint of ale barely touched at his elbow.

'I have nothing to say to you,' he said when Donal approached. 'I've heard about your version of the itinerary of Saint Finbarr through the town, and you know as well as I do that you have stepped into the realm of conjecture. I *strongly* recommend you reconsider. You shouldn't be giving tours anyway, but if you must, your information has *got* to be accurate.'

'Shut the fuck up, Cedric,' Donal retorted. 'This is Miley and his sidekick, Davey. Davey has a question about St Jude's.'

'Beautiful example of mid-Georgian architecture,' Cedric gushed. 'The gardens were laid out in the classic Arcadian style – I think old Brendan has done a marvellous job keeping them very much as they were. If the Devaneys ever stop operating it as a hospital, I would love to see the place opened to the public.'

'Are you aware of any underground chambers on the property?' Dunnigan asked.

'Of course. Almost all buildings of the era would have had root cellars, and there are old servants' quarters which were not part of the main structure in St Jude's, as I remember. They were separated from the hospital proper by an underground passage.'

'Do you know where on the property it is?'

'On the western side of the gardens. They would be marked by something – I think they had a stone folly above the access steps.'

'I know it,' Dunnigan said and stood up.

'Where are you going?' Donal called after him as he bolted from the room. 'You owe me a pint, you fucker!'

11

THE GATES WERE CLOSED, THE HEAVY CHAIN padlocked across them, when they got back to St Jude's, but Dunnigan didn't bother to ring the front desk – he had noticed a spot in the high wall where erosion had created some convenient footholds, and the pair used them to climb over.

'Are you sure this is a good idea?' Miley asked as they jogged through the trees, keeping to the perimeter to avoid detection.

'No.'

'OK. Just checking.'

Five minutes later they were standing at the low stone archway of the folly and could clearly see the steps that led down to a wooden door, obscured by some hanging vines.

'D'you think this is it?' Miley asked.

'I don't think it can be anything else,' Dunnigan said.

He descended to the door and tried the handle. Of course, it was locked.

'Stand back,' he said and delivered a kick directly to the place just below the handle. '*Ouch!* Oh, my gosh, that hurts!' The door didn't budge, and Dunnigan thought he may have fractured his ankle.

'Let me try,' Miley said, and slammed his foot into the barrier three times in quick succession, with no more success than Dunnigan had enjoyed.

Dunnigan tried using his shoulder, but with the wound Benjamin had given him, he could put no real force into it.

'Well, I knew I wasn't Chuck Norris or anything, but this is ridiculous,' Miley said ruefully.

'Come on,' Dunnigan said. 'I just thought of something.'

The below-stairs canteen was empty. Dunnigan went straight to the sets of keys he had spotted when he and Brendan had had their chat about Kettu (it seemed like a lifetime ago, now). He ran his finger along the labels and, sure enough, there was one with the words: *Private Wards*.

'Are you sure that's it?' Miley hissed.

'It's what Brendan called them. I don't see anything else that seems likely.'

It was getting dark when they made it back to the door. The grounds were completely deserted, but Miley had an eerie sense they were being watched. Every now and then the sound of a car from the road, or a snatch of conversation from the hospital, drifted their way on the wind, but they saw no one.

Dunnigan fitted the key into the lock and turned it: well-oiled tumblers did their work, bolts were released and the door moved easily.

'Open sesame,' Miley muttered, and followed Dunnigan inside.

The walls were painted a cracked pale green and the floor was of worn red tiles. Doors lined each side of the corridor, a metal grille at about head height set into each of them. Dunnigan peered inside one. At first all he could see was an empty room, but suddenly, with a snarl, a peeling, snot-smeared face was jammed into the space.

'You have my dog,' Benjamin screeched. 'They told me I could get it back from you! Let me out and I'll take it!' In a rush of movement he leapt back to his bed.

'This is your stabby friend, I take it,' Miley said.

'I don't think we're really friends,' Dunnigan said.

'He looks like he's pleased to see you,' Miley observed – Benjamin had taken his penis out and was masturbating thoughtfully.

Dunnigan moved on along the corridor. 'Kettu was right,' he said. 'This is a prison.'

'Have you ever been in an old-school asylum before?' Miley asked. 'Or even an old folks' home? This isn't what I'd call salubrious, but it isn't the worst I've encountered.'

'It's not right.'

'No, it's not.'

The next two rooms were empty, but the one after that held a figure Dunnigan took to be female, curled up on the military cot in the cell. The next one contained Kettu.

12

THE FISHERMAN WAS SITTING IN THE CORNER OF the tiny cell, his arms wrapped about his knees, staring into space. He looked up momentarily when Dunnigan knocked on the door, but then returned to staring at nothing.

'He's been drugged,' Miley said.

'We have to get him out of here,' Dunnigan muttered.

'How? You only have the one key.'

'Yes, because as luck would have it, only I hold the keys to these other doors,' Ressler's jolly voice said.

Dunnigan and Miley spun to see him standing in the middle of the corridor, a bundle of heavy keys held in his left hand.

'I want you to let Kettu out of there, *now*,' Dunnigan ordered. 'He's leaving with me this evening.'

'I do not think so, David Dunnigan.'

'I'm calling the police,' Dunnigan said, taking his phone from his pocket.

'Try. I will wait right here for you to make the call.'

Ressler made a 'go ahead' motion with his hand. Dunnigan dialled 999 and pressed the phone to his ear. It beeped once and the line went dead. He tried again.

'We are ten feet below the ground, with metal sheeting on each side to act as insulation,' Ressler said, slowly walking towards them. 'There is no signal in these rooms. What a pity, eh?'

The psychiatrist came to a stop a couple of feet in front of the pair.

'Well, I'm leaving,' Miley said, and went to push past him.

'No, I cannot have that,' Ressler said, and in one rapid motion walloped him across the head with the heavy set of keys.

Miley dropped immediately, stunned.

Roaring in outrage, Dunnigan rushed at the man, and in a lunge took him off his feet, grabbing him by the throat. He had every intention of throttling the life out of Ressler, but as he closed his fingers about the man's windpipe, he felt a sting in his bicep and realised that the psychiatrist had stabbed him with a hypodermic syringe.

'That's a drug we've been testing,' Ressler said, pushing Dunnigan off him – the criminologist was already losing any feeling in his muscles. 'You'll sleep for a little while, and when you come around, it will take about an hour for the strength to return to your limbs.'

He sat on the floor beside the prone man.

'Believe me, David Dunnigan – I can make an hour feel like a very, very long time.'

Reality was a point of light with darkness all around it.

'While you're having a pleasant nap, I think it's time I introduced your disabled friend to Benjamin. I believe they're going to get along like a house on fire, don't you?'

Dunnigan tried to say something, but no words would come.

13

WHEN MILEY CAME BACK TO CONSCIOUSNESS HE was propped up against the wall of the stone folly, looking out over the night-time gardens of St Jude's. Ressler was gazing down at him, and Benjamin was squatting on his haunches, the lower half of his face covered in slobber and mucus, his tongue lolling out obscenely. He was making a high keening noise, almost like a kettle boiling.

'Why did you come here, Mister Miley?' Ressler asked him.

'I heard it was a nice place to visit,' Miley said, feeling the golf-ball sized lump that was coming up on his head. 'And I must say, you don't disappoint.'

'In times gone by, people with your condition would have been locked up in places like the one down those steps.'

'That fact did not escape me.'

'You would have been shackled naked to the wall like a fucking animal.'

Miley cast a glance at Benjamin, who was now jiggling up and down like a Mexican jumping bean.

'Is there a point to this story, because I have somewhere I need to be?'

'Please forgive me, I am always so fascinated by the history of my profession. Sometimes, I quite lose the running of myself. Ha!'

'Well, it's good to have a hobby. But if you're done, I'll be on my way.'

'You see, that was precisely what I was trying to say: time has passed and we live in a more enlightened era. One hundred years ago, you would have been caged like the monkey in the zoo. Now, you come as a valued guest and can leave with our blessing. Is that not the truth, Benjamin?'

'I can taste the wind,' Benjamin keened. 'I can feel the blood in my skin.'

'You must pardon my beloved ward here – I gave him a little shot of something that has exaggerated his adrenaline and testosterone production. He is in what you might call a heightened state of arousal.'

'How nice for him.'

'Oh, yes, he will be having a very good time shortly. Now, Mr Miley, the gate is half a kilometre to the west as the pigeon flies.'

Miley got to his feet. 'I'm taking Davey.'

'That is most loyal of you, but I regret that David Dunnigan and I have some unfinished business which I am anxious to resolve tonight. I promise you he is most comfortable.'

Miley seemed uncertain.

Ressler put a hand on his shoulder. 'Mister Miley?'

'Yes?'

'*Run.*'

'What?'

'Benjamin, he's all yours.'

With a howl of pleasure the crouching man sprang forward, but Miley was already sprinting as hard as he could through the trees.

14

HE RAN MORE ON INSTINCT THAN ANYTHING ELSE –
he could hear the jabbering and wailing of Benjamin behind him,
and he had no idea where he was going, so he just tried to keep in
a straight line and not charge in to anything.

Miley was not overweight, as people of his age with Down
syndrome often are, but neither was he a runner, and within a
few minutes his lungs were burning and his legs aching in protest.
He did not know how close the wall and escape were, but he
understood he was going to have to make a stand or everything
was finished.

A huge oak tree loomed to his right, and he staggered around
it, using the trunk for cover. Casting about, he spotted a fallen
branch on the ground and hefted it up, testing it for weight and
balance.

'They let my dog out and she never came back,' Benjamin
cooed, careening around the tree after him.

'I'm sorry about that,' Miley said, smashing the branch as hard
as he could right into his pursuer's face.

To his surprise, the man went down, but he was back up in a
second, his nose now at an interesting angle and blood adding its
colour to the coagulated mess on his chin.

'Gonna hurt you bad,' Benjamin intoned. 'Tear off your ears.'

'That's just wrong,' Miley said, and floored him with the branch
again.

Hating himself for doing it, he gave the fallen man another

thump for good measure, then stepped back, the club raised for further self-defence. Thankfully, there was no need.

'I don't know what they did to mess you up like this,' Miley said, squatting down beside the battered and bloody Benjamin. 'But I'm sorry for you.'

Trusty stick in hand, he started to jog back the way he'd come. Trying to find his way in the dark, it took him about ten minutes to get back to the stairs. Once there he squatted down, breathing heavily, peering at the door, which was slightly ajar.

Pulling out his phone, he made the call Dunnigan had been unable to complete.

'Yes, I'm at St Jude's Asylum, just outside Donbro. I've been attacked and my friend, who is a consultant with the gardaí at Harcourt Street, is being held hostage. I'm Miley—'

Before he could say another word the world was filled with an ear-splitting scream and something that smelt of sour milk, bile and blood landed on top of him. He dropped the phone and it skittered down the steps.

'Sorry, so sorry.' Benjamin began to drag Miley back towards the trees. 'Gonna mess you up, yes I am.'

Miley fought like a man possessed, but Benjamin, his face barely visible now beneath the blood and gunk, kicked him in the throat and he suddenly couldn't breathe. They had just reached the treeline, and all seemed lost, when, silently, a tall figure stepped out of the shadows.

'I'm going to ask you one time: let him go.'

Miley recognised the voice, but in his pain and terror thought he must be wrong.

'Bad man. Very bad. Kill you, too.'

'Have it your own way,' the figure said and, in a blur of savage motion, knocked Benjamin into the air – he landed on his back five feet from where he had been standing. Knowing he was outmanned, the tormented soul fled into the trees, sobbing bitterly.

'Are you all right, Miley?'

Strong hands lifted him to a sitting position and pounded him on the back until his breath was flowing again.

'Am I dreaming?' he asked, grabbing his saviour in a fierce hug.

'You're not,' Father Bill Creedon said. 'Now let's go and get Davey while there's still time.'

15

DAVID DUNNIGAN REGAINED CONSCIOUSNESS TO see Miley's grinning face hovering over his. 'Where am I?'

'You're safe. We put you lying on the grass – the door leading to the private wards is right behind you.'

'Where's Ressler?'

'He's still down there. Father Bill is reasoning with him.'

Dunnigan passed out again at this point, and when he came back around, police were milling about, and he was being loaded into an ambulance.

'Kettu,' he said to the paramedic who was inserting a drip into his arm. 'Don't forget him.'

'Just rest now, you've had a rough night,' the man said.

And Dunnigan drifted.

Brendan

The police interviewed him three times about the events at St Jude's, and he had told them what he'd told Dunnigan – things had gone wrong in the place years ago and had never really righted themselves.

He'd always had his suspicions about Ressler – something about that man jarred with him, and he thought Olive Jules was a proper snob. But then, it was his job to do the gardens and change the odd fuse, not to pass judgement on all these people with college educations.

He should have kept his mouth shut about Kettu. Gossip never led you anywhere good, and he had permitted himself to indulge in a bit of tattling. Maybe he'd been showing off – he was probably getting a bit soft in his old age, trying to look like the big lad in front of his grandson, sitting down and taking tea with the gardaí.

He lived in a cottage on the outskirts of the asylum's property. His wife had died ten years ago, and he was proud to say that he had kept the place as clean and tidy as it always was when she had tended it.

He was a precise man, and he liked things to be in their place.

Which was why he was surprised to see the kitchen window was ajar when he went to get his glass of water before turning in for bed. He was sure he had closed it earlier, when the dew was coming down. He loved the old cottage, but it was always prone to damp.

Shutting the latches, he ran some water into his glass and switched off the light, his stockinged feet making soft padding sounds as he walked up the hallway to the room he and his wife had shared for forty-five years.

He got the smell as soon as he opened the door – sour milk with an underlying hint of aniseed. Benjamin was on him before he had time to hit the switch.

'Time to play,' he said, before sinking his teeth into the gardener's throat.

16

WHEN NEXT DUNNIGAN OPENED HIS EYES IT WAS morning. He gathered by the white walls and bedclothes that he was in hospital. Detective Chief Superintendent Frank Tormey was asleep in a chair by his bed. The door opened and a blonde nurse came in.

'Nice to see you back in the land of the living,' she said.

Tormey stirred and sat up with a start.

'I'm just checking on the patient,' the nurse said, winking at him.

'Is he going to live?'

'Oh, I think so. Would you eat something, Mr Dunnigan?'

'Please call me Davey. Yes, I'm quite hungry.'

'I'll have some tea and toast sent down.'

'I think she likes me,' Tormey said when she was gone.

'You're old enough to be her grandfather.'

'So? How are you, anyway? Seems you and the Boy Wonder managed to start World War III and almost get yourselves killed in the process.'

'It all escalated rather quickly in the end. I really didn't see it coming.'

'Mmm. Well, we have Doctor Ressler in custody, and seeing as the asylum is now in the middle of an investigation into false imprisonment and a number of other crimes, some of which I have yet to formulate, we've been able to bypass that law they were hiding behind. I've had a few keen young officers working on it through the night, and some interesting things have come up.'

'Where's Miley?'

'He's gone to meet Diane. She should be here shortly.'

'Oh.'

Tormey looked at him quizzically. 'Trouble in paradise?'

'Not really.'

'The accountants have got back to me too, after I set a fire under their arses.'

A woman came in with a tray loaded with a teapot, cups, hot toast, butter and jam.

'I thought you might like some too, Chief,' she said.

'God bless you, Harriet. Your blood's worth bottling, d'you know that?'

She giggled like a schoolgirl and scuttled out.

'She likes me too.'

They applied themselves to breakfast.

'Kaiser Care, which I'm sure you remember owns St Jude's, is owned, it turns out (after much digging), by a conglomerate called Composite Holdings, who happen to be an umbrella firm owned by none other than Eastwich Industries, who operate out of London.'

Dunnigan spread another slice of toast with jam. 'And?'

'Eastwich Industries is run by a board of trustees. Guess who the chairman of the board was, up until three months ago?'

'You know I'm not going to guess.'

'Ernest Frobisher. Ressler is directly employed by Kaiser Care and was sent by them to run the asylum when they bought it after it foundered financially. The deaths in the late nineties were due to psychotropic drug trials he was carrying out – basically, he was testing a new anti-depressant which ended up making the subjects even worse than they previously had been, to the point that quite a few of the poor buggers couldn't cope anymore. He claims the families of the patients he used agreed to it, but, see, the Mental Health Act prohibits the use of psychiatric patients in drug trials, so we have him.'

'Good.'

'You said you thought there were very few residents in the place, and you were absolutely right. Besides the three that were in the underground cells, only two were resident in the main building.'

'So how the hell were they keeping afloat?'

'Right now, we're assuming these poor fuckers were being subjected to drug trial after drug trial, and that was the main business St Jude's was engaged in. But, to be honest, even that looks suspect. Let's just say half a dozen agencies are going to be picking through every level of the asylum's operations for the foreseeable future.'

Tormey leaned in to Dunnigan and spoke to him quietly. 'I think Frobisher lured you down here with the intention of killing you. He nearly succeeded. If Miley hadn't been able to get away from that psycho Ressler sent after him, and had the good sense to dial 999 and get the local constabulary over there, I dread to think what might have happened.'

'But what about Kettu? And the children being brought by bus?'

'The company Kettu worked for paid for him to be sent to St Jude's when he went doolally after his boat sank — they thought they were being decent employers. It was the closest private sanatorium to their offices, and they believed they were helping him get over the trauma he'd experienced. Being Inuit, though, he presented Ressler with a new biological profile, and he jumped at the chance to use him as part of these pharmaceutical trials. He must be made of stern stuff because he seems to have fared better than most of the others. His being there is just what it seems — a coincidence. And poor old Mrs Tarbuck doesn't know up from down. I'm sorry, Davey. You did as much as anyone could have, and you stopped some bad people doing some awful things. That's going to have to be enough.'

Part Six

SECOND INTERLUDE

1

DIANE CAME IN AN HOUR LATER AND HELD HIM and cried and called him an asshole, and he held her back and cried some too and asked her not to call him rude names.

'They say I can bring you home,' she said when they were finished making up.

'I'd like that.'

'Miley tells me you have some odds and ends at this house you've been renting, so we can stop by there and collect them.'

'All right.'

Miley met them at the door of the house.

'You saved my life,' Dunnigan said, giving him a quick hug.

'Well, I contributed to it, but it was actually this guy.'

'Who?'

'You don't remember, do you?'

'Remember what?'

Father Bill, looking pale, tired and far too thin, came out of the living room. 'Hello, Davey.'

'I need to sit down,' Dunnigan said.

Miley made them tea and they arranged themselves around the small living room and listened as Father Bill told his tale.

'I'd probably be dead if they hadn't dumped me in the river,' he began. 'The shock of the water revived me, and, weak as I was, I knew it was my only chance. They'd tied my legs to a bundle of breeze blocks, but not tightly, and when I hit the bottom I was able to get loose. I just allowed myself to go limp and let the currents take me. The Liffey spat me back out an hour later near Clontarf, and I found a space behind the bus depot and waited for it to get dark.'

'You'd lost so much blood,' Diane said. 'We didn't think you could have survived at all.'

'I'm not going to lie to you, it was touch and go,' Father Bill said. 'I was pretty much delirious and operating more on instinct than anything else. I had some money in my pocket, and I got the last bus into the city. They thought I was dead, so no one would be looking for me, but I took off the dog-collar and turned my jacket inside out for good measure. The river had washed most of the blood out of my jeans, so I looked just like a homeless person who needed a wash and some fresh clothes. I tore a sleeve off my shirt to wrap the wound in my gut, and staunch the blood, so I didn't stand out too much.'

'Where did you go?' Miley asked.

'To a friend of mine, Kevin, who has an apartment near the IFSC. He's a former Christian Brother who left the church to work for Doctors Without Borders – thought he could do more good with them. Thanks be to God he was home for a couple of weeks before heading back out to Syria. I arrived at his door at midnight – another ten minutes and I wouldn't have made it at all. I stayed with him for a week. He stitched me up, gave me antibiotics, even managed to find blood somewhere to replenish what I'd lost.'

'Why didn't you call us?' Dunnigan asked curtly. 'Things were awful enough as it was without throwing your death into the mix.'

'I'm sorry.'

'You're not forgiven!' Dunnigan said. 'We needed you and you weren't there.'

'I thought I could be more effective under the radar with

Frobisher's people thinking I was dead. If no one was watching me, I could move around with complete freedom and try to get to the bottom of what was going on.'

'That's hard to do when you're laid up in some hippy doctor's flat!'

'While I was with Kevin, I sent out feelers to see what was going on with all of you. I heard about the shoe, and about Miley going to Forensics Ireland, and what was found on it. I knew you'd gone to West Cork, and it didn't take me long to find out why and where.'

'How in the hell did you learn all of this?' Diane asked him, incredulous. 'I mean, no one knew, other than us and the police!'

'You and Miley need to be more careful about where you have your private conversations.' The priest smiled.

'Someone at the project?'

'Gizzy.'

'That bollix spoke at your memorial service!'

'I heard about that. Sorry I couldn't be there.'

'You *asshole*!' Diane said, but she was grinning, and hugged him again.

'I also called Tim Pat and asked him to make sure the physical threat was eliminated.'

'So Rogers knew you were alive, too?'

'He did. I asked him to keep it to himself.'

'It wasn't him who got the gangs off our backs, it was me!' Diane spluttered.

'I suggested he point you in the right direction. I had complete confidence that you could manage the rest by yourself.'

Diane actually blushed. 'Thanks, Father Bill.'

'I made my own enquiries about St Jude's. An old college friend of mine is a Church of Ireland minister down here, and he visited the place from time to time in the late nineties. He informed me that they stopped allowing him in in the early years of the new millennium. He said that the entire ethos of the place changed when Ressler came. He also said he had concerns about the conditions the patients were being kept under. He lodged some complaints, but apparently some archaic piece of law, combined with the usual apathy, stopped the powers that be from doing anything about it.'

'We ran into the same problem,' Dunnigan said, still a bit sniffily.

'He did tell me, though, that he had been there late one evening, around the time of one of the suicides – the family had asked for a prayer service to be held on site, and Devaney had given permission. He stayed on a little after everyone else had gone, chatting to a few of the other patients, who were very upset at another death. One lady, Jenna, was particularly bereft. It was about two, two thirty, in the morning when he was leaving, and as he was pulling out of the gate, a minibus with blacked-out windows was going in.'

Dunnigan sat bolt upright. 'A minibus?'

'That's what he said.'

'Nurse Tarbuck told me that the children came by bus.'

Father Bill nodded. 'If you want to know anything about the comings and goings in any place, speak to the homeless people. There weren't so many around Donbro in the late nineties, but I found one, who is still in the area. Maurice used to do casual labour on some of the local fishing boats during his periods of sobriety, and when he was drinking, he used one of the sheds down by the pier to sleep. He told me that, on more than one occasion, he was woken by trawlers coming in in the middle of the night.'

'Is that out of the ordinary in a working fishing port?' Miley asked.

'If the boats were only carrying fishermen and fish, no,' Father Bill said.

'And these weren't?'

'Maurice said he saw them unloading boxes of fish, all right. But the strange thing was, they had women and children on board too.'

Everyone went deadly silent.

'Maurice said these boats came from the island. So I went out and had a look. There's a large shed on the eastern end. It doesn't look like it's used regularly, but there are several old cots in there. Tins of food. Clothes.' He looked at Davey. 'And some toys. An old doll.'

'Show me,' Dunnigan said.

2

NO ONE WAS SURPRISED THAT FATHER BILL already had a small boat at his disposal.

They sat pensively while he steered out into the sound.

The shed was situated on a flat piece of land almost at the furthest eastern point. Father Bill did not go to the main docking on Tully Island, but navigated to a thin strip of beach and, with Dunnigan and Diane's help, dragged the boat up onto the sand.

The structure itself was made of corrugated iron and old boards and had a sliding metal door that was padlocked shut. Father Bill had kicked one of the boards at the back loose and he held it up so they could all squeeze inside.

The place had a fine layer of dust, but everything was as the priest had said. Dunnigan squatted down and picked up the doll. A sad-looking teddy bear and a red plastic truck lay there too.

'We have to tell Tormey,' he said. 'This is another trafficking hub, isn't it?'

'I think so,' Father Bill said. 'But there's more. Look.'

He walked to the back of the structure, where some crates had been stacked against the wall. They had clearly been used to hold fish at one time, but now contained boxes of dehydrated mashed potato, tins of creamed rice and other non-perishables. Stapled to the side of one of the crates was a faded piece of paper, dated March 3rd, 1999, listing the fish that had been transported in it. Dunnigan ran his eyes down the names: silver hake; winter flounder; king mackerel; and, just at the bottom, Arctic char.

'The fact it's at the bottom of the list means it's the least common catch,' Father Bill told him. 'But they would have *occasionally* caught one or two. Global warming had brought them into the outskirts of our waters, of late.'

Dunnigan looked at the piece of paper and then at the priest. 'What are you saying?' he asked, his voice tight with emotion.

'You need to go and speak to Doctor Ressler,' Father Bill said.

3

RESSLER WAS BEING HELD IN THE CELLS AT THE
police station in Donbro. He was due to be transferred to Cork
Prison later that day, but Dunnigan was permitted to see him
before he made the trip.

The psychiatrist looked as if he had been mauled by a grizzly
bear: his face was swollen and bruised, his nose was packed where
it had been broken and Dunnigan saw that several fingers on his
left hand were in splints. Father Bill, it seemed, had not been gentle
in his ministrations.

'Hello to you, David Dunnigan,' Ressler said through scabbed
and torn lips.

'I know about the buses and I know about the shed on the
island,' Dunnigan said. 'Now I want to know one thing from you,
and one thing only: was Beth ever in St Jude's?'

'I would really love to be able to give you an answer in the
definitive, Davey, but alas, I cannot.'

'But children were trafficked into the asylum?'

'Women and children passed *through* St Jude's,' Ressler said. 'You
see, the real business we had was the grooming and the preparation
of young women and little boys and girls before they were sent
to perform their duties in other parts of the world. They were
brought to us from all over Ireland and the United Kingdom by
boat. The ships drop anchor in the waters just off the island, where
they don't have to worry about the coast guard, and a couple of
the local fishing-boat captains would bring the cargo into port, and

from there to the asylum. We used boats that were part of the fleet our dear friend Kettu was once captain of.'

'So his being in St Jude's wasn't just a coincidence.'

'We both know there are no such things as coincidences, David Dunnigan. My employers have many interests all over the world, and Kettu was, unknown to himself, working for them long before he came to Ireland.'

'Why did the children come here? Why the asylum?'

'For some very good reasons, Davey. The children, in particular, need a lot of work – they can be time-consuming, you know? They are often most upset when they are taken, so they require sedation. On some of the little kids, we have to perform surgical alterations to their appearances to avoid identification, but the most important thing is that they be *conditioned*.'

'What do you mean by that?'

'They need to learn to be obedient and compliant. Kids these days, lots of them are used to getting their own way, to living comfortable lives where they have lots and lots of choice over what they do and don't do. At St Jude's, we made sure these little children knew that when they are asked to do something, they should just do it right away or there will be consequences they don't like.'

'You frighten them.'

'We teach them fear, yes. The smarter ones understand very quickly, and the others learn in time. Kaiser Care runs homes for the mentally ill all over Europe in which we carry out this service for several different organisations who require a regular supply of children. I mean to say, David Dunnigan, it is the perfect cover for us. You have already learned about the confidentiality laws, but also we must consider the most convenient fact that nobody listens to the mentally deranged, and if they do, they take what they say with pinches of salt.'

'Where do the children go from here?'

'Everywhere.'

'Be more specific.'

'I am tired of this now, David Dunnigan. I will be out of custody very soon, and I wish you to know that, when I am, I will be dedicating all of my energies to making your life and the lives of your friends very uncomfortable.'

'You're not going anywhere. After what you've just told me?'

'I will deny every word of it. Your friend beat and brutalised me last night, and nothing I said then will be admissible. My solicitor has already ensured there are no recording devices in this room, so what has passed this morning is between you and me. That means all I can be charged with is the alleged false imprisonment of you and the drugs trials. I have a feeling the lawyers Kaiser Care keep on retainer will make short work of the matter of the trials – particularly as every single one of their families gave us leave to carry them out (with the small inducement of a cash payment for any pain or suffering their relatives might experience). That leaves the issue of you being drugged and held against your will.'

Dunnigan laughed. 'You were planning to torture me to death.'

'I was going to start and let Benjamin finish. Speaking of dear Benjamin – has he been captured yet?'

'No. He's still at large.'

'They won't find him, you know. He is a remarkably bright young man. He will only surface when he is ready to.'

'What are you getting at, Doctor Ressler?'

'I honestly do not know whether your niece was in St Jude's – is it possible she was there? Yes, it is certainly a possibility. Can I say for definite? No, I cannot. There have been *hundreds* of little girls in the hospital over the last eighteen years. This shoe that was sent to you, I had no part to play in that business, of that I give my word. You came to my asylum and you started to ask questions that would lead to aspects of our business being discovered and I had to deal with you. It is my job to do so – you have to understand that. It's not personal at all.'

'Maybe not to you,' Dunnigan said.

'Pish and posh, David Dunnigan, you are too sensitive. Anyway, we are at something of an impasse, are we not? Here is my proposal to you. Make the charge of false imprisonment go away, and I will tell you where I think your niece would have been sent if she was in my care.'

'You just said she could have been sent anywhere.'

'Yes, but the shoe is a puzzle, is it not? A mystery? If we look at the clues, I think they tell us a story. And it is a tale I know very well.'

Dunnigan looked at the battered and bloodied man. He was in no doubt that this was a deeply evil and dangerous individual, who should spend the rest of his natural life behind bars. And yet …

'All right. I'll say I gave you permission to try out a new drug on me.'

'You will sign the paper stating that?'

'An affidavit, yes.'

'Very good, David Dunnigan. When it is done, and I am no longer in custody, I will give you the information you wish to know.'

'No deal. Tell me now.'

'Those are my conditions, Davey. If you do as I ask, I will help you solve this most interesting puzzle. If not: *pow*! The truth you wish to discover goes away forever. The choice is yours.'

And Ressler lay down on his bunk, turned his back on Dunnigan and went to sleep.

4

'YOU'RE NOT GOING TO LET HIM OFF, ARE YOU?'
Diane said as they drove back to Cork city.

'No. He admits that Beth may well never have been at St Jude's.
I'm not letting him loose to do more damage based on a "maybe".'

'A part of you wants to, though, doesn't it?' Miley asked from
the back seat.

'Yes. And a year ago, I would have done it in a heartbeat. But
not now. I honestly don't believe Beth would want me to.'

They were stopping at Cork University Hospital on the way
home to say goodbye to Kettu. Dunnigan didn't feel he could leave
without paying his respects, and Miley agreed they owed it to him
to at least say goodbye.

He was sitting up in bed watching *Loose Women* when Dunnigan
went into his room.

'I have never seen this show before, but it is very funny,' Kettu
said. 'This one, Janet, she says mean things but with a smile on her
face. I don't always understand it, but it makes me laugh.'

'I don't understand it either,' Dunnigan said.

'You are a good man, Davey,' Kettu said, muting the sound
with the remote control. 'I am told they put poisons into me in St
Jude's, and these made me sick in my body and in my spirit. Now
they give me good medicine to take the poison away, and I am not
afraid anymore. But for you, this would not have happened.'

'So you're not worried about the devil?'

'That is hard to speak of. I did bad things – I did not abide by
the omens and signs. I thought I saw the demon when I was in the
dungeons, but now, I wonder if it was a dream.'

'A dream?'

'Yes.'

'The first time I met you I asked you about my niece, and you said the Inuit word for dream.'

'I don't remember that.'

'I asked if you had seen a little girl at St Jude's.'

Kettu suddenly went very pale. 'Sit, please, Davey.'

Dunnigan did as he was asked.

'I do not know if what I am going to tell you is real or if it was a dream,' Kettu said. 'When I was so sick in my spirit that I lost who I was, they brought me to the dungeons. You saw them – you have been there. One night, when I had been there a long time, I heard footsteps, and I looked out of the hole in the door, and I saw a small, dark-haired girl.'

Dunnigan suddenly felt as if he was watching the two of them from somewhere above.

'I thought this was a vision,' Kettu continued. 'I believed it was a spirit-child. But she saw me, and she stopped, and she spoke to me.'

'What did she say?' Dunnigan asked, his voice breaking.

'She said she was looking for the Doctor, that he would take her away from the monsters.'

'That's what she said?' Dunnigan gripped Kettu's arm. 'This is very, very important – you have to think hard and make sure you are absolutely certain.'

'Yes. She said it was not *a* doctor she wanted, but *the* Doctor. And something about a blue box.'

'It was Beth,' Dunnigan said, and tears he could not stop streamed down his face. 'Oh my God, it really was her.'

'I told her to run away, to find the door and get out, but I was too late. The devil came – he looked like an old man, but he wasn't. He was something else.'

Even through his pain, Dunnigan knew who Kettu was talking about. He had seen Ernest Frobisher.

5

HE SAT IN THE GARDA STATION IN CORK CITY AND
signed a sworn affidavit that he had, freely and of his own volition,
given Doctor Phillipe Ressler permission to try a new sedative and
muscle relaxant on him.

Dunnigan knew he was different from other people. He
knew people often talked about him being 'on the spectrum' or
exhibiting 'autistic tendencies'. In fact, his mother, an educational
psychologist, had tested him herself when he was younger and had
sent the results to a colleague of hers for an impartial analysis.

Apparently Dunnigan 'exhibited symptoms of obsessive
compulsion combined with tendencies characteristic of a mild form
of anti-social personality disorder'. His mother had gleefully told
her son, who was ten years old at the time, that he was a sociopath.

He had spent his teenage years trying to prove her wrong but
could not sustain the effort to be sensitive and caring about anyone
other than Gina and, later, Beth.

Every now and again, someone would ask him outright if he
had Asperger's (which he would always point out to them 'wasn't
even a thing anymore') or if he was 'one of those *Rain Man* guys'.
It always rankled. It was nobody's business, and he did not like
discussing his psychological self, not even with Gina or Diane.

So it was with a sense of bitter irony, now, that he used his
Achilles heel to have the charges against Ressler dropped.

'I have certain personality traits I wished to modify,' he wrote
in his statement. 'Doctor Ressler showed me peer-reviewed
studies which outlined how psychiatrists in Eastern Europe

have had success with patients exhibiting sociopathy using new pharmacological treatments.'

'Are you absolutely certain about this?' Father Bill asked him when he joined the priest, Diane and Miley in a pub once the deed was done.

'Yes. I am in no doubt that Beth was there. After eighteen years, I have sight of her. Ressler says he knows where she was sent next. This is the only way he'll tell me.'

'Give me ten minutes with him and I'll have him talking,' Father Bill said.

'But could we believe anything he said?' Diane asked. 'This is all some kind of game. I just wish I understood the rules.'

'So what do we do now?' Miley said.

'We wait,' Dunnigan replied.

Diane Robinson

Father Bill arrived at the Homeless Project one evening shortly after they brought Davey home. He came into the office where she was working, and took out the bottle of whiskey and two glasses he kept in the desk drawer, then sat across from her and poured them both liberal measures.

'I'm going to be gone for a bit,' he said. 'Can I ask you to continue running this place for a while more?'

'Of course. Can I ask where you're going?'

'It might be better if you didn't. Let's just say that I have some leads I want to follow up on. Some stuff I learned about Beth and Davey that might shed some light on everything that's been happening.'

Diane sipped her drink.

'How much danger are you exposing yourself to?'

'Some. But I've asked the police to keep up the charade that I'm dead, so the threat will be minimised. A bit, anyhow.'

'I don't want to lose you again.'

'I know that, Diane. And it means a lot to me.'

She sighed and rubbed her eyes.

'I don't know about this, Father.'

'About what?'

She downed what was left in her glass and poured some more. She noticed the priest had hardly touched his.

'You know I care about Davey. I mean … I love him.'

'Yes, of course.'

'Miley would give his right arm for Davey, and you've already gotten yourself almost killed for him …'

'What are you getting at, Diane?'

'When I was in the army, every campaign, every mission, was weighed up closely to establish whether or not it was an achievable goal: did we have the numbers, the skills and the necessary firepower to get it done with as few losses as possible.'

'I see.'

'Going up against the people who took Beth is not an achievable goal.'

'I'm still here. So are you. And Davey, and Miley.'

'Since we started this business we've gotten by on luck. When do we accept that this is as much as we're going to know, that this is as close as we're going to get, and walk away?'

Father Bill turned the glass in his hand and nodded slowly.

'Whether we like it or not, Diane, we are in this and we have no choice but to see it through to the end.'

'Have you never heard of a tactical retreat?'

'This isn't the military. These people do not abide by the Geneva Convention. The only rules of engagement are that you keep on going until the other side are all dead.'

'Is that what you're planning? Go out there and kill them all?'

'I like to think I'm a little more subtle than that.'

She snorted and downed her second glass.

'You know what's driving me mad?'

'No.'

'He's not even grateful.'

'You're talking about Davey?'

'Who else?'

'You don't believe that. This is your pain talking. Your fear.'

'I used to tell myself there was something more buried beneath all his weirdness. I thought that, even though he couldn't tell me how he felt a lot of the time, that there were other ways he showed me. But the last while, ever since that fucking shoe showed up, he has proven time and time again that I was wrong.'

'He's been going through an awful lot.'

'What about me? And Miley? Haven't we been going through a lot as well?'

'That's not the same ...'

'Yes, it is! I thought you were dead, Father! Goddamn it, you're my best friend! I was grieving, and all I wanted was for him – the man who was supposed to love me and be there for me – to hug me, or even take a moment to ask me how I was doing. But he didn't. Not once. Now, he's looking for us all to go off on some other fucking expedition, and what worries me is that I don't think he cares one way or another who comes back alive so long as he gets what he wants.'

'You don't mean that.'

'I do. I'm not saying I don't love him. I'm just trying to acknowledge the reality of who David Dunnigan really is.'

'He's a lot more than that, Diane.'

'True. But we can't deny that, right now, the part of him that is prepared to march his friends into the mouth of hell so he can find his niece is front and centre.'

Father Bill swallowed what was in his glass and placed it empty on the table.

'I can't help you with this,' he said. 'I believe David Dunnigan is a good man – a damaged man, and a man with a lot of ghosts, but a good man for all that.'

'You're going anyway, aren't you?'

'Yes. And I suspect you are too. You won't let Davey and Miley go into danger again by themselves.'

'You're right. What that means for me and Davey, I don't know.'

'You'll do what's best. I know you will.'

She rubbed at her eyes with her sleeve – somewhere in the middle of the conversation, tears had come, unbidden.

'Please be careful, Father. Wherever you're going, just promise me that.'

'I promise.'

And standing, he leaned over the desk, kissed her on the forehead, and was gone into the night.

Frank Tormey

The priest came to see him shortly after Dunnigan and Miley came back out of the west. He walked into Tormey's office unannounced and sat down uninvited.

'I see they didn't kill you.'

'Hard to do away with a bad thing.'

'I hear that.'

'I need a favour.'

'And why would I grant you one of those? I have long been of the opinion that you are as much a fucking menace to this city as that gangster you keep company with. The fact that Davey and Miley and Diane, whom I happen to think are good people, have been taken in by your Father Trendy routine doesn't alter that one little bit.'

The priest smiled in a tired kind of way. Tormey saw that he had lost a lot of weight, and he hadn't been carrying much to begin with.

'You don't think I've done any good, then, in my ministry?'

'I have no doubt that you have, but you've an awful habit of bending the law when it suits you, and far too bloody often people who have stepped over lines of propriety you've drawn in the sand end up dead. I'm a simple copper, and I don't make distinctions between good laws and bad laws – I simply uphold the law. You seem to have a very loose view of it, and that makes me uncomfortable.'

'I didn't come here to argue ethics with you, Frank.'

'What do you want, then?'

'To stay dead.'

'What?'

'Davey, Miley, Diane and a few gardaí know I'm alive. Ressler met me, but he doesn't know who I am. The people who tried to kill me think they succeeded. For now, I want it to stay that way.'

'Why?'

'Because I learned a few things while I was in the wind trying to help

Davey. I want to be able to follow up on them without looking over my shoulder.'

Tormey narrowed his eyes. 'I don't like the sound of that.'

'All I'm asking is that you put the word out among your people that my missing-presumed-dead status stays in place for a while.'

'Am I going to regret this, Bill?'

'I hope not.' Father Bill stood up and left.

It was two months before Tormey saw him again.

6

THE CALL CAME TWO WEEKS LATER.

Dunnigan was in Dunnes Stores at Stephen's Green buying groceries. He glanced at the screen, and it was a number he didn't recognise.

'Hello?'

'I know you,' came a querulous, gurgling voice.

Dunnigan pulled the receiver away from his ear as if Benjamin might actually climb out of it like some kind of foul snake, then thought better of it and put it back carefully.

'Hello, David Dunnigan!' Ressler came on, all jubilance and merriment. 'Our little scheme worked, and I am again a free man! I expect you are very pleased that I have been reunited with my close friend Benjamin! He cannot wait to meet you again at the earliest opportunity.'

'We had a deal,' Dunnigan said, making his way to the very end of the store and walking along the top of the aisles, peering down each one to make sure the psychiatrist had not followed him.

'Yes, we did, and I am a man who always honours his agreements.'

'Well?'

'Faringen.'

'I beg your pardon?'

'Write it down or send it to yourself in a text or have it tattooed on your dick, Davey, I don't care. That is all I am saying to you.'

'Come on, you can do better than that!'

'Oh, Davey, Davey, Davey – it is lucky I have a soft spot for you. All right, I will throw you a bone, so to speak. A fish bone! The Faringen Processing Plant. That's it. Until we meet again, David Dunnigan. And I think that will be very soon!'

And the line went dead.

Gina Dunnigan-Carlton

She had met Davey in Wagamama near the Stephen's Green Centre the day before he left for Greenland. He sat and did his best to make small talk (probably not his greatest talent), but she could tell he was already gone.

She loved him – she always had – but these past few months she felt they had never been further apart. It was as if something in him had died all over again, and no matter what she said or did, she could not bring it back to life.

He was shrinking right before her eyes.

He told her that he was going to the Arctic to find Beth, to follow some lead he had been given by one of the monsters who had taken her in the first place, but it seemed to Gina that, by chasing this spectre, he had allowed them to take the child from him all over again.

And she was sharing in that loss.

'Diane is going with you?'

'Yes. And Miley.'

'Well, I'm glad. Miley will keep you human and Diane will keep you in one piece.'

He made a sort of half-smile.

'I need to say something to you, Davey.'

'What?'

'If, when you get out there, you find yourself in a position where you have to make a choice between finding out what happened to Beth and saving yourself, save yourself. Every time, Davey, save yourself.'

He looked at her over his soup spoon, and in that instant she knew he would, gladly, give his life in this quest to find the child he had allowed to be taken.

Her great fear was that he would gladly give everyone else's lives too.

Part Seven

ICE TOWN

1

THE PLANE BANKED AND STARTED ITS DESCENT towards the airport of Faringen in northern Greenland. Dunnigan peered out of the tiny window at a snow-covered tundra far below. Beside him, Diane was asleep, her head lolling on one side. Across the aisle from her, Miley was plugged into Chris de Burgh's *Crusader* album, a book on the Arctic open on his lap, his face creased in concentration.

A month had passed since Dunnigan had received the phone call from Ressler, and that time had been spent trying to work out what to do with the information the psychiatrist had deigned to give them.

Tormey was furious with Dunnigan for striking such a bargain, putting it to him that this was not the behaviour of a person who worked for the gardaí. Dunnigan responded by pointing out that had he not, they wouldn't have anywhere to go at all, but Tormey was not convinced.

Since an army of lawyers had secured his release from prison, Ressler had disappeared completely, and while Father Bill had his sources hard at work trying to locate him, Dunnigan suspected the man would surface, Benjamin in tow, when he was good and ready and not before. In the meantime, they would all have to be as watchful and prepared as they could be.

Various phone calls were made, by Tormey as well as the Garda Commissioner, to the authorities in Greenland in an attempt to start a dialogue, but very little help was forthcoming. The Faringen Fish Processing Plant was owned by Kohlberg Industries, which, it did not take Dunnigan long to discover, did a lot of business with Composite Holdings, Frobisher's umbrella company.

Dunnigan had managed to get a satellite map of the plant, which, to his amazement, was the size of a small town. It was the main source of income for the people who lived in the area and held a cannery, a dehydration and freezing factory, fish and cephalopod farms and a plant for rendering blubber from whales and seals into oil of various denominations.

According to information Dunnigan had been able to access online, the plant employed about sixteen hundred people at a time, working two shifts across a twenty-four-hour period. Another army of drivers, engineers, fishermen and local guides came and went as required, and Kohlberg Industries owned about half the buildings in the nearby town of Faringen (the town was named after the plant, from which it had grown), and these they rented to their workers.

'You've got to remember, this is not the West,' Davies, an agent with Interpol, had told Dunnigan over the phone. Davies worked in the Anti-Trafficking Unit for the international police force. 'The rules are different, and the expectations people have are not what you're used to. Somewhere like Faringen, people are not just prepared to work outrageous hours in the most appalling conditions for well below minimum wage – they *expect* to. These are people whose parents worked in places that would make a Middle Eastern sweat shop look like Disney World.'

'So why do they need to traffic people, then?'

'Because, even though it might be a pittance, your average local *does* want to be paid *something*. And this isn't Willy Wonka, Davey. If a plant of this magnitude doesn't have a lot of the locals working there, serious questions are going to be asked. We also have to consider the fact that the polar regions of Greenland are sparsely populated, and they might not be able to find *enough* locals to run the plant. So you ship in slave labour, work them until they drop, and then ship in some more.'

'But an initial outlay is necessary.'

'Within reason. A lot of companies in the Arctic still use scrip and their workers are happy to take it.'

'What's scrip?'

'A currency printed by the company themselves – Monopoly money that only has value at the company store.'

'That can't be legal!'

'It's not, but in these very remote locations, a huge operation like this will more than likely have the local police and the local government in their pockets. I wouldn't be surprised if Kohlberg scrip is the main medium of exchange somewhere like Faringen.'

'I've been told a child who was abducted in Dublin back in 1998 may have been trafficked there.'

'It's not unlikely.'

'Do you think they use child labour?'

'They may – it's common enough all over the world. But even if they don't, with a workforce of that size out on the ice, they need to provide some recreation.'

'You're talking about prostitutes.'

'I'm talking about sex slaves, Davey. Prostitutes get paid.'

Tormey had, eventually, refused to send him.

'On what grounds?' the chief superintendent asked. 'Every single piece of information you have is useless to us from a legal point of view.'

'So what am I supposed to do?'

'It's not my job to answer that question.'

And that seemed to be that.

Dunnigan wasn't the only one looking for a ticket to the Arctic.

Something had been niggling Miley since the day he and

Dunnigan had sat with Kettu in the garden of St Jude's, and he couldn't put his finger on what it was. Every now and again, he felt he was getting close to it, but then it would dart away once more, elusive as smoke. It was one evening when Harry was over and the two of them were cooking dinner together that it came to him.

One of the boy's favourite dinners was fish pie: prawns, cod and smoked haddock in a creamy béchamel sauce, topped off with mashed potato and served (Miley could never understand why it worked, but somehow it did) with baked beans.

Harry was mashing the spuds and Miley was stirring the sauce and adding just a pinch of nutmeg (he'd seen this suggested by Donal Skehan, an Irish chef he liked to watch on TV) when the boy said, 'Where did you say they took my dad?'

Miley played for time because, in reality, he could not remember. He knew Tom and Pauline, Harry's mother and father, had been trafficked to two different locations, and he seemed to recall Pauline had been destined for Amsterdam. He thought Tom's fate had something to do with forestry but was ashamed to admit he had not actually noted the names involved.

'I'll call Davey and find out for you,' he said, and when the pie had been constructed and put in the oven and the beans were bubbling away in their pot, he did just that.

'I have the details here,' Dunnigan had said, tapping a couple of times on the keyboard of his ageing laptop. 'Pauline was probably sent to Amsterdam, but we believe she may be in Rotterdam right now, and Tom was initially shipped to the Czech Republic, and from there to –'

There was silence for a moment.

'You OK, Davey?'

'I'm sorry,' Dunnigan said. 'I just … I can't believe we missed this.'

'What?' Miley asked, worried now.

'One of the locations Tom may have been shipped to was Faringen, northern Greenland,' Dunnigan said.

Miley didn't go into the nitty-gritty of what this meant when he talked to Harry, but later that night he lay awake for a long time thinking about it. The following day, he went around to Dunnigan's flat.

'I'm going with you,' he told the criminologist.

'To Harcourt Street? I'd love to bring you, but you'd probably be bored.'

'No. To Greenland.'

Dunnigan paused in packing books into his shoulder bag. 'I don't know for sure that I'm going yet.'

'You are. And I'm coming too. I owe it to Harry.'

'You don't owe that lad anything.'

'Yes, I do, and we both know it.'

'Do you have the money to go?'

Miley's face fell. 'No. But I'll get it. Somehow.'

'Have you any idea how much it is?'

'Uncle Frank won't pay?'

'He has been quite firm on that issue.'

Luck stepped in the following morning, in the form of Davies from Interpol.

'Did you know that Danish is the official language in Greenland but that virtually everyone speaks English too?'

'Why are you telling me this?' Dunnigan asked him.

'I hear on the grapevine you're looking to go to Faringen.'

'Well, I did indicate as much when we talked last.'

'I also heard that the girl you're looking for is your niece.'

Dunnigan made a non-committal sound down the receiver.

'We've had an interest in that particular area for a long time, but this is the first hard lead we've ever encountered. I've gone out on a limb and had a contract drawn up for you to be employed as a consultant for our department. I've also called your university and had them agree to say they've sent you out there on a research trip. That means that, if you run into difficulties, you've got a cover story, and, of course, we can offer you some support, even if it only means a stern phone call with whoever is closing doors in your face. I'm emailing over the paperwork right now.'

'Thank you.'

'I hope you find something, Davey,' the agent said. 'And I hope, whatever it is, it doesn't hurt too much.'

It was agreed that Diane and Miley could travel with him as 'research assistants'. Father Bill went to the airport with them. 'I've got some leads to follow up here,' he said. 'Now will you for God's sake be careful.'

'I'll look after him, and Diane too,' Miley reassured him.

'I'm pleased to hear that,' the priest said, hugging them each in turn. 'Be sure to keep me posted.'

As the plane taxied along the runway and Dunnigan looked out at the windswept, snow-caked buildings, he could not remember ever feeling further from home.

Kettu

They told him it was supported accommodation – this meant a woman called to his flat twice a day to make sure he had not killed himself. He didn't mind – she was nice enough, and she usually forced him to make dinner, which he was often inclined to skip.

One morning he got up to find a tiny figure sitting on top of his television set. He didn't have to inspect it closely to know it was carved from whale bone, just as he knew before picking it up and turning it over in his hands that the figure resembled a man, but with scales and webbed feet, lines on the neck resembling gills.

It was a Tupilak, an Inuit demon.

That it had made its way into his new home meant only one thing.

He found the card Dunnigan had given him and rang the number on it.

'Hello, Kettu.'

'You said you are going to my homeplace?'

'Yes.'

'Go to my people. Tell my chieftain and my brother Showashar they were right – I should never have gone across the sea. I wish I had not.'

'Didn't you say you had a daughter? Won't she be glad to hear from you too? She's going to want to see you, I'm sure.'

'I will not be going back, Davey. I thank you, but this is where I will meet my end.'

'Nonsense. I'll ask when I see her.'

'You are a good friend, David Dunnigan, but you do not understand.'

'Well, is there anything else you'd like me to say?'

'Tell them I am full of remorse.'

'OK. I think you're wrong, but I'll do that.'

'Travel well, David Dunnigan.'

'Goodbye, Kettu.'

That night, when the moon was at its peak in the sky, he got up and went to the window. On the green outside the flats stood a man in blue overalls. Kettu opened the door, and let him in.

Death had found him again, and this time, he welcomed it.

2

THE COLD WAS LIKE BEING GRIPPED BY A HUGE FIST made of liquid ice. It was shocking in its intensity, a physical experience none of them had ever encountered before.

The main street of Faringen was wide and furrowed, the ice carved with deep ruts from the four-wheel drives that passed up and down on their way to God knows where. The shops and houses that lined the thoroughfare all looked like they had seen better days – blasted by the cutting winds, most needed a lick of paint and some tender loving care. Snow-devils – miniature whirlwinds of ice and snow – whizzed here and there on the raised footpath as if they had minds of their own.

It was as desolate and unwelcoming a place as Miley had ever seen.

Dragging a suitcase that was both far too heavy and totally impractical for the terrain, David Dunnigan stomped up the street, his teeth chattering violently and two streams of snot frozen to his face. Diane followed him stoically, Miley bringing up the rear.

'I think we're in for a *long* few days,' she said ruefully.

The Hotel Faringen, like every other building in town, was constructed without character or artifice and looked like an office block from the outside. It was a small family-run establishment, and the trio were given adjoining rooms. Dunnigan refused to make any small talk with the girl at the reception desk, glowering at her comments about it being 'mild today' and how there should be a 'lovely aurora' later on. Rather than speaking, he simply scribbled his name and address on the page she gave him and paid in advance by shoving crumpled euros across the desk. The girl patiently took them and explained that, for everywhere else in town, the legal currency was kroner. Dunnigan grunted in response and stomped away towards the stairs.

Diane just smiled sympathetically and accepted the key they were given.

She and the criminologist had been in their room for three minutes when he rang reception with his first complaint.

'The room is too cold.'

'Is the heating turned on, sir?'

'It's not turned on enough!'

'If you give it a few minutes, I'm sure the room will heat up nicely.'

'If you say so.'

Five minutes later: 'Why is it still so cold?'

'Like I said, sir—'

'I have waited and I am still cold.'

'Maybe if you stand next to the heater until you warm up a bit? If you're not used to the Arctic, it can be a bit of a shock to the system.'

'I *am* standing next to it.'

'I'll send you up an extra heater.'

'Good.'

Ten minutes later: 'I don't think this heater works.'

'Mr Dunnigan, I turned it on when I was in your room a few moments ago and it worked just fine.'

'Then why am I still cold?'

Pause. Then: 'Perhaps if you eat something and have a hot drink?'

'All right. Could I have some tea and a ham and cheese sandwich with Colman's English mustard on the side? *On the side* – all right? Not on the sandwich. On the side.'

'Very well, sir. It'll be with you in about fifteen minutes.'

Twenty minutes later: 'What did you send me?'

'I believe you ordered a pot of tea and a ham sandwich.'

'A ham and *cheese* sandwich, yes, but … I mean, is this bread *stale*? And this isn't English mustard – it isn't even *Colman's*! What kind of a hotel is this?'

Knock, knock, knock, knock.

Miley opened his door. Dunnigan was standing there dejectedly. 'Diane says I can't stay with her because I'm an asshole.'

'She only noticed that now?' Miley said.

'Can I stay in your room?'

'Come on in! I'm listening to Chris de Burgh's *Spanish Train and Other Stories* album.'

'Not anymore you're not.'

'My room, my rules, asshole!'

Diane Robinson

Diane stared out the window at the frigid world below and wondered what had possessed her to come to this God-forsaken place with a man she no longer truly understood.

Finally, she decided she had come because the trip to West Cork had almost killed Dunnigan and Miley, and she was not prepared to stand aside and allow two people she loved be harmed (the likelihood of Father Bill leaping from a snow bank and saving the day here seemed slim).

She had hoped that the journey might do something to bring her and Dunnigan closer, that his struggles in St Jude's might have sated the desire in him to make amends for losing Beth, but if anything he was more distant, more distracted since coming home, and his behaviour with the hotel staff was the last straw.

It was as if he was going out of his way to be abrasive and unpleasant, and she simply could not stand it anymore. She wanted to help him find out what had happened to his niece – heaven knows, she was pretty invested in it herself at this stage. But she didn't know whether she and David Dunnigan would still be a couple by the time they returned to Ireland. If things continued as they were, she was fairly certain they would not.

In the meantime, Miley could spend some quality time with Dunnigan. For whatever reason, he seemed to find his most irritating traits funny and charming.

As she heard 'Lonely Sky' playing through the thin wall between the rooms, she couldn't help but smile. She doubted that Dunnigan was being so indulgent of Miley's eccentricities.

3

WHILE MILEY STARTED TO PLAY CHRIS DE BURGH'S
second studio album from the start for the third time, Dunnigan
rang for extra towels. He thought it likely he would be spending
more time with Miley than Diane on this trip, and while he knew
he should be upset by this, in truth it didn't bother him all that
much.

He was glad she had come because she was good at what he
thought of as 'the physical stuff' – she knew guns, she could make
bombs and she could fight hand-to-hand very well. Dunnigan was
no good at any of these things, and he knew it was foolish of him
to have gone running off to Donbro without that kind of backup
in place.

So her presence was welcome in that regard. What he couldn't
focus on just then was her moping over the emotional side of their
relationship. He couldn't devote his energy to such a triviality, not
while he needed to be thinking about Beth and Harry's father and
what they might find at the processing plant fifty kilometres from
this awful forgotten town.

With that in mind, he and Diane were probably better apart, at
least until he had this business wrapped up, and then he could go
back to trying to navigate the complex world of their romantic
entanglement.

Miley was unpacking his clothes, shaking them out, refolding
them and putting them in the wardrobe. While he did this, he sang
along to the music he was playing from his phone.

Miley was totally committed to the Chris de Burgh song,

putting what Dunnigan assumed were supposed to be harmonies to various lines. The criminologist thought it sounded cacophonous.

'Can't you listen to that through earphones? And sing quietly? Or, perhaps, just in your head?'

'Father Bill says music should be shared,' Miley said matter-of-factly.

'He's wrong,' Dunnigan replied.

'I agree with him.'

'I don't.'

'Well, my good friend, we will have to agree to disagree, won't we?'

'Maybe we could agree to some house rules relating to the playing of music.'

'This is my room, and the rule is that the music stays.'

There was a knock on the door at that point, and, still trying to come up with a compelling argument for the benefits of listening to music through headphones, Dunnigan got up and opened it. A petite dark-haired girl was standing outside, some fluffy white towels in her arms.

'Thank you,' he said, taking them from her.

'If you're in this room now, the manager says I have to check the heating,' the chambermaid said.

'Well, yes, that makes sense,' Dunnigan said.

The girl, who was dressed in black trousers and a waistcoat with an open-necked white shirt underneath, went in and, nodding at Miley, put her hand on the radiator and then began to fiddle with the settings.

'Um ... hello,' Miley said, turning the music off (to Dunnigan's delight).

The girl glanced up at him, nodded and smiled. 'Hello there.'

'I'm Miley.'

She nodded again and, taking a radiator key from her back pocket, began to loosen one of the nuts on the underside of the heater. She was perhaps five feet tall and very slim, and her skin was a dark brown. Her jet-black hair was loosely plaited, and she had chestnut-brown eyes. Miley thought she was the most beautiful thing he had ever seen.

'What's your name?'

'Oh – sorry. I'm Leeza.'

'It's very nice to meet you, Leeza.'

'Likewise. I think that's working fine. We've turned up the thermostat for the whole building, but if we crank it up too much, the other guests will complain.'

'Why, do they like being uncomfortable?' Dunnigan asked, deadpan.

'No, they understand the value of a good jumper,' Leeza replied and, winking at Miley, left them to it.

4

MILEY PERSUADED HIM TO GO TO DINNER IN THE
hotel's restaurant later that evening.

'The menu has pictures of the food,' Dunnigan said, as if Miley
perhaps had missed them.

'I know. I suppose there are people here who speak lots of
different languages, so this is the handiest way of making sure they
have all the bases covered.'

'None of it looks good.'

'I'm having the mixed grill,' Miley said, ignoring him.

Dunnigan ordered fish and chips. 'Hard to mess that up,' he said
to the waitress, who ignored the comment.

'Aren't you at all happy to be here?' Miley asked him when she
had gone. 'You've been like a bear with a sore head ever since we
got on the plane.'

'I want to get out to the plant and find Beth – or at least start
trying to work out what happened,' Dunnigan said. 'This is all just
… time-wasting.'

'And we will get there, but in the meantime, you have to eat,
and you are in an amazing place very few people get to see, with
your best friend and the woman you love. So stop behaving like
someone took your last Rolo!'

'I'll try,' Dunnigan said, and Miley knew him well enough to
know this was as close to an apology as he was going to get.

To Miley's delight, Leeza brought their food.

'Hello again,' she said, smiling at him and making him blush
right down to his socks.

'You are from an Inuit tribe,' Dunnigan said to her as she set down their plates.

The girl gave him an odd look, and Miley cringed internally – he wasn't sure whether or not his friend was making a cultural faux pas, but he figured they were about to find out within the next second or so.

'Yes,' the girl said.

'Are you from the reservation?'

Leeza seemed uncomfortable, and Miley was about to apologise and tell Dunnigan (who seemed to have completely lost the run of himself) to shut up, when she said, 'I grew up there, but I live in town now.'

'One of the reasons I am here is to meet your people and speak to your elders.'

The girl looked from Miley to Dunnigan and back to Miley again. 'Why?'

'I work for the police in Ireland, and I met a man called Kettu while I was working on a case there. He asked me to deliver a message to Showashar, your shaman.'

The girl seemed to blanch and looked at her feet uncomfortably. 'Kettu is dead,' she said.

'No, he isn't,' Dunnigan replied.

'I have to get back to work,' she muttered and hurried away, casting one last look back at the pair.

Miley followed her with his eyes until she disappeared into the kitchen.

5

AFTER DINNER (WHICH PROVED MUCH BETTER than Dunnigan had expected) he and Miley decided to explore the town. It was becoming clear to them both that Faringen was in the grip of an economic and social meltdown. Store after store was boarded up, and the dock (upon which they could only tolerate standing for a couple of minutes so biting was the wind from the ocean) was empty save for one very rusty tug.

Miley did find himself marvelling at the electric-blue icebergs that floated past, ghostly apparitions seemingly out of place amid the black waves. Dunnigan remained unimpressed.

'They're that colour because they're made of fresh water.'

'But they're pretty.'

'They're just very big ice cubes.'

'But they're pretty!'

The Faringen General Store was the only place still open at eight o'clock, other than the hotel bar, and they went in to get a few odds and ends they needed. Miley chuckled when the store's ATM paid out kroner when he put his card in.

'We're not in the EU anymore, Dorothy,' Miley said.

'Don't call me Dorothy.'

Dunnigan, to his delight, found some Colman's English mustard and added some fresh(ish) bread, some ham and a block of Swiss cheese to the trolley. Miley threw in Pringles, Snickers bars, a six-pack of Diet Coke and a bag of Haribo jellies.

'Do you sell Irish newspapers?' Dunnigan asked the grizzled man at the cash register.

'Do you see any Irish newspapers?'

'I wouldn't have asked you if I had.'

'Don't get much call for them.'

'English ones, then?'

'I get the *Daily Mail* maybe once a month. Usually by accident.'

'Would you call the *Mail* a newspaper?'

The man finished punching the prices of their items into his antique-looking till. Sighing wearily he said, 'Know what I sell more than anything else?'

'No.'

'Liquor and pornography. Want any of those?'

'Well, now that you mention it …' Miley piped up.

'No. We'll just take these.'

'There's the damage,' the man said, indicating the amount showing on the register's screen.

Dunnigan tried to count out the amount – he had never used kroner before – but finally gave up and just handed over the largest note he had.

'It's a while since I've been given one of those,' the shopkeeper said.

'What?'

'A hundred-kroner note. I usually only get these.' He held up a dull brown piece of paper.

'Scrip,' Dunnigan said, as if the man didn't know what it was.

'We call them scales. And I don't have change in kroner, so you're getting some.'

6

THE WIND HAD UPGRADED FROM A PIERCING whistle to a dull roar when they came out of the store, and they hurried back to the hotel, which was at the other end of the street and on the other side. They were crossing the rutted ice when Miley stopped dead.

'Hey!'

Dunnigan turned in irritation to see what had distracted his friend and saw, back in the direction from which they had just come, two figures engaged in a scuffle. As he looked more closely, he saw that one was doing most of the scuffling while the other was lying on the ice, curled into a ball.

Miley dropped his bags and ran, slipping and sliding across the uneven surface towards the altercation. The man on the ground was dressed almost completely in furs and Dunnigan realised he was Inuk. He also spotted (and probably too late) that the man kicking him was dressed in what appeared to be a police officer's uniform.

If Miley registered this detail, it did nothing to deter him, and he slammed into the cop and pushed him aside. 'He's on the ground and you've made your point!' he said, standing over the prone figure.

The uniformed man was a good foot taller than Miley, making him perhaps six feet four or five.

'Who the hell are you?' he demanded to know.

Dunnigan had arrived at this point and put his arm around Miley.

'We're researchers from the National University of Ireland,' he said. 'We've come to study the Inuit community – my friend here is very excited about having the opportunity to meet them.'

'*He's* a university researcher?' the giant cop asked, nodding at Miley.

'Why wouldn't I be?' Miley sidled up to him again, seemingly unmoved by the other man's bulk.

'We believe very much in diversity in Ireland,' Dunnigan said, pulling Miley back. 'Mr Timoney here is very well read in the field of crime and minorities, as it happens.'

'What's going on here?'

Dunnigan turned to see a rotund figure picking its way delicately towards them. Also clad in police garb, this person seemed to have the proportions of a bowling ball, set atop oddly bowed, skinny legs. A furry hat with ear-flaps finished off the ensemble.

'What seems to be the trouble, Officer Berinson?'

The huge man began to say something in Danish, but the newcomer held up his hand.

'Our friends here aren't local. Let's not exclude them from the conversation.'

'Jojun here was drunk again, Chief. I caught him pissing on the street outside the credit union. I tried to get him to come with me, and he resisted, so I was forced to subdue him. Then this pair decided to get involved.'

The chief bent down and gave Jojun his hand, helping him to his feet. 'Is this true? You know what I've told you before about public drunkenness, and I could lock you up for a month for urinating on the street.'

Jojun squinted at the policeman and said something none of them could understand.

'You know I don't speak Inuk,' the chief said, 'but I'm going to take that as an apology and let you go this time. Do you have somewhere to sleep? It's too late to make the trip back out to the res.'

The man slurred something incomprehensible and staggered off.

'I'm Fendarr Lorrinsen,' the chief said, offering his hand to Dunnigan and Miley in turn. 'Let's go and have some coffee.'

7

THE POLICE STATION WAS A SINGLE-STORIED building that sat between the library and the schoolhouse. It consisted of a lobby waiting room, two offices, an interview room and a pair of cells divided by carbon-steel bars.

Lorrinsen brought them into his office and poured them each a cup of something black that smelt awful.

'I received an email from an Agent Davies from Interpol,' the chief said, removing his hat and coat.

Dunnigan was surprised to see that he had a thick head of red-blond hair, long eyelashes and pristine porcelain skin. His nose was long and delicate, and gave him a thoughtful look, and his lips were full and almost feminine.

'He tells me you are here as a representative of that organisation.'

'I have information that at least two people from Dublin – an adult and a child – have been trafficked here to work at the processing plant,' Dunnigan said. 'I need to get out to see the place.'

'Yes, I have heard stories, of course, but in my time I have never seen hard evidence of any sort of corrupt activity. The plant is run by a man called Flemens – Gunder Flemens. I'll give him a call and see if I can set up a meeting for you.'

'Thank you.'

'Davies says the official line is that you're here to research the tribes.'

'We're going out to the reservation tomorrow,' Miley said.

'If there's something dodgy happening, I would think it more likely you'll find it out there,' Lorrinsen said. 'Most of the crime I see from day to day involves the fucking ice people. I'd watch my back out there if I were you.'

'Isn't that something of a generalisation?' Dunnigan asked.

'Not if it's true,' the policeman said. 'You've seen this place – Faringen is hanging on for dear life. When whaling was allowed freely this was a boomtown, but since people started looking down their noses at it and getting all touchy-feely, we've been dying on our feet a day at a time.'

'I thought whales were still killed in this part of the world,' Dunnigan said.

'They are, but the restrictions make it hardly worth our while. The plant processes blubber for oil, but the vast majority of that comes from seals. Last year 175 whales were caught by Greenland vessels and only five of them from out of Faringen. It's going to finish us if something doesn't change.'

'What does this have to do with the Inuit?' Miley asked.

'They're allowed hunt whatever they fucking well please to feed themselves. Most of us believe the restrictions on commercial whaling are an attempt to keep numbers up so the cunting First Nation Peoples can swan around in their skin canoes and take as many minkes as they like – you don't see inspectors checking on them. Our community is being choked to save theirs.'

'And you're observing these quotas to the letter?' Dunnigan said.

'We don't have any choice. We're here, eking out a living hand to mouth so our native brothers can continue to live a fucking stone age existence out in the ice fields, and what do they do with this freedom? They drink themselves into oblivion and fight and kill one another at every available opportunity – which is the only thing I like about them, because it saves me some work. Then they bitch and moan and complain that the Greenland government isn't giving them enough subsidies – money taken right out of the taxes the rest of us pay. It makes me sick.'

'That's what I've heard people in Ireland say about the Travellers,' Miley said, 'and you'll come across a similar complaint about blacks and Hispanics in the US, Aboriginals in Australia. I've had people tell me on a regular basis that individuals with special needs are a drain on the taxpayer's money too. It all sounds like prejudice to me.'

Lorrinsen poured himself some more coffee – neither Dunnigan nor Miley had touched theirs.

'I tell it like I see it,' the chief said. 'They're fucking evolutionary throwbacks. Sorry if it offends your sensibilities. I'll effect an introduction with Flemens out at the plant. But please remember, that place is the only source of employment for people around here, and it supports almost all of the other businesses you see in town. I don't know if the people you're looking for were ever there – but I do know we can't afford to have production stopped. Not even for a day.'

'I won't promise anything,' Dunnigan said.

'Somehow, I didn't think you would,' Lorrinsen said ruefully.

8

THE POLICE CHIEF'S PARTING SHOT AS THEY LEFT
the station was to remind them to check in with the local librarian,
who was the usual contact for academic researchers coming to the
area.

'If you're meant to be here for some university or other, it'll
look weird if you don't at least say hello to old Iorek,' he said.
'He's half-Inuk – luckily, it's the smaller half – and he knows more
about them than most people care to. He has pictures and books
and all sorts of shit about life on the res going back a couple of
hundred years, before it even was the res.'

Diane met them for breakfast the next day and seemed in
a brighter mood, and after they'd eaten, they strolled over to
the library to introduce themselves. The librarian was a short,
blocky man with a dense white beard and the lined, quizzical
face of someone who has seen everything. 'You're the three from
Maynooth,' he said, greeting them warmly. 'Haven't had any Irish
out here in a long while. You're welcome.'

'Thank you, Iorek,' Diane said. 'You have a wonderful collection
of photographs. Did you take these yourself?'

'Some. But there's prints here dating back to the early 1900s – I
surely didn't take them! These ones here are by Robert Flaherty,
the filmmaker from the twenties. He was going to make a movie
here, but the ice was too harsh for him, and he ended up making
his film in Canada. I think most of it was staged.'

'*Nanook of the North*?' Miley asked.

'That's right.' Iorek seemed surprised at Miley's knowledge, a reaction the young man was well used to.

'The ice here was too harsh?' Diane asked. 'Isn't ice just … well … ice?'

'That's the first mistake people make,' Iorek said. 'They've experienced a few cold snaps wherever they're from, and they might even have done some training with the military in Sweden or wherever, but it just doesn't prepare them for what they find this close to the pole. You have to have all your faculties about you out there. If you're a bit off, or feeling delicate in yourself, you won't stick it. You'll come back into Faringen shaking like a baby, or worse. We've had other researchers head off, and it doesn't always end pretty for them. What gets some people is the isolation. You're going to be near one hundred miles from civilisation, if you can call Faringen civilised. The closest proper town is Uummannaq, which has 1,300 citizens and is considered quite the metropolis for this part of the world – that's three hundred miles to the south of here, and that's where you'll find the nearest hospital. You're going to be living in an environment people aren't meant to be in – if we were, we'd have a darn sight more fur than we do. That can be scary. Last one of your kind came out – he couldn't hack it: went crazy after three months, started seeing all kinds of shit out in the snow fields. One mornin' they found him buck nekked, wanderin' across the glacier. He had to have three toes removed and spent a year in a sanatorium. I don't know if he's right in his head even now.'

'We'll be fine,' Dunnigan said, leafing idly through a book. 'I promise you, we're well prepared.'

'Really?' Iorek said, his eyes twinkling and dancing merrily. 'Well, let me put it to you that you *ain't*. There's these clothes, to start with – I bet you bought them in some hikin' store that caters for Irish winters. Fuckin' Gore-Tex or some such nonsense. You're leakin' heat faster 'n' your body can produce it. That'll get you killed.'

'Our gear is wrong?' Miley asked – he had been quite proud of his cold-weather outfit.

'We were assured this would more than suffice,' Dunnigan said testily. 'We didn't come here for fashion advice.'

'That's another thing,' Iorek said, jabbing at Dunnigan with his finger. 'I suppose you've spent a good deal of your life gettin' by on bein' just a bit of a dickhead, but that won't work with the tribal people. I reckon they won't even notice. There's no rules or laws on the ice. The tribes just sort of operate some basic ideas of how people should behave towards one another, and none of 'em relate to what you should say – they're all about what you should do. That's a little different to how it's done in your part of the world.'

'I think that's different to how it's done everywhere,' Diane said, glaring at Dunnigan.

9

'ARE YOU MAKING AN EFFORT TO ALIENATE PEOPLE or is it all just some horrible joke?' Diane said as they walked back down the footpath towards the hotel. 'That man was trying to help us, and you were unbelievably hostile.'

'We don't have the time or the money to get a whole new set of clothing,' Dunnigan said evenly. 'And we're being picked up to go to the res in two hours. We have other stuff to do.'

'They have clothes at the general store,' Miley suggested. 'Thermals and the like.'

'There's a factory outlet at the other end of the street,' Diane said testily. 'I don't think this is something we can afford to be flippant about.'

'You go. I'm going to review my case notes.'

'David,' Diane said, her teeth gritted. 'What bloody use are you going to be to Beth or anyone else if you keel over of exposure?'

'Get me a jacket, then,' he said. 'I don't care what colour.'

'Oh, suit yourself!' Diane said. 'Come on, Miley. Let's leave him to his files.'

Diane walked briskly away, and Miley, mouthing an apology to him, followed her.

Dunnigan was just crossing the road to go into the hotel when he heard shouting, and a group of people charged past him looking alarmed. Glancing about, he realised they seemed to have come from a narrow laneway about halfway down the street. Never inclined to follow a crowd, Dunnigan walked quickly in the direction everyone else was fleeing from and peered into the alley.

There, at the end of the narrow walkway, rooting through a dustbin like an over-sized dog, was a huge adult polar bear.

Dunnigan was utterly fascinated. The bear did not look in any way ferocious or even dangerous – he had seen far more frightening-looking dogs. It made snuffling, grunting noises as it nosed through the trash, and every now and again it stood up on its two hind legs like a massive, furry man.

'They're coming into town more regularly,' a voice at his shoulder said, and he turned to see the ungainly figure of Lorrinsen. He had a pump-action shotgun held at court arms. 'The ice caps are melting more every year. We can't fish for whales, so we fish for seals instead, and that's what the bears are supposed to eat. So they come into town looking for food, and that scares the daylights out of most people. And so it should. Y'know how they say if you leave them alone, they'll leave you alone?'

'Yes.'

'That don't tally with a polar bear. They're hunters, and they come in here to find food. On the ice or in the ocean, they'll take seal and porpoise and even small shark if they come across them. In town, it's going to be people they go for, cause that's what's here. So don't go following them down any dark side streets. Or you'll end up the meat course.'

Dunnigan continued to watch the animal.

'You should go on now,' the police chief said.

Dunnigan nodded and left him to it.

10

THE POLICE CHIEF HAD GRUDGINGLY MADE arrangements for them to be picked up by some of the local tribal people and brought to the reservation, and at one that afternoon they were waiting outside the hotel with their luggage. Diane and Miley were decked out in their new snow gear, which both admitted was remarkably warmer and more comfortable than the stuff they'd brought with them. If Dunnigan felt the same way about his new jacket, he kept it to himself.

One o'clock passed. The criminologist paced up and down the path, checking the time on his phone, looking left and right the street, going in and asking at reception if there were any messages for them.

Leeza came out and sat next to Miley. 'You're going to the res?'

'We're supposed to be. Our ride is late.'

'What time was he meant to be here?'

'One o'clock.'

'It's only twenty past. He'll be late when it's four o'clock. Do you have somewhere else to be?'

'No.'

'So what's the hurry?'

'Try and tell Davey that.'

'That guy scares me. Why is he so angry all the time?'

Miley laughed, glancing at his friend, who was now standing in the middle of the ice-rutted road trying to get a signal on his mobile phone. 'He's actually a really good guy. He's just … a bit *stressed* at the moment.'

'The hotel staff won't be sorry to see him go.'

Miley looked crestfallen. 'What about the rest of us?'

Leeza placed a conciliatory hand on his shoulder. 'My mother lives on the res, and I'm a regular visitor. If you're going to be out there for a while, maybe you'd have a drink with me or something?'

'Um … yeah … I mean … sure I would! Definitely I'd like to have a drink with you. Or something. Or anything!'

'Great. I'll find you.'

'I'll wait to be found.'

The girl grinned and walked off towards the general store. Miley sat back on the bench outside the hotel, thinking Greenland might just be his favourite place in the world.

11

AT HALF-PAST TWO THREE SNOWMOBILES CAME UP
the street and parked outside the hotel. They were driven by two
men and one woman, and the leader dismounted and approached
the trio.

'I'm Quin'ta,' he said. 'My cousin, Showashar, he says he knew
you was coming. I think he talks shit a lot of the time, but the
whole bloody place is waiting for ya now. We best go.'

Quin'ta was tall by Inuit standards, probably a little under six feet
in height. He had a broad, handsome face and very straight, very
long black hair. Diane took him to be perhaps thirty years old.

'You're late,' Dunnigan said. 'We are severely delayed now.'

'Sun don't go down till nearly eleven o'clock tonight, matey,'
Quin'ta said. 'Loadsa time.'

'I am here on very important business,' Dunnigan said sharply.
'I will not be kept waiting.'

'They've got a big feast going in the community centre. Lots
of bigwigs coming to show you honour. After the eating and
drinking and singing, there'll be a talk about why you're here and
how we can help. Won't start till you get there, and it won't finish
till you're done.'

'Please stop talking and help me to load up our bags. I am out
of patience.'

Quin'ta surveyed Dunnigan, looking him up and down with
some amusement. 'Well, you're gonna be a handful, eh, matey?'

With that, he punched Dunnigan so hard on the shoulder that
he sat down hard on the ice.

'Now,' Quin'ta said, turning to Diane. 'Let's pack up your stuff.'

Diane, doing her best to stifle a grin, went to help him.

12

THE INUIT VILLAGE WAS SITUATED ON A PIECE OF protected government land one hundred kilometres north of Faringen. The Inuit had lived there, according to Quin'ta, for more than a thousand years, so how the government could think they owned it he could never quite work out.

'But I don't reckon it hurts to let them think they do,' he said philosophically.

They drove across the tundra on the snowmobiles, Dunnigan perched behind Quin'ta, Miley behind an older man named Uumaq and Diane behind the woman, Aguta. Their belongings had been placed on sleds pulled behind them.

The ride was unlike any experience Diane had ever had, awful and beautiful in equal proportions. The wind was so loud it drowned out everything else, and even with her new coat and a balaclava worn under her hood, she thought her ears might actually drop off so numb did they become. Yet for all this, everywhere she looked she saw amazing beauty: the snow was a hundred different types of white, with the incredible blue of icebergs a startling contrast. Every now and then Aguta would point to something they passed which might be of interest: a polar bear and cub lolling on the ice; an Arctic fox standing stock still by a fishing hole; a hawk hovering above the half-eaten carcass of a porpoise something had left on the ice.

Looking across at her friends, she saw that Miley and (amazingly) Dunnigan were experiencing the same joy, their faces beatific inside fur-lined hoods.

They had been travelling for an hour when two vast trucks

emerged from the shimmering haze that came off the ice, their great wheels wrapped in chains to better cling to its surface. The sound they made as they approached was remarkable – a high, jangling singing.

Quin'ta signalled and the convoy of snowmobiles pulled over to allow the trucks to pass. 'Trucks running all day back 'n' forth, back 'n' forth,' he said. 'There's only one road in these parts – it was built so trucks and SUVs could travel from Faringen to the plant.'

'Will we be passing it?' Dunnigan asked. 'I wouldn't mind getting a look.'

'Naw, not today, matey,' Quin'ta said. 'We'll be leaving the road and heading out on the ice sheet in about five miles. You'll get there soon enough. Today, we see beautiful sights and then give you a bloody good feed, answer your questions.'

'It would really help if I could –'

But the Inuit had already revved their engines, and the little party were off across the ice again, making for the reservation and a meeting of the elders.

13

THE INUIT VILLAGE WAS MADE UP OF A HODGE-
podge of gaudily coloured government-built flat complexes,
mobile homes in various states of repair and quite a few tents of
varying sizes, all made of different kinds of hide.

Quin'ta led the train of snowmobiles to a cluster of new-looking
caravans and pointed to two which had been placed so the doors
faced one another.

'If you need anything let me or Aguta know,' he said. 'Maybe
we'll get it for ya, maybe not. But no harm in asking us, eh?'

Diane thanked their drivers and, picking up her rucksack, went
inside one of the mobiles and closed the door.

'Looks like it's you 'n' me again, roomie!' Miley said, slapping
Dunnigan on the back and following Diane's lead. 'I bags the top
bunk!'

When they had stowed the gear, the three Irish visitors made
their way to the community centre, which Quin'ta had said was
in the middle of the res and impossible to miss. He was right: it
was really just a big hall – no offices, no crèche, no café – just a
very big prefabricated building where the whole village met and
mingled. Gazing around its single room, Dunnigan could see that
various groups were gathered in clusters, each doing a different
activity. On closer inspection, it was the women who were being
active (setting tables, preparing food, laying out chairs) while the
men seemed to be lolling about, smoking, chatting and reading
out-of-date newspapers. In the centre of it all was a tiny man who
could have been any age from forty to eighty. He had a shrivelled
face of dark walnut, a shock of greying hair, tiny black eyes and
almost no teeth.

This was Tuntuk, the village chief.

As soon as Dunnigan, Miley and Diane entered, the place settled down to eat. Tables were laid out all across the big room, and food and drink was served to everyone. The fare consisted mainly of fish – grilled, fried, in stews, with rice or noodles. Most of it was pleasant enough, but the fermented whale blubber, which was served in a kind of a pickling liquor as a digestif, was a bit much, even for Diane, who had quite an adventurous palate.

No one seemed to mind, though, and the meal was a merry, convivial experience for them all.

Quin'ta explained to Dunnigan that the tribe were called the Inughuit, whom many once had described as Polar Eskimo – they numbered the smallest group of Inuit in Greenland and were fiercely proud of their heritage.

Tuntuk made a great fuss of the three travellers. Despite having very little English, he spoke rapidly in Inuktun and used sign language to let them know how pleased he was to have them as his guests. Dunnigan, who had learned a few words of the language while working with Kettu, still found Tuntuk utterly incomprehensible. Tuntuk, for his part, seemed to find Dunnigan hilariously funny, laughing every time he said anything and tousling his hair as if he was a cute child.

'Why is he laughing at me like that?' Dunnigan said to Quin'ta, who was on his other side at what amounted to the top table.

'You're the star guest,' the young man told him. 'You're expected to keep everyone entertained and happy. With all the noise in the hall, no one can hear that you're a miserable old bugger and that you haven't even tried to be nice. Anyone looking on will think you're the life and soul of the party. Tuntuk is doing you the honour of *pretending* you're good company. He's a nice bloke, is Tuntuk. A great man, really.'

For the first time in a long time, David Dunnigan felt a twinge of guilt about something other than Beth.

14

WHEN THE HALL HAD BEEN CLEARED A CIRCLE OF beanbags and cushions was set out and Tuntuk, Quin'ta and an assortment of Inughuit elders, all of whom seemed to be smoking cigarettes or pipes, sat for a council meeting. Dunnigan, Miley and Diane were given positions of honour to the left of Tuntuk.

The chief spoke for a few minutes first, and each of the three heard their names mentioned. Then Quin'ta said, 'Tuntuk wants you to say why you come here. He's already told 'em, but wants it in your own words. I'll say it again in Inuk, but I'll make the words as close to what you say as I can. Course, you got some words we don't got, but I'll do my best.'

Dunnigan told the story as plainly and simply as he could: Beth being taken, the After Dark Campaign, Harry's parents, the shoe, St Jude's, Kettu, Doctor Ressler and Benjamin, and finally the Faringen Processing Plant.

When he was finished, Tuntuk looked at Dunnigan and pointed to a grey-haired man in a huge fur coat sitting directly opposite him, the butt of a rolled cigarette pinched between his thumb and forefinger.

'This Showashar – Kettu brother,' he said. 'Showashar very powerful shaman.'

Dunnigan was not sure what to do or how to react to this introduction, so he bowed low, pressing his forehead against the carpeted floor, and said, 'Showashar, Kettu is my friend. He has asked me to tell you that he is well in his body and that he has been freed from a terrible devil. He is full of remorse for not heeding your warnings when he left Greenland as a young man.'

'You do us great honour by coming here, David Dunnigan of Ireland,' Showashar said – his voice was deep and rasping, almost a growl. 'When my brother left us, the omens were very evil. I saw red lights in the sky, and we pulled strange, misshapen fish from the ocean. I told him that leaving would only cause him pain and would bring shame on our clan, but he was young and he wished to find fame and glory. Instead he found pain and death.'

'None of which was his fault,' Dunnigan said.

Tuntuk barked something.

'You must be silent,' Quin'ta said.

'Kettu's boat was caught in a storm—'

'*Silence!*' Tuntuk shouted, and this time Dunnigan obeyed.

'My brother Kettu found his time of dying,' Showashar continued as if he had not been interrupted, 'but he tried to cheat the Gods, and they cursed him and locked him in a prison of bad dreams and evil things. We thought that would be the end of his story. But we did not know a warrior would find him and slay the devil and set him free.'

'Do you mean me?' Dunnigan could not remain quiet.

'But these demons were wily and clever, and they sent another after the first was defeated. My brother Kettu spoke to me from the other side. He asks that our tribe aids you. A great darkness has come to the north, but Kettu says you can fight it and bring back what has been lost.'

'What do you mean "the other side"?' Dunnigan asked, but no one heard him because the group were all applauding Showashar, who had now produced a bottle of cheap whiskey and was taking a generous slug.

'I have a prophecy for you, David Dunnigan,' the shaman continued. 'You will lose what was found and find what was lost – but what you find will not be what you thought you needed.'

A hush fell over the group. All eyes were on Dunnigan, who blinked at the old shaman confusedly. 'That doesn't mean anything,' he said, finally.

'Its meaning will be revealed to you in time,' Showashar said sagely.

'Thank you very much,' Diane said, elbowing Dunnigan hard in the ribs. 'You do us a great honour.'

Tuntuk spoke in Inuktun again, and Quin'ta translated. 'Our tribe has been dealing with the people at the processing plant for many years. We know the compound, and we know of the people who are brought to work there – the slaves. You will stay here with us, and we will help you.'

He said something else, and Quin'ta nodded.

'He tells me to draw you a map of where these poor buggers live. If you manage to get in, this is where you'll find them.'

The young man produced a piece of paper and a pencil from one of the pockets of his coat and drew a rough diagram of what looked like a small town. 'There you go, Mighty Warrior,' he said to Dunnigan.

'I'm not a warrior,' Dunnigan said.

'It's better than the other name you're getting called.'

'What's that?'

'You don't have an English version, but it more or less means "tiny penis".'

'I'd stick with Mighty Warrior if I were you,' Miley said.

When they got back to their mobile home, Dunnigan checked his messages and found an email from Tormey, informing him of both Brendan and Kettu's deaths. It was clear from what was left of both corpses that Benjamin had been responsible, although no one had seen hide nor hair of him since the events at St Jude's. He was also more than a little bit puzzled that, somehow, Showashar had known about Kettu's death before he had. He lay and stared at the ceiling, feeling awful for the two men who were gone, and wondered what it all meant.

Part Eight

THE WALKER
IN THE SNOW

1

DUNNIGAN RANG LORRINSEN THE NEXT morning, but the police chief informed him that, so far, he had not been able to secure a tour of the plant.

'Give me one more day,' he said. 'They can't really refuse – I'm the law around here, after all.'

'And that means something to them?' Dunnigan asked.

'How's things out with the snow gypsies?'

'We're being looked after very well.'

'I wouldn't get too comfortable if I were you. The second you do, they'll steal the lead out of your fillings to sell for hooch.'

'I'll call you again tomorrow, Chief Lorrinsen.'

'Don't bother. I'll ring when I have something.'

With nothing else to do, Quin'ta suggested he and Tuntuk take Dunnigan and Miley ice fishing. Diane, to Dunnigan's surprise, seemed happy to remain behind and work with the women curing some skins. Miley warned him that this might well be the calm before the storm.

'It's when she stops being mad at you, that's probably the time to be most worried,' he said to his friend.

Dunnigan just shrugged it off and followed Quin'ta to the snowmobiles.

They travelled to a spot about ten kilometres outside the village, and Tuntuk used a hand drill to expertly bore a hole in the ice. While he did this, Quin'ta was baiting a line that had already been equipped with seven large hooks. When the hole was complete and the slush scooped away to stop it freezing over again, the men squatted around it. Miley, who had brought a flask, passed around some tea.

Minutes crawled by as they waited in silence. Finally, Dunnigan asked Quin'ta, 'What do you call that sort of snow?'

Quin'ta translated what he said to Tuntuk, humour evident in his voice. The chief chuckled, then said something rapidly, gesturing at the ground, the hills and the sky. Quin'ta looked at Dunnigan and answered solemnly. 'He says he calls it ... snow.'

Miley slapped his forehead with his gloved hand, but Dunnigan shook his head irritably. 'No – Inuit have many different words for snow! Everyone knows that.'

'Aw, Davey, can't you see when you're digging yourself in all over again?' Miley said in exasperation, but it was too late – the game was afoot.

'Really?' Quin'ta was saying, reeling Dunnigan in. 'How many words do we have for snow then, according to all your academic pals?'

'I don't remember exactly – but I do know it's several hundred.'

Quin'ta appeared very interested in this nugget of information. 'That so? Well, what would you call this here snow then, matey?'

Dunnigan considered the clump of white powder he had indicated. 'Well ... well, it's sort of a snowdrift, isn't it?'

Tuntuk rattled something at Quin'ta, who burst into deep guffaws of laughter.

Dunnigan watched the exchange. 'What? What's so funny?'

Quin'ta wiped his eyes. 'He was agreein' with you. The Inuk word for drift is *qimuqsuq*. Tuntuk was just sayin' as how he couldn't think of the word. He doesn't use it very often.'

Dunnigan was beginning to smile himself now. 'So you don't have hundreds of different words for snow?'

'Naw. We got snowdrift. Snowball. Fallin' snow. Snowflake.

We sometimes comment on the snow gettin' compacted. Then of course there's slush and meltin' snow.'

Tuntuk stood up stiffly and began to walk towards the drift which had been the subject of their discussion, talking as he went.

Dunnigan looked quizzically at Quin'ta. 'What's he saying?'

Quin'ta was barely keeping it together – tears were streaming down his face again, and he was having trouble speaking. 'He just told me not to forget one important type of snow, which he is off to find.'

'What sort is that?' Dunnigan asked, genuinely interested.

Miley seemed to have worked out what was going on at this stage and burst into laughter himself.

'Yellow snow!' Quin'ta said, and collapsed in a heap, leaning against Miley, who was similarly in bits.

The sound of flowing water could be heard from behind the drift, from which a plume of steam was now rising.

'Never ... eat ... the ... yellow snow,' they heard Tuntuk saying in his laboured, broken English, and, despite himself, Dunnigan burst into a fit of giggles too.

Miley Timoney

Greenland began to weave a spell on him almost as soon as he stepped from the plane. His life had been a series of small rooms, of locked doors and stern faces. What struck him within moments of leaving the airport was the sense of space, of huge skies and vast pastures of snow. He found them terrifying but also achingly gorgeous.

He had spent his life feeling out of place, disenfranchised, never quite belonging. So why did he somehow feel this was a place where he just … fit?

He was grappling with the concept, turning it over in his mind as he lay on his bunk in the mobile home.

He began by admitting that he had never been truly comfortable in his own skin.

Every time he glimpsed a reflection of himself in a shop window he was surprised at what he saw because the image he carried in his head was so different: in his mind's eye, he was not 'disabled'. Yet he was painfully aware that if his condition was what he saw when he looked at himself, then what must others see?

Somehow, though, the Inuit looked at him with eyes that saw deeper.

From the moment he met the girl, Leeza, he had been conscious that his appearance was unimportant to her. She had talked to him, smiled, even asked him out, and had never once made reference to his being … unusual. He had been worried this was just wishful thinking on his part, but over a lifetime of being patronised, spoken down to and insulted, Miley had a laser-like ability to sense discrimination, and try as he might, he could find none.

It was the same when he got to the reservation: Quin'ta, Tuntuk and the others greeted him with the same respect – reverence, even – with which they met Davey and Diane. No one tried to dumb down their conversation, no one spoke too loudly when he was around and no one asked the person sitting beside him how he took his tea.

For the first time in his life, Miley seemed to have wandered, quite by accident, into a world where people were blind to disability.

And he was not sure he wanted to leave it.

2

THEY WERE ALMOST BACK AT THE RESERVATION, A sled loaded with fish, when Dunnigan's phone, which had a weak signal, buzzed.

'They'll see you at ten a.m. tomorrow,' Lorrinsen said. 'Don't be late.'

'I never am.'

'No, but those savages you've fallen in with always are.'

Dunnigan didn't know what to say to that, so he just hung up.

Leeza came out to visit that evening, and when she had finished seeing her parents, she found Miley, sitting at a table in the almost empty community centre, reading an old *X-Men* comic he had found among the magazines and newspapers.

'You like comic books?' she asked as she sat down.

'I like this one, yeah,' Miley said.

'What's good about it?'

'Do you know *X-Men*?'

'I've seen some of the movies – I like Hugh Jackman!'

'OK, well you know how the X-Men are mutants, right?'

'I do.'

'Well, a lot of people have interpreted that as an allegory of race – when the *X-Men* comics came out first in the 1960s, it was right in the middle of the civil rights movement in the US and England – Watts, Brixton, all that stuff. The idea of mutants, who were seen as different and were the victims of all sorts of prejudice, even by the government, that was a perfect parallel for racial unrest and the politics of colour.'

'But you don't see it that way?'

'Some of the X-Men are blue – Beast, Nightcrawler, Mystique – but you kind of know that the families they come from are all white. You don't actually see a lot of black or Asian faces in *X-Men*. So I struggle with the idea that it's a commentary on ethnicity. When I look at the series, though, I do see a lot of people who have grown up physically and mentally different from everyone else. Kitty Pryde, Storm, Rogue – these guys are from ordinary families, but they're marked out as different within their communities because they were born different to everybody else.'

'You see disability.'

There it was – so she wasn't blind, after all.

'Yes. Professor Xavier sets up a special school for these kids. There's an island off the coast of Scotland where some of them go to live in peace. In the Marvel Universe, the general population looks at mutants and is disgusted by them or afraid of them, so society's response is to lock them away.'

'And you understand that?'

'I do. I mean, I wish I didn't, but … well, there you go. Sorry for going off on one.'

'You don't have to be sorry, Miley. I get it too.'

Miley took her hand. 'You do?'

'Every time I go into Faringen, I know people are looking at me and seeing a filthy snow gypsy from the res. My tribe makes up one per cent of the population of Greenland. That's a small minority, no matter how you look at it. So, yes, Miley, I know very well how it feels to be marginalised.'

'I wish you didn't.'

'Me too. There are people in the village here who spend their whole lives among our people or out on the ice – they never go into town unless they absolutely have to. Others just get out of Greenland altogether. My father ... he left, and he never came back.'

'Your father?'

'Kettu was my dad.'

Miley suddenly saw the similarity – something about her eyes – and he knew her grief and her loss, and he sensed she knew his too.

They stayed like that, holding hands in the quiet room, as night fell on the Arctic.

3

QUIN'TA AND TUNTUK BROUGHT THEM TO THE
Faringen Processing Plant the next morning, delivering them right
to the vast gates just before ten o'clock (Dunnigan had nagged them
so much the previous evening about the necessity for punctuality
that neither man wanted to have to deal with him if they were
late).

The first thing that struck the three Irish was the sheer size of
the place – it took up several square kilometres of land and was
surrounded by high walls on every side. It was more like a military
compound than a factory.

The second thing that struck them was the smell – the stench of
burned fish hung in the air for miles around the place, and all three
found it more than a little nauseating.

'They're doin' everythin' you can do to a fish in there,' Quin'ta
explained. 'They're bein' frozen, smoked, tinned, rendered, turned
into dogfood, catfood, medicine, soap – if you can do it with a fish,
those buggers are.'

'Soap?' Diane asked in disgust. 'What kind of person washes
themselves with fish soap?'

'Dunno,' Quin'ta admitted. 'I just give meself a rub down with
snow now 'n' again. I don't think Tuntuk has washed hisself in
about five year.'

Diane narrowed her eyes at him. 'You're winding me up,' she
said finally.

'Had you goin' though, din't I?'

A door in the gate opened, and a tall man in an anorak and

woollen hat came out. He had steely blue eyes and was clean-shaven, the blue shadow of a dark beard just held at bay showing about his jaw line.

'You are the people Chief Lorrinsen called me about?'

'I am David Dunnigan. This is Miley Timoney and Diane Robinson, my ... um ... team.'

'The chief only mentioned you.'

'We have come a long way.'

The man seemed to think about it for a moment, then said, 'They can come. Not the Inuit, though.'

'Hey, they have names, y'know!' Miley said, very annoyed.

'Those are my conditions. Please come now, I am very busy.'

Quin'ta seemed unmoved by this, and Tuntuk was paying no attention at all, looking off over the ice with his back to the group.

'You go ahead. Me 'n' Tuntuk'll go fishin'. Pick you up in two hours.'

'We may be a lot longer,' Dunnigan said.

'You won't be, but if you are, we'll wait. It's a nice day.'

Dunnigan thought it was a bitterly cold and deeply unpleasant day, but he kept the opinion to himself. 'Thank you,' he said, and followed their host into the plant.

4

'I AM GUNDER FLEMENS,' THE MAN WHO HAD COME out to meet them said. 'I am the coordinator of our operations here in northern Greenland. We came here because the materials we require – the various sea-life we utilise for our products – are generally caught in greatest volume in the waters around this area. We wanted to get as close to the source as we could to ensure absolute freshness. We were lucky, as the government was happy to lease us a large tract of land on which we were able to construct the facility you see here.'

As he was saying this, Flemens was leading them to a small three-wheeled van. He took three visitor badges from the glove compartment and handed them one each. 'How about a quick drive around the plant, and then you can see some of the areas visitors have found the most interesting in the past?'

Dunnigan, who was sitting just behind their host, pulled Quin'ta's map from his pocket as they drove. The building the Inuit had called the Blockade, where he believed the trafficked workers lived, was east of their current position and, if his sense of scale was correct, about three-quarters of a kilometre away.

They passed towering freezer units, massive ovens used to bake entrails down to be turned into pellets for cattle, colossal tanks full of seaweed that would end up as agricultural fertiliser. One football-field-sized area consisted of a series of tanks of frigid water where Arctic char – the fish that had kickstarted this adventure only a couple of months ago – were raised from fry to adult fish.

'We process and sell the wild char too, of course,' Flemens told them, 'but for the tinned product, the subtle distinction in flavour really isn't discernible. Farmed is adequate.'

He turned the van sharp left, and Dunnigan realised they were reaching the spot where the slave quarters should be. If Quin'ta's map was right, it would be a large warehouse-like structure. He took his mobile phone out to take a photo.

A series of smaller bungalow-type buildings gave way to a sprawling yard.

'Those are all staff quarters – our managers and their families live on site for some of the year,' Flemens said.

'And your other workers?' Dunnigan asked.

The yard, which they could see clearly behind a high fence, suddenly gave way, and they found themselves gazing at a massive hole in the ice – it was as if an entire building had been airlifted away, leaving nothing but a crater in its wake.

'Many of them rent properties in Faringen and commute out here – we do operate a shuttle service – by plane and truck,' Flemens was saying.

'What happened here?' Miley asked.

'Just a little routine maintenance to some of our storage facilities.' Flemens smiled and then they were on to the next location on their tour.

5

'AM I RIGHT IN THINKING YOU'RE AN AGENT FROM Interpol?' Flemens asked them over lunch in a very nicely appointed staff canteen.

They were tucking in to some poached char, served with prawns in beurre noisette and baby potatoes, some wilted sea lettuce on the side.

'Yes,' Dunnigan said. 'We received information that some Irish citizens had been brought here against their will as part of your workforce. Trafficked, to be precise.'

'My gosh,' Flemens said. 'How awful. Do you have photographs of these people?'

Miley took a shot of Tom Gately from his pocket. 'Let's start with this guy,' he said. 'Tom is his name.'

Flemens studied the picture closely. 'I don't recognise him at all,' he said, 'but we do have a very large workforce.'

'He would have been brought here within the past year,' Dunnigan said. 'Could you tell me which of your facilities received a batch of new workers around twelve months ago?'

'We have a large turnover of casual workers, Mr Dunnigan,' Flemens said. 'There is a lot of seasonal work, and we have people coming and going all the time at all levels of our business.'

'OK, which of your units has the highest turnover?'

'I would say ice-packing.'

'Would you mind if we went out there and showed your workers this photograph? See if any of them recognise him?'

Flemens shook his head. 'I could not allow that, as it is a dangerous place and there is also the issue of contamination, food hygiene – that sort of thing.'

'We could suit up,' Diane said. 'I don't mind showering or going through whatever procedures you have in place – treat us just like your workers.'

'I have an alternative,' Flemens said. 'In one hour, we have a team coming off shift. You could meet them and talk to them and show your photograph about. Then I will make a copy of the snap and have it posted on all the staff noticeboards, and I will even offer a reward if anyone can give us information – what do you say to that?'

'That is very generous,' Diane said.

'Thank you. Now, who is for coffee?'

6

THE STAFF THEY MET COMING OFF SHIFT LOOKED to be primarily food scientists – they were dressed in white overalls, wore protective masks over their mouths and gauze caps on their heads and some carried clipboards. Dunnigan saw a mix of nationalities, but most of them spoke excellent English, and they were all happy to look at the photograph. They discussed it between themselves – there was some talk about it bearing a resemblance to a German marine biologist they had worked with a couple of years previously.

No one had seen Tom Gately.

'I will call you if I hear anything,' Flemens said as he unlocked the door to the outside world. Through it, Dunnigan could already see Tuntuk and Quin'ta lounging on their snowmobiles.

'Today was just an initial reconnoitre of your facility,' Dunnigan said dismissively. 'Tom Gately is one of the people we are trying to trace, but there is another, a young girl called Beth Carlton. She was sent here, we have been told, in the late 1990s, possibly early 2000.'

Flemens took a breath, and some of his charming façade slipped, momentarily. 'Mr Dunnigan – the allegation that we have illegal, trafficked workers in the plant is one thing. I will admit we utilise the services of several employment agencies from across Europe, and it is not unheard of that some of these companies behave unscrupulously at times. I am willing and able to help you address that, if I can.'

'Good,' Dunnigan said.

'But to add to this that we might be engaging in child labour –'

'I never said she was working on the floor,' Dunnigan said, his gaze now fixed on the man. 'It has been suggested that she may have been brought here to ... entertain some of your workers.'

Flemens glowered at Dunnigan, then at Diane, then at Miley. He looked beyond them to the Inuit waiting in the snow.

'You come here with a fucking retard and two savages, and you make these kinds of accusations, and you expect me to be all nice and helpful and say "yes, sir" and "no, sir" – get out of my plant before I call security and have you dragged out.'

Diane was leaning against the doorframe, and she spoke calmly and without moving. 'Don't make threats you can't back up,' she said. 'And if you ever use terms like that about any of my friends again, you and I will be having a whole different kind of discussion.' She began to walk towards the snowmobiles.

'Fuck you very much,' Miley said, and followed her.

'I'll see you soon,' Dunnigan said, offering his hand to Flemens – to his great surprise, the manager shook it.

7

TUNTUK AND QUIN'TA HAD BEEN WAITING FOR them for ninety minutes, and the snowmobiles were cold. While they allowed the engines to idle, Dunnigan wandered along the fence, following it for a quarter of a kilometre. Looking through the wire mesh he saw, through some low buildings that could have been storage sheds, a taller construction, seemingly made of better materials, with several satellite dishes and what he took to be a mobile phone mast protruding from the roof.

Just below this tower was an enclosure full of sled dogs (Dunnigan counted fifteen, and they had passed four similar packs during their tour). Flemens had said that, while trucks, planes and snowmobiles were used to transport people and materials to and from the plant, dogs were probably the most common and effective means of getting about.

As he watched, two workers came to the door of the enclosure with large buckets and fed the animals: their meal seemed to consist of a kind of gruel but Dunnigan saw what he took to be a seal carcass or some other kind of game tossed into the enclosure too.

He stood, both fascinated and appalled, as the huge animals fought and squabbled with one another as they stripped the carcass to the bone, leaving a gory pattern of blood on the snow about them. There were dogs out at the res, but he had never had cause to go near them, and Quin'ta and Tuntuk seemed to travel everywhere by snowmobile.

'Them dogs, see, people come here and think them's pets – but they surely are not.' Quin'ta had come up behind him. 'They're kind of a workforce. And we make sure they grow in a partic'lar way.'

Dunnigan turned to look at him. 'You mean selective breeding?'

'Yup. Every litter of puppies is gone through to get rid of any weakness, and puppies that do not show strong and fierce are drowned. Usually only one or two live on to become members of the pack.'

'I see.'

'Lotta Westerners don't like that. Think it's cruel.'

Dunnigan continued to watch the pack tearing the carcass to shreds in their enclosure, the ground about them a muddy red slush. 'It probably is,' he said, 'but if it comes down to that or dying out on the tundra because one of the team has had enough … I suppose I can see the merit in it.'

Quin'ta laughed and punched him on the shoulder again – this time, Dunnigan didn't budge at the blow.

'You're a strange one, Mighty Warrior. You ain't as soft as you seem to be.'

'Thank you for noticing.'

'The snowmobiles are ready.'

'So am I.'

8

BACK AT THE RESERVATION, THEY GATHERED IN Tuntuk's cluttered tobacco-smelling apartment to assess what they had learned and what the next step was.

'Well, the building where they used to sleep just isn't there anymore, for a start,' Miley said. 'How do you move a whole building?'

'It's not that hard,' Quin'ta said. 'You can't dig foundations in the permafrost, so most buildings are on wooden or metal pallets. Dependin' on the size, you can either bring the whole bloody thing on a truck or transport it in sections and just drop it in with a crane. Think of it like really big Lego blocks.'

'You think they just picked the blockade up and put it on the other side of the plant?' Diane asked.

'Could've. Or even outside it. It's a hundred kilometres from anywhere – no bugger's gonna run away, are they?'

'Flemens put on a show for us today,' Dunnigan said. 'He wanted to appear willing to help, but we only saw the parts of the plant he wanted us to see and we only met workers who would never in a million years be anywhere near the slave labourers.'

'He's not used to being challenged either,' Diane said. 'I think that little outburst at the gate was the real deal.'

'So what do we do now?' Miley asked.

'I need to go back,' Dunnigan said. 'Alone. It was a mistake to bring you two – he can refuse civilians entry, but not a representative from an international policing agency. I'm going to pull rank. I may give Davies a call and get him to bring a little pressure to bear first.'

'Haven't we warned them now, though?' Miley said. 'I mean, they know we're looking for Tom Gately – if he is there, won't they just drop him into a fishing hole or mince him up in one of their machines?'

'That's a possibility,' Dunnigan said. 'But we have to remember – they have hundreds upon hundreds of workers, and Tom will have been brought there under a different name, and probably doesn't look very much like he does in the picture anymore either. There's also a real possibility – and I'm sorry to point this out – that he's dead already. I think we have a little bit of time to make the next move.'

'I hope you're right,' Miley said. 'And I hope you're wrong.'

'So do I, Miley.'

'And what about Beth?'

'Our only hope is that there's someone who was around when she was brought here and remembers – or even has a sense of where the children are moved on to when this place is done with them.'

'That's a slim chance, matey,' Quin'ta said.

'I know. But I have to try.'

Tuntuk said something.

'He says if your faith is strong, that will give her strength too,' Quin'ta said. 'Your love for her, even from the other side of the world, will have kept her warm.'

'Thank you,' Dunnigan said, taking the chieftain's hand in his. 'Thank you, Tuntuk.'

The old man smiled a gummy smile and pressed his forehead against Dunnigan's. Diane marvelled at this – she had wanted so much to offer Dunnigan some form of physical comfort and every overture had been rebuffed, yet this strange old man seemed to be able to break down Dunnigan's emotional walls with ease.

'A cousin of mine, Oki, used to work out at the plant,' Quin'ta said. 'He was on the cleanin' crew, so he was all over the place. He lives in Faringen, but it might be worth our while talkin' to him – he might know somethin' that would help us.'

'You say he *used* to work there?' Dunnigan interjected.

'He got the sack.'

'Why?'

'The usual stuff.'

'What's "the usual stuff"?' Miley wanted to know.

'Drunk on the job. Stealin' supplies. You know. The usual stuff.'

'Can we believe him?' Dunnigan asked.

'He's an alcoholic and a thief. He's not a liar. I vouch for him.'

'That's good enough for me,' Miley said.

Quin'ta gave him a thumbs-up. 'Fuckin' A,' he said.

'Is that an old Inuit term?' Diane asked.

'You bet your sweet arse it is,' Quin'ta said.

9

THAT EVENING THERE WAS A STORY-GATHERING
in the community centre – Yura, one of the village elders and a
storyteller of great skill, with a store of hundreds of folktales and
songs, sat on a low wooden stool. The village gathered around her
as night fell, and she told them of Nukúnguasik and his brothers, a
great favourite of the tribe. Leeza was still there, and she sat beside
Miley, with Dunnigan and Diane just behind them, and whispered
the translation of what Yura said so they could enjoy the story too.

'Nukúnguasik had many brothers, and their clan had much
land and good waters to fish. When one brother made a catch,
he shared with the others, so they always had meat for the pot,
but Nukúnguasik was the best fisherman and the best hunter, and
he was the most respected warrior in his tribe. And so they lived
peacefully.'

It was warm and comfortable in the hall that night. With
everyone squashed in, Miley was pressed close against Leeza, and
he could feel the warmth of her and smell the soap she had used
to wash her hair. As the old woman wove her story, he eventually
heard only Leeza's voice as she recounted the tale, and the images
came to him like a dream.

'One day, Nukúnguasik rowed northward in his kayak and
he took it into his head to row over to a big island he had never
visited before. He landed and went up to look at the land, and it
was very beautiful. Down in a hollow he came upon the middle
brother, busy with something and whispering all the time. So he
crawled stealthily towards him, and when he got close, he heard

him whispering these words: "You are to bite Nukúnguasik to death; you are to bite Nukúnguasik to death."

'And then it was clear that he was making a Tupilak – a demon fashioned from the bones of dead animals – and he was telling it what to do. Suddenly Nukúnguasik took his hunting knife and held it before him and said, "It might not be so easy to bite this Nukúnguasik, for he is a fierce warrior!"

'And the brother was so frightened at this that his heart gave out and he fell down dead – for he had been a weak and cowardly man.

'Nukúnguasik saw that his brother had been letting the Tupilak sniff at his body to give it a taste of human flesh. And the Tupilak was now alive, and it lay there sniffing him and pawing at his skins. But Nukúnguasik, not being quite as fierce as he might have thought, was afraid of the Tupilak and went away without trying to harm it.

'Now he rowed home, and there his other brothers were waiting in vain for the middle one to return. At last the day dawned, and still he had not come. Daylight came, and as they were preparing to go out in search of him, the eldest of them said to Nukúnguasik, "Nukúnguasik, come with us; we must search for our brother."

'And so Nukúnguasik went with them, and they searched in all the places the brothers usually fished and hunted, but as they found nothing, the eldest said, "Would it not be well to go and make search over on that island, where no one ever goes?"

'And having gone on to the island, Nukúnguasik said, "Now you can go and look on the southern side."

'When the brothers reached the place, he heard them cry out, and the eldest said, "O wretched brother! Why did you ever meddle with such a thing as this!" And they could be heard weeping all together about the dead man.

'Nukúnguasik went up to them, and there lay the Tupilak, dying in the cold but nibbling at the body of the dead man who had created it. The brothers fell upon the demon and killed it and buried it there with their brother, making a mound of stones above them both. And then they went home. Nukúnguasik lived there as the oldest in the place, and died at last after many years.

'Here I end this story: I know no more.'

There were other tales that night, and singing, and some of the village children put on a play that seemed for all the world to be an Inuit version of Hansel and Gretel.

Later, when most of the village had gone home, Miley and Leeza sat side by side on a couple of beanbags.

'The story about Nukúnguasik,' Miley said.

'Yes?'

'What does it mean?'

'It is one of the oldest stories in our tradition. What do you think it means?'

'Well, at first I thought it was a version of Cain and Abel – one brother becoming jealous of the other.'

'Yes – in some versions of it, they make a big deal out of the fact that Nukúnguasik has no wife, and the wives of the other brothers have to care for him too. There is a suggestion they don't just wash his skins, if you know what I mean.'

'I see. I thought it might be that, but in the Bible version, Cain actually kills his brother – that doesn't happen in this one.'

'No. The brother is too afraid, and he has a heart attack when Nukúnguasik confronts him, then the demon he created eats him.'

'So it's a story about having the courage of your convictions?'

'It's about human frailty. The brother's demon – which could mean his flaws, his cowardice and jealousy – proves to be his undoing. And Nukúnguasik, for all his boasting, sails off and leaves the demon loose on the island, so he's a coward too. The story tells us that no one is perfect and that we all need one another to get by. Where my abilities are lacking, yours might be strong, so we balance one another out. Family, community, friendship – the three most important things for our people.'

'For any people.'

'Take your little gang – your Mighty Warrior is strange and rude, but he's smart and tough, for all that. Diane is fierce, and you have a great heart and people like you.'

'Do you like me?'

Leeza smiled and put her arms around him. 'I like you very much, Miley.'

As Miley was leaving the hall to go home for the night, Quin'ta beckoned him over.

'You and Leeza,' he said, speaking conspiratorially.

'What about us?'

'Do you have anything to report?'

Miley blushed a deep beetroot. 'She is a lady of your tribe and I am a gentleman,' he stammered. 'I would never ...'

'Never what?'

'You know!'

'Miley, my good, good friend! This is not the bloody dark ages! Things've changed here in the frozen north just like they have in the rest of the world. OK, when I was a boy they still arranged marriages, but these days the women are free to choose their men, and let me tell you, matey: *she wants you!* You must go to her room and be with her, or I will!'

Taking Miley in a bear hug, Quin'ta kissed him on the forehead and left him to his thoughts.

10

THEY WERE PREPARING TO GO INTO TOWN TO MEET Oki, Quin'ta's cousin, the next morning, when Dunnigan's phone buzzed.

'It's an email from Davies. He says I'm to go back over to the plant – they'll see me, but it's for today only.'

'You're going alone, I take it,' Diane said.

'Yes. It'll be OK – they know who I'm with.'

'That don't mean much,' Quin'ta said. 'People go missin' all the time out here. You don't need to shoot a bloke to kill 'im. Weather'll do it for you, if you're smart.'

'I'm emailing him back – I told him I'll check in every three hours. If he doesn't hear from me, something's up.'

'That's great,' Miley said. 'He's based where? London? I bet he'll be here post-haste, should make it in two days, tops.'

Dunnigan sighed. 'Do you have a better suggestion?'

Diane reached into her pack and took out a short, chunky handgun. 'I managed to procure this in Faringen,' she said. 'It's a SIG Pro 2022. Take it with you, please.'

'Diane, I'm useless with guns, you know that,' Dunnigan said, sounding not unlike a petulant child.

'The SIG Pro is really simple to use – there's no safety to worry about: you just point and squeeze. Even you can't mess it up.'

'I bet I can.'

'For fuck's sake, David Dunnigan! I've come halfway around the world to try and keep you safe, despite the fact that you've been nothing but rude and obnoxious for a very, very long time.

I have been patient, I have been tolerant and I have given you *miles* of fucking leeway, but I will *not* allow you to walk into the lion's den unarmed! Now take the motherfucking gun and say, "Thank you, Diane!"'

He took the SIG gingerly from her, as if touching it might infect him with something, and dropped it into his bag.

'Put it in your pocket before you go into the plant,' she said in a tired voice.

'I will.'

'Here's some ammunition. Make sure there's a clip in it.'

'Thank you.'

She suddenly hugged him close, and he didn't fight her.

'I hope you find what you're looking for,' she said.

11

FLEMENS DID NOT EVEN TRY TO FEIGN A PLEASANT attitude this time.

'We have inspectors coming tomorrow. You'll have to be gone by then.'

'OK.'

'You can stay in one of the workers' bungalows tonight, and I'll have one of our drivers take you into Faringen in the morning. You can make whatever arrangements you want from there – you won't be my problem at that stage.'

'I would like to see the ice-packing plant.'

'I showed it to you on your last visit.'

'You showed me a building. I met some educated lab technicians. I want to see the factory floor and the people who work there.'

'Like I told you, it's dangerous – there are health and safety issues.'

'I'll sign a waiver. Just get me down there, please. If you obstruct my investigation one more time, I will have an army of police officers down here within a week, tearing the place apart. You don't want that, do you?'

Flemens looked as if he was about to say something, but he restrained himself. 'Anything else?'

'Casual workers' accommodation. I want to see where your lowest-paid staff members eat and sleep. I will be needing to interview some of them, and I'll choose who they are, not you.'

The manager studied his fingernails for a moment. 'Very well. It doesn't look like I have much choice.'

'You don't.'

'Let's go to ice-packing, then,' Flemens said. 'You'd best get suited up. You think you've experienced cold? Where we're going, it's *really* cold.'

12

OKI DID NOT LOOK LIKE QUIN'TA AT ALL. HE WAS short to the point of dwarfish and was built like a barrel. His dark hair had shafts of red running through it, and his cousin seemed to find this very funny and kept suggesting he might have some Irish in him – Oki was half-Inuit (his mother was Norwegian), so it may have been possible somewhere down his genetic line.

When Diane, Miley and Quin'ta met him at the hotel bar the little man seemed to have been there for a while already, as his cheeks were rosy beneath their natural weathering, and his speech was slightly slurred.

'I know they were in their rights to fire me,' he said, 'but if you put aside my bein' drunk on the job, and robbin' some overalls and some tools and a coupla tyres and a keg of heatin' oil and a snowmobile, I was a pretty good worker. You gotta give a man some elbow room in matters like this, don't ya, Sarah?'

He kept calling Diane 'Sarah', for reasons best known to himself.

'I'm sure they were very unreasonable in their treatment of you,' Diane said.

'Bastards,' Miley said sympathetically. 'Didn't know what they were throwing away.'

'You were a liability, Red,' Quin'ta said. 'And you bloody well know it!'

'Can you tell us anything about workers being shipped in from out of town?' Diane asked. 'We're looking for a couple of Irish people who we believe were abducted.'

'You're talkin' about the foreigners,' Oki said, motioning to the barmaid for another drink (he was drinking schnapps, which Diane thought was awful stuff).

'Yes. What do you know about them?'

'They kept to 'emselves, most of the time,' Oki said. 'Mostly 'cause they were put doin' all the crap hours and the shittiest, dirtiest, messiest jobs.'

'But you did see them?'

'Aw, yeah. Wasn't pals with 'em or nothin'. But they'd be around when I was washin' down the guttin' rooms. They work strippin' back the whale carcasses: hang 'em up on a bloody great hook in this refrigerated warehouse and use scaffolding to stand on as they cut off the blubber and meat, remove the liver and heart and such. Horrible bloody job.'

'Did you ever see any kids?' Miley asked him.

'What, out at the plant?'

'Yeah.'

'No. They don't got no kids out there.'

'Any Irish workers?' Diane asked.

'Could be. I wouldn't know for sure.'

'But these casual workers are definitely out there?'

'They come and they go. I don't know how long they keep 'em around, but when there's a whale or two in, or when the mackerel are runnin', they need a lot of hands to the pump, and that's when you see 'em.'

'Do you know how much they get paid?'

'Not much, I reckon.'

'Do they get paid?'

'Does anyone out at that place? It's all scrip, isn't it?'

'But do you think these workers even get that?'

Oki drained his glass and Diane got him another. 'Look, Sarah, even if they do get somethin' – let's say they pay 'em a few kroner worth of scrip – it don't amount to nothin'! They never leave the plant, and if they ship 'em off someplace else, they can't spend it when they get there. You're askin' me if there's slaves workin' out at the processin' plant?'

'That's what I'm asking you,' Diane said.

'Then I'm sayin' yes, there is,' Oki said. 'And there ain't a damn thing anyone can do about it.'

13

THE ICE-PACKING PLANT WAS LIKE HELL IF THE infernal flames had been replaced by gusts of freezing cold. Crystals of ice danced in the air, and great mountains of frozen shards sat all around. Men and women in orange overalls, rubber gloves on their hands and plastic coverings over their wellington boots shovelled the stuff into crates filled with fish of various kinds, and other men and women used their gloved hands to spread it over the top of the seafood, making sure everything was satisfactorily covered.

Dunnigan walked up and down the lines of workers, trying to see if any of them bore even a passing resemblance to Tom Gately, but none did. He showed the photograph as he went, but everyone simply shook their heads and went back to their work. Flemens marched right behind him, smiling at each member of the packing team in turn.

Dunnigan wondered if a smile, accompanied by no words, could be interpreted as threatening, and decided it depended on how well you knew the person delivering said smile.

Outside the freezer was a series of man-made ponds where squid and other cephalopods were kept alive while they awaited whatever treatment was required before being bottled or tinned. Two workers were in charge of each pool, checking the temperatures, making sure the water was clean and feeding the animals while they passed the time before their summary executions.

The workers on the pools and the staff in the freezer all looked painfully thin, dark-eyed and haggard.

'Seen enough?' Flemens asked.

'The sleeping quarters?'

'Of course.'

He was brought to a dormitory-type room lined with low beds. Most had people in them, all asleep. He noted that they were of mixed gender. 'When do these workers start their next shift?'

'Seven tonight.'

'I'd like to speak with them before they do.'

Flemens nodded. 'I'll take you to the breakfast room. You can wait there, unless you have something else you'd like to do?'

'I can wait,' Dunnigan said.

'As can I,' Flemens replied.

14

DIANE, MILEY AND QUIN'TA LEFT OKI TO HIS
schnapps and walked out to the street.

'What do we do now?' Miley asked.

'I'm inclined to go out to the plant,' Diane said. 'I'm really
worried about Davey.

'No point,' Quin'ta said. 'We wouldn't get in.'

'I've never let that stop me before,' Diane replied.

'What would you do once you got inside?' he asked her. 'They've
got a bloody army of security, and Mighty Warrior might not be
in any danger at all. It could be us who kick off a bloody row.'

Diane was thinking about this when their discussion was rudely
interrupted.

'I need to talk to you lot!' Berinson, the massive police deputy,
was stalking across the street towards them.

'What can we do for you, Officer?' Quin'ta asked, but before he
got a chance to say anything else, the giant had smashed his shovel-
like fist directly into his face.

Quin'ta went over like a tree that had just been felled.

Diane did not pause to take in what had happened and just
drove her boot into Berinson's genitals, causing him to gasp and
crumple over.

'Run, Miley,' she hissed. 'Make for the res and don't look back.
Get help!'

Miley did not need to be told twice. He dropped to his knees,
found the keys to the snowmobile in Quin'ta's pocket and slipped
and slid to where they had parked. He had never driven one of

these machines, but he had watched the Inuit do so often enough. He was thrilled and relieved to hear it roar into life, and he skidded out onto the ice-bound street. From the corner of his eye, he saw Diane trying to pull Quin'ta to his feet, the man, blood streaming down his face, swaying as if drunk. Miley noted Berinson was still on his side, clutching himself, but then he was past them and heading for the road that led out of town to the tundra.

The wind whipped him in the face and blew his hair back, and he suddenly realised he had no idea how to navigate the wilderness that lay between the town and the Inuit village. There was no compass on the dashboard of the vehicle – he knew he should be travelling north, but north was a big place.

And did he have enough petrol?

He gunned the engine and wondered if he was wrong to be considering such practicalities when he was on a rescue mission – shouldn't he be planning a jailbreak rather than worrying about the fact that he hadn't peed before leaving the hotel? He turned a corner in the narrow road and drove headlong into a police cruiser that was parked right across his path, sending him over the handlebars, across the bonnet and into the snow on the other side.

The last thing he saw was the round, slightly feminine face of Police Chief Lorrinsen smiling down at him. Then everything went black and he knew no more for a time.

15

THE INTERVIEWS WITH THE WORKERS WERE A complete waste of time. Few spoke English, and many waited for him to finish with his first question, then simply stood and walked away without saying a word.

They were all emaciated and dressed in ludicrously flimsy clothes (despite being inside, Dunnigan still wore his coat and several layers of jumpers and T-shirts, not to mention two thermal vests). One woman, who looked at him with hollow blue eyes, appeared to have the beginnings of frostbite on two of her fingers, which were blistered and black.

He spent an hour trying to get any of them to talk, shoving the photograph of Tom Gately under their noses, asking if they had ever seen any children at the plant, all to no avail. Flemens might not have been present this time, but he might as well have been – Dunnigan could see that these people were terrified.

When he knew there was no point in continuing, he went in search of the manager.

'You are clocking off for the evening?' Flemens said.

'Could you show me to my quarters, please?'

'Out the door, straight up the avenue, first right, third house on your left. The door is open.'

Dunnigan thanked him and followed the directions to one of the bungalows he had seen on the tour. Inside was spartan in the extreme – a small living room with a TV that only showed Nordic news channels and MTV Europe, a kitchen with a two-ring electric stove, a toilet and shower room and a bedroom that fit a single bed and little else. Tired from the disappointments of the day, he showered, got under the covers and sent Davies an email to let him know he was still at the plant and in one piece. Before drifting off to sleep he read some H.P. Lovecraft short stories on his phone.

Five hours later he was awoken by someone shaking him. His immediate response was to think it was Diane, then he remembered where he was and that he had gone to bed alone, and he fumbled for the light switch.

'Please, I do not wish to frighten you!'

Finding the lamp, Dunnigan saw his house guest was the woman with the frostbitten fingers. She was dressed in the same stained orange overalls he had seen on the other workers earlier, and she looked scared to death.

'What do you want?' Dunnigan said, sitting on the edge of the bed.

'You show me a photograph of Claude.'

'His name is Tom, Tom Gately.'

'Here, they call him Claude.'

'He is Irish.'

'I think so, yes.'

'You know where he is?'

'He guts the fish.'

'Can you show me?'

She looked about her, as if she was sure someone would rush in and attack her. 'You are police?'

'Yes.'

'I want to go home. I had a son. I had a husband. Can you help me find them?'

'I don't know,' Dunnigan said. 'But if you bring me to Tom, I promise you that I will take you both out of here with me tonight.'

'They will not allow me to leave,' she said. 'They say they own me. I have to work off my debt to them.'

'As of now, it's paid,' Dunnigan said, pulling on his snow trousers and reaching for his coat. 'What's your name?'

'I used to be called Urte. Here, I am Matilde.'

He reached out his hand. 'Take me to Tom, Urte, and then we'll all three of us go home.'

16

MILEY WOKE TO FIND HIMSELF STRETCHED OUT ON a cot in one of the cells in Faringen's police station. His head hurt and he felt giddy and nauseous, so he just lay where he was for a while, trying to get a sense of his situation.

Diane was sitting cross-legged on the floor, her eyes closed, as if she was meditating. He could see Quin'ta, blood dried onto his face, slumped on the cot in the cell adjoining theirs, and was pleased to see he was awake.

'Hey,' he said, and Quin'ta turned.

'Hello, matey. Good to have ye back.'

'Where's the Jolly Green Giant?'

'In the bathroom putting ice on his balls, would be my guess,' Quin'ta said.

Lorrinsen waddled in. 'Hello,' he said, smiling beatifically at them. 'Are we all comfortable this evening?'

Nobody said anything. Diane did not get up, but she opened her eyes and watched him.

'Not feeling very talkative, eh? Well, I'll talk and you listen. You are in some pretty serious trouble. A situation has developed this afternoon, and it's not good.'

'What kind of situation?' Miley asked.

'A crime has been committed,' Lorrinsen continued, 'and we have reason to believe you three might have some information to share with us about it.'

'We don't know anything about any crime,' Diane said.

'Oh, I think you do,' the chief replied.

'I want to speak to the Irish ambassador, and I am not saying one more fucking word until I do,' Diane said, closing her eyes again. 'Now waddle off and ring the embassy.'

'We are a little beyond that,' Lorrinsen said. 'There has been a murder.'

Miley felt a sense of dread creep into his gut. 'Who's been murdered?' he asked. 'And why do you think we know anything about it?'

The police chief laughed and pulled a chair up so he was sitting in front of the cells. He wagged a finger at Miley.

'Why don't you shut up, my retarded friend, and let the grown-ups talk?'

As if on cue Berinson came in, limping slightly and very red in the face. He began flexing his neck and shoulder muscles – the joints popped as he slowly moved his head in a circular, swaying motion. Taking a key from his pocket, he opened a cupboard above one of the desks and retrieved a thick wooden truncheon from inside, which he swung in a few practice arcs through the air.

'Start with the Inuk,' Lorrinsen said. 'Let's see what we can learn when a little bit of pressure is brought to bear.'

Slapping the club against his knee, Berinson walked to Quin'ta's cell and unlocked the door.

17

DUNNIGAN HAD TO JOG TO KEEP UP WITH URTE,
who walked at such a speed through the maze-like avenues of the
plant that he became quite dizzy hurrying along behind her.

'We must get to the other side of the complex,' she said. 'Claude
works in the last building in the west wing. There will be security
at this time of the night, but I know a way in where we will not
be seen.'

It took them ten minutes to make the journey. She took his arm
and pulled him into the narrow space between the buildings and
the fence, and they walked about a hundred and fifty yards. Urte
pushed open a narrow window.

'Is lucky you are skinny,' she said and climbed in.

They were in a locker room that reeked of sweat and fish oil.

'Please to put on one of these,' she said, indicating a line of
overalls hanging on hooks.

'Are they clean?'

'If you walk in dressed like you are, you will be thrown out
right away and then we are both in trouble and you will not ever
find Claude.'

Muttering darkly, Dunnigan did as she suggested.

'Now, follow me and say nothing, please.'

She opened a door and the criminologist was almost blinded by
light.

The room was vast – the ceiling was perhaps forty feet above
them, and a spaghetti-junction-like network of conveyors brought
a constant flow of fish to line upon line of figures, gutting knives in

hand, who deftly removed their insides, dumping the viscera into troughs where water sluiced it away to be used in other processes in other parts of the plant. The only sound was the whirring of machinery and the sloshing of water.

Urte did not wait but began to walk at a great pace along the line of gutters, Dunnigan still being pulled along behind her. Down one row, up another, halfway down a third.

'Here,' she said and stopped dead.

Dunnigan was staring at the back of a tall person, hard at work on his station. 'Excuse me.' The criminologist took the man by the shoulder, turned him about and found himself staring into the face of Harry's father, Tom Gately: a thinner, paler, ill-looking Tom Gately, but undeniably the same man.

'I'm here to take you home,' Dunnigan said.

And then an alarm suddenly started wailing, and all the lights went out.

18

QUIN'TA STOOD TO MEET THE GIANT POLICEMAN, who barged into the cell and hit him three times in rapid succession on the right arm with the wooden truncheon. Diane, who knew what to listen for, heard bone break.

Quin'ta tried to protect himself by striking Berinson with his left, but the man grabbed his wrist and twisted it, then brought the club down on the elbow, breaking that arm too – it gave with a loud crack.

'Jesus Christ, stop, for the love of God!' Miley wailed, flinging himself against the bars, tears streaming down his face. 'What do you want to know? Tell me what we're supposed to say!'

'Ah, the half-man has had enough already,' Lorrinsen said, still sitting in his chair observing them. 'Officer Berinson is very thorough, is he not? He used to be Särskilda – do you know what that is?'

'No,' Miley said, still sobbing.

'Swedish special forces,' Diane said almost to herself.

'Please don't hurt him any more,' Miley said desperately. 'I'll say anything. Just leave him alone.'

'You're no good to me, my simple friend.' Lorrinsen grinned. 'I don't think your testimony will stand up in court, and let's be honest, no one would believe you had it in you to hurt someone, let alone kill them.' He grinned at Diane. 'Her, though. She's a different matter. Ex-soldier. Medical training. History of mental illness ...'

'Been checking up on me, I see,' Diane said.

'Isn't it wonderful what you can do from the comfort of your office, even in a place as remote as this?' The chief smirked.

'What crime am I supposed to be guilty of?'

'The vicious murder of a love rival.'

'You what?'

'You and the skinny detective, you're an item, aren't you?'

'If you could call it that.'

'What would a woman with your skills and talents do if, out on the ice, your sweetheart was to have his head turned by a native girl? It's been known to happen. Now, you add to that the fact that it's not so unusual for researchers to go a bit nuts out there in the wilds, and I think we have our case solved.'

'You're off your head,' Diane said.

'Which native girl?' Miley suddenly asked.

'I am not agreeing to anything,' Diane said. 'I would like to make a phone call, please.'

'Which girl has been killed?' Miley asked a second time, his voice high-pitched with anxiety.

'Little Leeza from the hotel.' Lorrinsen's voice was full of regret. 'We suspect her dalliance with Mr Dunnigan might have begun when he stayed there. It was bound to happen – he knew her father back in Ireland before that man's unfortunate demise.'

'*No!*' Quin'ta roared and charged into Berinson, who tumbled through the open door of the cell onto the floor of the office.

Quin'ta tried to headbutt him, but the cop drove the narrow end of the club into his attacker's eye, blinding him, and then dealt him a ferocious blow across the temple. Quin'ta slumped onto his side, his skull fractured.

'You bastards!' Miley was on his knees, gripping the bars as if he was trying to bend them, his knuckles white. 'I am going to fucking kill you!'

'I need a signature on a piece of paper, Ms Robinson, and all this can stop.'

'What have you got planned for Davey?' Diane said, pushing herself into a standing position in one fluid movement.

'Am I going to get my confession, Ms Robinson?'

'Fuck you, you fat, evil cunt.'

Lorrinsen tutted and looked at Berinson sadly. 'Take the mongoloid and tenderise him a bit.'

Berinson grinned and fumbled for the key. Diane shrugged off her coat.

19

DUNNIGAN, TOM AND URTE WERE BROUGHT TO
the locker room by a team of security men. Ten minutes later,
Flemens arrived.

'This is Tom Gately,' Dunnigan said.

'Are you?' the manager asked.

'Yes, sir,' Tom said, staring at the floor, his arms folded across
his chest. 'Or I was, once.'

'You are down on our books as Claude Maes, a Belgian national.'

'I'm Irish, sir. I don't even speak French.'

'You have come to our plant under false papers, then?'

'Not by his choosing,' Dunnigan said. 'This is the man I came
to find. Can I please contact Chief Lorrinsen and bring him and
Urte into Faringen – I need to contact Agent Davies immediately.'

'Of course. I will arrange transport.'

'Thank you.'

'Could you take these three to the executive canteen and give
them something warm to drink while I make some calls?' Flemens
said to one of the security men and strode out the way he had
come.

They sat on plush seats and drank steaming mugs of tea.

'Harry is being cared for by a lovely family and is doing very
well at school,' Dunnigan told Tom. 'A friend of mine has been
taking a real interest in him – he came to Greenland with me. He
can't wait to meet you.'

'My wife ... have you found Pauline?'

Dunnigan shook his head. 'I'm sorry. The trail went cold in Holland. They're still looking, though.'

'I don't know what to say.'

'You don't need to say anything,' Dunnigan said.

'You saved my life.'

Dunnigan waved it off tetchily. 'It's my job. Tom, did you ever hear anything about any children being here?'

'Sometimes, yes.'

'As workers?'

'No. Sometimes, on special occasions, they bring in whores. It's like a treat. There are all kinds: men, women, he-males, she-males ... and sometimes kids.'

'Is there anyone who has been at the plant a long time?'

'A couple,' Urte said. 'Isaac has been around since the 1980s.'

'Thank you. I'll ask Flemens if I can see him before we go.'

They slept for a while and were woken by Flemens returning.

'Mr Dunnigan, you will travel in one of our trucks. This is Halbert – he will bring you directly to the Faringen police station.'

A broad man in a filthy anorak, his cheeks stubbled and his mouth obscured by walrus-like moustaches, waved from the doorway.

'Claude and Urte will be brought by helicopter to the hospital at Uummannaq. My company wishes to ensure they are given a full physical. When they receive a clean bill of health, we will pay their fares first class to wherever they wish to go.'

'I would prefer if they came with me,' Dunnigan said.

'Come now, Mr Dunnigan.' Flemens smiled. 'I feel partly responsible for their situation. Allow me to make amends.'

'I will be calling the hospital as soon as I arrive in Faringen,' Dunnigan said.

'But of course.'

He nodded at Urte and Tom, who seemed uncertain about this new turn of events, and followed Halbert out to the snow.

'Up you go,' the driver said, indicating the passenger side of the cab of his truck – it was one of the ones they had pulled over to allow past on their way to the res.

'How long will it take us to get to Faringen in one of these?' Dunnigan wanted to know.

'An hour and a half, maybe. It's not like there's a lot of other traffic.'

Two workers pushed open the vast gates and, snow falling heavily, they turned out onto the ice.

'Mind if I turn on the radio?' Halbert asked.

'Yes.'

'Oh, you're a card, aren't you?'

Patsy Cline came on, singing 'I Fall to Pieces'. Halbert sang along. Dunnigan tried to sleep. He dreamed about being in a boat, trying to get to an island that always seemed to be further and further away, no matter how hard he rowed. Somewhere, in the distance, he could hear whispering.

'Rise 'n' shine, sleepyhead!'

He didn't know how long he'd been asleep. The truck had stopped and Halbert was grinning at him. The snow fell so hard outside, he couldn't see anything through the windows.

'Are we here?'

Glen Campbell was signing now: 'Wichita Lineman'.

'This is your stop.'

'Thank you.'

He pushed open the door and climbed down. The wind seemed terribly strong – usually, the buildings in Faringen's only street created some kind of shelter. The truck pulled away, and Dunnigan tried to get his bearings. He couldn't see more than a few feet in front of him but started to walk towards where he thought the police station should be. He staggered on for what felt like five or six minutes and found that the snow was getting deeper and deeper, so he turned and walked back the way he'd come. The tracks of the truck were almost covered up by drifts, and he could not remember ever being so cold in his life.

He knew, suddenly and in a moment of utter clarity, that Halbert had let him out in the middle of the tundra – miles from either the plant or the town.

He pulled the phone from his pocket – he had one bar of coverage. He took his hand from his heavy glove and tried to punch the touch-screen to make a call but his fingers were too frozen to function. He tugged the glove back on and tried to think what to do.

Just as he was about to give up hope, he thought he saw two lights coming through the gloom. He held his hand above his eyes to shelter them from the blizzard and squinted against the onslaught. Coming towards him through the snow was an SUV, complete with thick snow tyres and chains.

With the last strength he could muster, Dunnigan jumped up and down and waved his arms. The vehicle swerved slightly towards him, then came to a halt. He half-ran, half-fell to the door, which was pushed open, warmth and light spewing out of it.

'Thank … God!' Dunnigan said, his teeth clacking together so loudly he could barely get the words out.

'Peekaboo, I see you!' came a familiar, gurgling voice from inside, and Dunnigan saw that Ressler was at the wheel and Benjamin, still wearing his blue jumpsuit, a scarf wrapped loosely around his neck the only compromise for the cold, was beside him.

The freezing man pushed himself away from the Range Rover, lunging desperately into the snow and the darkness, but he could hear Benjamin's whooping laughter as he leapt from the vehicle and scuttled after him.

'I want my dog back,' he said, as his hands closed around Dunnigan's hair and began to drag him back towards Ressler. 'But we need to have a talk with you first.'

Part Nine

FINDING YOUR TRIBE

1

BERINSON OPENED THE CELL DOOR AND MADE A grab for Miley, but Diane kicked his arm in a movement that looked slow and easy, but which he seemed completely unable to avoid, and popped it out of its socket.

'You bitch!' He tried to swing the club, but was unable to do so now.

Miley, a red mist descending on his vision, smashed his elbow into the huge man's throat, causing him to choke, and Diane swept his legs from under him. He went down, cracking his skull off the edge of the bunk, and landed with his head at an awkward angle. He did not move again.

Turning, Miley saw that Lorrinsen was holding a shotgun.

'Bravo,' the police chief said. 'That really was very impressive. I've seen him take down three big men without breaking a sweat.'

The shotgun boomed, and Diane was flung against the wall of the cell.

Miley screamed for all he was worth, cowering in the corner despite himself.

'Don't worry, little man. I just winged her. I still need someone to stand trial.'

Diane's shoulder was a mess of flesh and shredded material. She raised her head and grinned at the fat policeman. 'Shit. You've shot me in my writing arm.'

He raised the gun again, but before he had a chance to shoot, something came flying through the door and embedded itself in his wrist. Miley blinked, unsure what he was seeing, and realised it was a small axe. Wailing, Lorrinsen dropped the gun and tried to pry the projectile out.

As he did so, Tuntuk walked casually in. 'I take my friends,' he said amiably.

'You fucking savage!' Lorrinsen spat, finally levering the axe from the bone where it had stuck. He raised the weapon to strike at Tuntuk, but he smoothly stepped out of the way and, as if he were plucking an apple from a tree, snatched the tool from the chief's grip.

'One last time,' Tuntuk said, with enviable patience. 'Take my friends now.'

Lorrinsen roared and lumbered at the fur-clad chieftain, but Tuntuk slid around his body, grabbed him by the collar and used his own weight and momentum to drive him into the wall. Stunned, the rotund man staggered backwards and sat down hard on the office floor.

Tutting and saying gentle words in Inuktun, Tuntuk went to where Quin'ta lay on the station floor. He squatted down, still murmuring what Miley now understood were prayers. He touched the younger man's cheek, stroked his long hair and finally placed a hand on his forehead.

'Will he be all right?' Miley asked, already knowing the answer.

'He is gone now,' Tuntuk said.

Miley sobbed.

Giving Quin'ta one last look, Tuntuk stood and went to Diane and, to Miley's amazement, lifted her in his arms. 'Come,' he said to Miley. 'This bad place.'

Miley spotted that, while their backs were turned, Lorrinsen had fled. 'I have to go after him,' he said. 'For Leeza.'

Tuntuk paused for a second, then nodded. 'She you woman.'

'I think she was,' Miley said. 'I never got the chance to ask her.'

'She you woman,' Tuntuk said again, nodding at each word.

Miley smiled. 'Yes.'

'Go,' Tuntuk said.

And Miley did, though he was terrified and had no idea what he would do when he caught Lorrinsen.

2

BENJAMIN SAT BESIDE DUNNIGAN IN THE BACK OF
the SUV as they drove back to the plant, his arms wrapped about
him, his head on his shoulder.

He was cheerfully singing a song about going on a summer
holiday. Dunnigan had a sense it had originally been recorded by
Cliff Richard, but he wasn't certain – at that moment, though, it
didn't seem important.

'He has always loved the music, has my Benjamin,' Ressler said
as he drove. 'When I found him first, he was like a wild animal. I
believe that music has been instrumental in civilising him.'

Dunnigan glanced at the snot-caked face and remained silent.

They did not go in the front gate but used a smaller entrance
to the rear. Ressler made his way to the tower Dunnigan had seen
the first day he had visited, with its satellite dishes and phone mast.

'This is the penthouse suite,' Ressler said as they got into an
elevator. 'No expense spared, you know.'

'What are you doing here?' Dunnigan asked.

'All will be revealed,' Ressler said. 'You must have patience, as I
have had, as Benjamin has had.'

The lift opened onto a luxuriously decorated apartment: deep
carpets, a wide-screen television, leather upholstered furniture.

'Benjamin, please search our friend for any weapons, and take
away his phone.'

With deft hands, Dunnigan's pockets were gone through.
Ressler tutted as he saw the SIG dangling from Benjamin's hand.

'You surprise me, Davey. I do not see you as a violent man. But enough of that. Can I get you something to drink?'

'No.'

'I insist. You know my weakness for Scotch. I will not deny myself, and I do not wish to drink alone this evening.'

Dunnigan sat while the psychiatrist made their drinks. Glass in hand, he watched as Ressler sat opposite him while Benjamin prowled about the room like a restless animal, the gun still held loosely by his side, which Dunnigan found deeply unnerving.

'Here we are,' Ressler said. 'A long, long way from home, from work, from all that is familiar. We are at the ends of the earth, wouldn't you say?'

'I like it here,' Dunnigan said.

'I am heartened to hear that,' Ressler said. 'So many do not. Have you discovered the fate of your niece yet? Have you been able to follow the trail of breadcrumbs?'

'No.'

'You have not? Mr Flemens informed me you did track one lost sheep. Good for you, David Dunnigan. At least I do not find you completely empty-handed after all of your efforts.'

'Is Tom still alive?'

'What? The man you took from the gutting rooms? Oh, yes, we just gave him a beating and sent him back to work. He is a commodity, Davey. We are not going to do away with someone who has so much left to give us! That would be biting the nose off in spite of our faces!'

Dunnigan watched Benjamin as he ran the tip of his tongue along the glass of the windowpane, leaving a glistening trail in its wake. Dimly, he could hear the snarling of the pack dogs in their wire-mesh cage three floors below.

'After you and I crossed our paths, and you told me of your niece and what had become of her, I did some research on your behalf – I hope I did not overstep the lines?'

'No, not at all,' Dunnigan said, wondering where this was going.

'I spoke to some of my employers and they to the people above them and ... well, I won't bore you with the managerial hierarchy. Finally, we reached the top of the heap, and I had the very great honour of talking to Mr Ernest Frobisher. I believe you made his acquaintance?'

Dunnigan nodded.

'He certainly remembers you! He asked me to extend his regards and to say he wishes so much that he was here, but that his health really does preclude him from making any strenuous journeys at the moment. You understand – he is not a well man.'

'In every sense of the word,' Dunnigan said dryly.

'Ah – the rare flash of humour.' Ressler laughed. 'I admire that. You do not smile enough, or exercise your gift for the bon mots.'

'You were telling me about Frobisher,' Dunnigan interrupted.

'Yes, back to the business of the hour. I asked Mr Frobisher about your lovely niece, Beth. And do you know, he had some things to say about her.'

Dunnigan shifted on his seat. 'What did he have to say?'

'Well, you have always believed she was taken from the streets of Dublin by an opportunistic predator – in your version of events, this man saw the pretty little girl through the crowd and wanted her, so he took her. We both know from our respective fields of academia that criminals of this type are very, very hard to catch. There is no planning and no real thought behind it. It is a crime of instant passion. *Pow!* Just like that! In most cases, and please pardon me if you find this upsetting to hear, the child is killed very soon after the relationship is consummated.'

'That is the accepted wisdom, yes,' Dunnigan said.

'What if I were to tell you that was not how it happened?'

'I'm listening.'

'Mr Frobisher, for many years, ran a business which specialised in abducting children *to order* – if I am a gentleman who is attracted to a certain type of child – a little girl of about four years with brown hair and blue eyes, for example – Mr Frobisher's people would source that child. Your Beth was one of these. Our agent had been on the lookout for a girl who matched her profile for one of our regular clients, and he had been watching her for some time. Your shopping trip provided just the opportunity needed to take her.'

'If she was abducted for a client, how did she end up here?'

'Other procedures were needed to make such a commodity like your Beth viable – I have already told you of the services Kaiser Care supplied. In most instances, these methods worked, and the child, suitably malleable and conditioned to be obedient, could be sent to the client who had placed the order. Sadly, the conditioning did not work with Beth. She was too wilful, and she would not give up the belief that she would be rescued.'

'You couldn't break her.'

'Alas, no. And added to that, you generated a lot of media attention around her disappearance, so the decision was made to send her to a place where she would not cause too great a disturbance.'

'The Arctic Circle.'

'You can't get much further away than that, don't you agree?' Ressler laughed and got up to have another drink. 'This is where the untameable are sent – to the frozen arsehole of the world.'

The psychiatrist turned back to Dunnigan, his fresh drink in his hand. 'I want you to think about this, Davey. Your Beth would have been used by every filthy, inbred roughneck in whatever way they wanted. And no one, not a soul, would have given a fuck how hard she screamed.'

Dunnigan eyed the gun that Benjamin was now holding with only one finger looped through the trigger guard. He had done as

Diane had asked and made sure a fresh clip was in the gun before going in to the plant the previous day. It wouldn't take much to knock it from Benjamin's grasp. He seemed barely aware he still had it. Dunnigan tried to remember what she had said about the safety – did it have one or not?

'Mr Frobisher was very anxious you knew that before you died,' Ressler said pleasantly. 'Now, it has been lovely chatting with you, but it is way past dear Benjamin's bedtime, so I believe it is time to wrap up our evening's entertainment.'

'I have one more question,' Dunnigan said.

'One more, but then I really must allow Benjamin to have his fun.'

'Of course. Actually, it's Benjamin I want to talk to.'

'What?'

Dunnigan turned so he was facing the drooling man, whose tongue was still pressed to the windowpane. 'Benjamin?'

The mucus-wet visage turned to look at him quizzically.

'I know where your dog is.'

A grin spread over the strange face, and Dunnigan threw his glass of whiskey as hard as he could, and hoped for the best.

3

MILEY STOOD IN THE MIDDLE OF THE ROAD, THE snow falling thick and fast all around him, the wind coming in strongly from the west causing the flakes to fall in hard diagonal lines. He turned in a steady circle, looking for tracks that might tell him where Lorrinsen had gone, but the flakes were covering any markings as fast as they had been made – a fact that made his job both easier and more difficult all at the same time (there were no tracks for him to follow, but his own movements also left no trace).

Running wasn't possible, so he began to trudge back up the street. He hadn't gone more than a few steps when a gunshot rang out from his left, and he dove to the ground, rolling over and over until he was in the ice-clogged gutter.

'Come out, little man,' the police chief called over the roar of the wind. 'There's nowhere you can go now.'

Miley looked around desperately. He was hemmed in, and he had no idea where the fat cop was holed up. The mouth of an alley loomed behind him, and on hands and knees he scuttled backwards until its shadow swallowed him up.

'You should not be so sad about the Snow Savage,' Lorrinsen shouted after him. 'You think he gave a shit about you? His kind leave babies born with faces like yours out on the ice to die. What d'you think of that, Little Man?'

As soon as he was in darkness, Miley stood and made his way to the end of the laneway. The passage itself was a cul-de-sac, but it ended in a kind of T-junction, and Miley saw that one of the buildings had a cellar, the window of which was open a crack. He got his fingers in just enough to pull it fully open and squeezed through just as his pursuer waddled up the alley, his gun and torch held before him.

4

THE GLASS WAS A THICK, CUT CRYSTAL AFFAIR, AND as soon as Dunnigan threw it, he flung himself forward in an awkward rolling motion. The glass connected with Benjamin's arm just above the wrist, and the gun dropped onto the floor with a dull thud. The criminologist did an artless forward tumble and somehow managed to scoop up the weapon, coming to a stop with it held in front of him with both hands. He had no time to aim – he just squeezed the trigger and counted on luck.

An essential truth David Dunnigan had learned about himself very early in his time with the police was that he was an absolutely terrible shot. He understood the mechanics of how guns fired. He could appreciate the intellect that had gone into making them, and he could even see how some of them were quite beautiful, if you were into that kind of thing.

But what he could not do, for love nor money, was hit what he was pointing at.

His first shot went completely wide of the grinning Benjamin, and instead caused the window, which was made of reinforced Thermaglas, to explode outwards in a single sheet, which the wind caught in its fury and carried away instantly. This seemed to have little effect on Benjamin, who looked once over his shoulder and then back at Dunnigan – as if to say: *I believe you were talking about dogs?*

The window gone, the slavering of the dogs could be heard loud and clear, rising above even the roar of the wind. Benjamin cocked his head to one side, recognising something in the sound. Dunnigan took the opportunity and fired again, hitting him squarely in the stomach – this time purely by accident (he had been trying to hit him in the knees). Benjamin looked down at the bubbling wound for a second, then back at the window and the sound of the dogs.

'Take him, Benjamin,' Ressler said, keeping well back.

'Can you hear them?' Dunnigan asked.

Benjamin nodded. 'Mother?' he said in the voice of a frightened child.

'Your dog is out there,' Dunnigan said. 'She's been here all along – Ressler didn't want you to find her.'

Looking at the psychiatrist in pained disgust, Benjamin turned and in two galloping steps flung himself through the open window frame. The sound of the hounds falling on him, mixed with his howls of joy, reached a sickening crescendo.

Getting to his feet, Dunnigan fired in the vague direction of Ressler, who made a valiant dash for the elevator. By the time the criminologist got to the lift, the doors were already closing and the psychiatrist was gone.

5

LORRINSEN CAME DOWN THE ALLEYWAY AND stopped at the end, scanning both directions with the gun held out defensively.

He didn't think the retarded boy had a firearm – and he probably wouldn't have a clue how to use one even if he did – but he wouldn't put it past him to chuck a brick or a piece of wood, or even a snowball with a piece of shit in it. He'd been a cop for twenty years, and he'd seen it all.

The end of the alley was a clutter of bins and rubbish, some in bags and some just strewn here and there: he was always telling the fucking roughnecks who rented these houses, packed in like sardines in a can, that they needed to take better care of their trash, on the grounds that it looked like crap and was liable to attract all sorts of vermin.

Taking a tentative step forward, he moved aside a sheet of cardboard, revealing a patch of white/grey fur. Just the type the mongoloid kid had on his jacket. He jabbed the exposed area with the torch, hard.

'Come on out and take your medicine like a man, you fucking cretin,' he said, stepping back to give the boy some room.

In a rush of noise and motion the boxes and bins exploded outwards and the enormous polar bear that was sleeping beneath them crashed forward, decapitating the police chief with one swipe of its massive paw, then pounced on the twitching body and shook it like a rag doll.

From his hiding place in the cellar, Miley watched silently.

And smiled.

Tove Olssen

The call came to Uummannaq that the police chief in Faringen, the furthest outpost to the north, had been killed by a polar bear, and his deputy, a former soldier named Berinson, had slipped on some spilled coffee and broken his neck – all in the same night. While the police were immolating themselves, some kind of riot had been taking place out at the fish processing plant.

Olssen was the chief deputy of Uummannaq, so it fell to her to go out and clean up the mess. What she found when she reached the company town was so ridiculously complicated that she spent the next week trying to piece together how complete madness had befallen a settlement that had reported nothing greater than fishing accidents in more than fifty years.

She was not slow about admitting that she could not make head nor tail of it.

Three days after she set up shop in the Faringen police station, a kid who looked like he was on a field trip from school arrived at her desk, introducing himself as Alain Davies and claiming to be an agent from Interpol. He was in the company of a tall, lean man with a thick moustache who might have just stepped out of the pages of a cowboy novel. This was Chief Superintendent Tormey, from Ireland's Sex Crimes Unit.

Both men wanted to talk to the strange character named Dunnigan, who had refused to leave the Inuit reservation and had been extremely reticent about answering her questions, although staff at the plant claimed he had been out there firing a handgun and had kidnapped two of their workers on the night everything had gone to shit in the frozen north.

Tormey tried to explain why David Dunnigan, who seemed to attract chaos like a flame did moths, had come to her part of the world. It was a bizarre story, but then bizarre seemed to be the flavour of the month in Faringen.

She put Davies and Tormey on snowmobiles, and the three went out to see if they could learn anything at the Inuk village.

They arrived as the tribe was holding a funeral for the two who had lost their lives in what Olssen had come to think of as the Craziness. The shaman was reciting prayers and chanting the incantations, and she noticed that the tokens – the items that had been special to one of the deceased (in this case a book of children's stories, some jewellery and a ukulele) – were given to a young man with Down syndrome, who, arm-in-arm with the deceased girl's mother, led the procession to the burial cave and was treated with great honour and affection by the community. At the feast that followed, he sat at Tuntuk's right hand, a position usually taken by clan elders or celebrated warriors.

It was late that evening before Dunnigan was free to talk. He brought them to one of the flats that were part of the village and introduced them to Tom and Urte, whom he admitted to taking from the processing plant by force.

'You found him,' Tormey said, beaming beneath his moustache. 'You nearly broke a whole town to do it, but by God, you found him.'

'I believe Beth was here,' Dunnigan told them (Olssen understood now this was his niece, who had been taken from him years ago). 'Urte tells me there is a man out at the plant who has worked there since the eighties. I know they won't let me in again without a police presence – I only got out last time by waving a gun around. With you three at my back, they'd have to be more cooperative.'

'What do you say, Chief Olssen?' Davies said. 'Do you want to see this through to the end?'

'Why the fuck not?' Olssen said.

'When do we leave?' Tormey asked.

'Now,' Dunnigan said.

6

FLEMENS WAS NOWHERE TO BE SEEN WHEN THEY
arrived – the house he had occupied was empty, and a man who
told them his name was Mikhail brought them in and told them to
wait while he went to get the man Urte had called Isaac.

When he arrived to the meeting room where the police had
been told to wait, Dunnigan saw he was very old and bent almost
double with arthritis. What work he could possibly be doing was
anyone's guess.

'A girl who they call Nathalie, but she tell me her real name is
Beth, is brought here seventeen year ago,' the old man said. 'She
live here for three year, then is taken away.'

'What did she do here?' Dunnigan asked.

'She come here as a whore, but she bad at that. She fight. She
cause problem. They beat her, but it do no good. She still problem.
One time, they beat her so bad, I think she die, but we take her to
our house, my wife and me, and we nurse her, and she live. In end,
she get job caring for other children who come, and this she does
well.'

'But they still sent her away?' Tormey said.

'She make them think she be good, but this lie. Hides in truck,
tries to go on boat. They find her, bring her back. She locked up
and then sent away.'

'Where?' Dunnigan asked.

'One day I hear oil rig in North Sea. Another mines in Chechnya.
I wish I knew. I liked her very much.'

'I'll check the databases, see what we can learn about trafficking to those locations,' Davies said. 'This is good, Davey. It's a lot more than we have on 99 per cent of the cold cases on our books. You've pulled off a miracle here.'

'But I don't have her,' Dunnigan said.

'Yet,' Davies replied.

Dunnigan turned to the old man. 'Sir, I owe you a great debt.'

'No debt. Nathalie, your Beth, she make me happy. Good girl. Brave and strong. She always think someone will come for her. I think that how she stay alive. It why I no surprise you here now. She was right, you see.'

'If you'd like to go and get your wife, I'd be glad to take you both away from here,' Tormey said, placing his hand on the old man's twisted shoulder.

'My wife is dead ... long time,' Isaac said.

'I'm very sorry for your troubles,' Tormey said. 'Just you, then.'

'Where I go? This my home. I no leave my home.'

And turning, he left them where they stood.

Miley Timoney

'Quin'ta was your assistant,' he said to Tuntuk.

The old man looked puzzled.

'Your captain?'

The chieftain's face brightened. 'Yes.'

'He died well. He was very brave.'

Tears were running down his face as he spoke. He felt like he had been doing nothing but crying since the night everything had gone to hell.

'Quin'ta strong,' Tuntuk said. 'Warrior.'

'I wish I could have done something to stop him being killed,' Miley said. 'I tried. I swear to you that I did.'

The chieftain reached over and hugged the youngster tight. He smelt of tobacco, soft, old leather and the sea.

'You have father?' Tuntuk asked him when they broke the embrace.

'My father is dead,' Miley said. 'He died when I was little.'

Tuntuk nodded and went to an old chest he kept behind the sofa in his apartment. He took out a well-used axe and a harpoon head and gave them with great seriousness to Miley.

'I you daddy now,' he said. 'You my son.'

'Yes,' Miley said. 'I'd like that.'

7

DIANE WAS DEEMED FIT TO TRAVEL A FORTNIGHT later. Olssen, who turned out to be a strong, friendly woman, quick to laugh, quick to anger and proudly and loudly lesbian, organised a helicopter to bring her from Uummannaq to the reservation.

'The plant is being taken apart a brick at a time,' Dunnigan told her over cups of the thick tea they brewed in the community centre. 'The Greenland government has had to come in and inject a colossal amount of capital into the town, but Kohlberg Industries, scrip, slave labour and everything else that went along with it is a thing of the past, for the moment anyway.'

'And Ressler has disappeared?'

'Everyone at the plant is claiming they never heard of him, and, of course, no one saw anything that night. Benjamin, or what was left of him, was pulled out of the dog pen, but the plant are saying he's an employee who had too much to drink and fell in.'

'So it's your word against theirs.'

'They're running DNA tests on his remains, but we both know they'll come up blank.'

'Where does that leave us?'

'Tove has her people checking all the airports the good doctor might use to get out, but we suspect he'll go to ground here until it all blows over. I think the sting has been taken out of his tail, for the moment at least.'

'We thought that about Frobisher.'

'I know. But a lot more people, a lot higher up the police

food chain, are involved in this. I think we can rest easy – for the immediate future, anyway.'

'You mean that?' she asked. 'You're going to rest easy?'

Her arm was held tightly in a sling, and her shoulder was still packed, but on a more positive note, she was on enough painkillers to stun a horse, so was reasonably comfortable.

'That's the plan,' Dunnigan said, without an ounce of conviction.

'I don't believe you.'

'Why not?'

'Did you find what you were looking for here?'

'No.'

'So, with that in mind, you're going to walk away and "rest easy"?'

Dunnigan lowered his eyes. 'No.'

'What are you going to do?'

'Keep looking.'

She smiled sadly and put her mug down. 'I don't know if I can keep looking with you, Davey.'

'I don't expect you to.'

They both knew what that meant, but didn't want to face the bleak reality of it yet.

'How's Miley?'

Dunnigan shook his head. 'Miley's changed.'

'I'm not surprised. He went through hell that night.'

'I know.'

'No. You don't.'

8

DIANE FOUND MILEY SITTING ON A ROCK AT THE burial cave.

He stood when he saw her, and his eyes filled with tears for the fifth time that day, and he held her for a long time. When they were done, she sat next to him and they looked at the distant hills.

'I'm sorry about Leeza,' she said.

'Me too.'

'And I'm sorry about Quin'ta. I know you loved them both. But I understand that you and Leeza had something special that was just getting going.'

'Tuntuk says we were together because we both wanted it and we understood that each of us wanted it. So in our hearts, it was real. We had already bonded.'

'He's a great man, is Tuntuk.'

'He has adopted me.'

Diane looked at him askance. 'Aren't you a bit old to be adopted, Miley?'

'Not in the Inuk culture. It means I'm a member of the tribe and that Tuntuk has obligations to me and I do to him. It's a great honour.'

'Well then, I'm pleased for you.'

'It's the first time in my life a family has *wanted* me to be a part of them.'

'That hurts, Miley. I kind of thought we were like a family. You and me and Father Bill. Davey, maybe, in his own weird way. And you and Harry, of course.'

'Not anymore. Davey found Harry's dad.'

'That doesn't mean he won't love you, Miley. You and him will still be as close as anything!'

Miley put his arm around her waist (he didn't want to hurt her shoulder). 'I'm not going back, Diane. I'm staying here.'

'You're doing what now?'

'Tuntuk has asked me to stay, and I've said yes. When you and Davey fly home, I won't be going with you.'

9

DUNNIGAN, DIANE, TOM, TORMEY AND DAVIES SAT
on the narrow benches of the tiny airport that served Faringen. A
plane would take them to Uummannaq, from there to Stockholm,
and then from Stockholm to London, where they would part
company with Davies before taking a final flight to Dublin. The
entire journey would take twenty-three hours, and none of them
were looking forward to it.

Urte had flown to Prague the previous day.

They had all bid emotional goodbyes to Tuntuk and Miley, who
came all the way to the terminal with them but then headed back
into town to buy supplies for the res. Dunnigan was concerned for
his friend's welfare, and neither he nor Diane were certain whether
he had made the decision based on some sense of loyalty to Leeza
or a feeling that he had to fill the gap left by Quin'ta as Tuntuk's
right-hand man.

In the end, it didn't matter. The result was the same. Dunnigan
had hugged his best friend before parting, but neither man spoke –
there was nothing that needed to be said between them.

'Things won't be right without him,' Diane had said as they
watched the two diminutive figures disappear around the corner
of the street and out of their lives.

'He's a brave soul, you've got to give him that,' Tormey said.

'He might be the bravest person I've ever met,' Dunnigan
said.

Now, on the benches, they sat in silence, each trapped in their
own private thoughts.

Dunnigan's phone rang, Father Bill's name flashing on the screen.

'Did one of you tell him about Miley?' Dunnigan asked, looking around at the group, expecting to receive an earful from the priest.

Everyone shook their heads.

Assuming Miley had emailed him to say goodbye, Dunnigan answered the call, preparing for a difficult conversation.

'Davey, can you talk?'

'Yes. I'm on my way home. Just starting the first leg of the journey.'

'Good.'

'How are things back home?'

'Davey, I've got some news.'

'Well, so have I. You'd better go first.'

'OK. Davey, I think I've found Beth.'

'Me too – well, possibly. We have two locations. My friend Alain is running checks on them right now.'

There was some static across the line.

'What did you say, Father?'

'I said I've *actually* found her. I have her in a hotel room in Ballsbridge. She's waiting to see you, Davey.'

Dunnigan swallowed – his mouth seemed to have gone dry all of a sudden. 'Are you saying what I think you're saying?'

'Yes, I am, Davey. Beth has come home.'

ACKNOWLEDGEMENTS

When She Was Gone had a painful birthing. I knew exactly what story I wanted to tell, but for the first time in my life as a publishing author, I found myself seriously blocked. I have to admit, I was terrified. The screen of my laptop, with its winking cursor, which I normally greet like an old friend, took on a threatening, judgemental air, and I spent two days gazing at it helplessly. As usual, it was my wife, Deirdre, who realised something was up, and when I finally admitted to her that I believed I may never write again, she suggested I abandon my computer with its accusatory screen and go back to basics.

She was right, of course. With pen in hand, I spent an afternoon filling page after page of an old notebook with character sketches, names, addresses, plot beats – over one wet Tuesday in June the world of the book took shape. Suddenly I could see the gardens about St Jude's and feel the chill in the Greenland morning air.

Thank you, Deirdre, for giving me the kick in the arse I needed.

I spent many long hours during the summer of 2017 walking the tracks and trails of the Forth Mountain with my two dogs, George and Lulu, pondering the characters, plotlines and pacing of the story. Benjamin made his first appearance during one of those walks: as my dogs and I moved through a patch of dense woodland, I thought for a moment I saw a figure loping towards us through the brush. I was mistaken – it was a trick of the light as dusk fell, but as we made our way back to the path, I found the image playing in my mind's eye, and before that hike was over, I knew his back story and how he fitted in to the novel.

In many ways, *When She Was Gone* was written as much on

those mountain walks as it was in my study. George and Lulu aren't great readers but the walks were much more fun with them for company.

Thanks are due to Marnie, Richard and Rhys, who have to tolerate me disappearing into my study and off up into the woods for hours on end while a book is percolating. Without their patience, the process would be infinitely more difficult.

I owe Brian Gibson, from Forensic Science Ireland, and Detective Sergeant Jonathan Hayes, from the Sex Crimes Unit of an Garda Síochána, a debt of gratitude for their time and patience during my research for both this book and its predecessor. They granted me access to their places of work and answered my questions without ever making me feel stupid or naïve, and Dunnigan's role as a consultant within the police force was very much shaped by Jonathan's explanation of how such an individual might work (and be paid) in the world of modern Irish policing.

It goes without saying that, where I get the details right, Brian and Jonathan should take credit. Where details are incorrect, I have simply opted to serve the story, and these two gentlemen are in no way to blame.

The Arctic has long held a fascination for me, and I knew Dunnigan would somehow function quite well there. For anyone interested in exploring the region and Inuit culture in general, Barry Lopez's *Arctic Dreams: Imagination and Desire in a Northern Landscape* is a really beautiful book.

The move from non-fiction to fiction has been a surprising journey: the literary world has opened to me in ways it never did before. I want to particularly thank my writing tribe from Wexford and the south-east: Carmel, Sheila, Adele and Caroline have become a very valuable resource for advice, support and friendship, and have shown me that this strange thing we do doesn't have to be a solitary occupation, as I had once believed.

Ciara, Joanna and all the folks at Hachette, thank you for taking a chance on a pretty off-kilter story about a weird criminologist and his even stranger friends, the central plot conceit of which involved a missing child whose story barely even featured in the first book of the series. Your faith and confidence in me has been very humbling.

Thanks to Jonathan Williams, my literary agent, for keeping the fires burning and the ship afloat when the waters got rough.

Finally, I want to express my deep gratitude to my readers. I never underestimate how lucky I am to be able to do what I do: to share my stories (both fiction and non-fiction) with a group of people who are so enthusiastic in their appreciation is a true privilege. Rarely a day goes by without someone contacting me via social media to tell me how much one of my books has meant to them, and the fact that the vast majority have followed me to crime fiction has been really touching.

If you keep reading, I'll keep writing.

Wexford
November 2017

IF SHE RETURNED

David Dunnigan comes home from Greenland to discover a young woman who may be his niece, Beth, being cared for by his friend and mentor, Father Bill Creedon. Is this damaged shell of a person the girl he has spent the last eighteen years searching for? And, if she is, can they rebuild their lives?

Meanwhile, five university lecturers from all over Ireland have, seemingly at random, come across a strange, frightening book that tells of a shadowy figure called Mother Joan – a character many believe is simply an online ghost story. The academics, however, insist the creature is real, and is stalking them.

The strange mystery leads Dunnigan to the crowded streets of London, and from there to the sprawling forest of Kielder in Northumberland, where urban myth and reality become terrifyingly linked, and where Dunnigan must fight to save Beth from an evil far more terrifying than any he has faced before.

Coming April 2019